Also by Barbara Nattress

Dreams in the Mist
Hannah' Search

CLARA
LOYALIST OR PATRIOT

BARBARA NATTRESS

Order this book online at www.trafford.com
or email orders@trafford.com

Most Trafford titles are also available at major online book retailers.

Print information available on the last page.

ISBN: 978-1-6987-0347-3 (sc)
ISBN: 978-1-6987-0349-7 (hc)
ISBN: 978-1-6987-0348-0 (e)

Library of Congress Control Number: 2020918397

Trafford rev. 10/21/2020

www.trafford.com

North America & international
toll-free: 844-688-6899 (USA & Canada)
fax: 812 355 4082

Thank You to all my friends and family for their encouragement and assistance over this past year.

Author's Notes

Writing historical fiction is exciting as the writer becomes the observer in the daily lives of families in a period of history. Their lives reflected their beliefs, fears, joys and struggles.

Researching this time period revealed many events that took place during the Patriot War in Lower Canada. Growing up in York Region in Ontario and having a Loyalist background I was somewhat aware of the Mackenzie Rebellion but not the Rebellion in Lower Canada. The references listed were filled with fascinating material describing the lives of both Patriots and Loyalists during this time period.

Discovering the similarities of injustice, inequality, poverty and elitism that took place during the 19th. Century and the 21st. Century reinforced my belief that knowing history is important and similar mistakes must not be repeated. During the 1800's, the decisions made by government were based on the values and beliefs of the day and what they thought were in the best interests of the people. Our country's past history will always be there and cannot and should not be erased. Our country today reaps the many benefits of all those past decisions made by both Loyalists and Patriots.

This book is a work of fiction. Reference to historical characters, places, events and phrases are used to provide an authentic historical sense. All other characters, dialogue and events are the imagination of the author.

Author's Notes

PART I

NEW BEGINNINGS

ONE

'CHANGE IS INEVITABLE. CHANGE IS CONSTANT.'

Benjamin Disraeli

Clara awoke to loud voices just outside her bedroom window. There seemed to be several men all talking at the same time, but she was unable to determine how many. The first light of dawn was just staring creep above the eastern horizon so she knew it must be about 7. She quickly got out of bed and dressed in her warmest clothes knowing this was likely the day she would have to leave the warmth of the house forever.

As Clara opened her bedroom door, Gabrielle St-Pierre was hurrying along the hall towards her. "Quickly Clara, we must leave right now. Go to the barn and hitch the horses to the wagon. Louis is out there already and he can help you. I am getting the younger children ready to leave. The soldiers are just a few miles away and if we stay here we will be killed or taken prisoners."

Clara grabbed her coat and boots, her small packed suitcase and ran out of the house. She saw about ten or twelve men at the side of the house, all carrying guns and talking loudly. They must have been the voices outside her window. They were still all talking at once so it was difficult to hear what they were saying, but the words *soldiers* kept being repeated. She recognized Jacques St-Pierre, her older brother Sean, and some men from a neighbouring farm. She knew it must be serious as these men were usually attending to farm chores at this time of the morning.

When she reached the barn, Louis had the harnesses on the horse and was just hooking them to the wagon. "Jump up into the seat and take the wagon to the front of the house and wait for Gabrielle," said Louis. "She will tell you where you are to go. But you will have to drive as fast as you can to get away from the soldiers. Do not go near the river as the messenger says the British have crossed near St-Antoine and have met up with another unit coming down from the north. You know how to drive the wagon don't you?"

"Yes I have done it several times," replied Clara. She hoped her voice sounded more confident than she felt at that moment. She had driven the horse pulling the smaller cart a few times but at a much slower pace than she suspected she would be taking it today. Clara managed to guide the horse out of the farm yard around the corner and up to the front of the house just as Gabrielle was ushering the three young children out the door. They all looked very frightened and still somewhat sleepy. Marie, the youngest at just 3 years old, was crying and almost being dragged by her older sister.

Gabrielle climbed up to the seat beside Clara after she had arranged the children in the back of the cart. "Sit close together and hang on to each other and keep low, Marie stop crying and hang onto your sister. Clara, drive as fast as you safely can toward St-Charles," she ordered.

The partially frozen road was very bumpy but at least there was no snow on the ground. Heading into the wind brought tears to Clara's eyes. Her thin woolen coat certainly did not keep the chill away from her body and the heavy grey sky promised more cold and probably snow by the end of the day. The small group had no choice but to leave their home and find shelter in a safer place away from the advancing soldiers. "How far will we have to go to be safe?" asked Clara.

Gabrielle did not answer but just shook her head. Clara had many more questions but this was not the time to ask so she concentrated on the bumpy road, her driving and taking an occasional glance across the field toward the river running parallel to the road.

They had travelled several miles along the road when what looked like a group of people appeared ahead of them. It did not look like soldiers in uniforms and some of the group were small children. "Should we stop? Do we know who they are?"

"I believe they are from the village to the west of us. Yes it is the Bisset family. Stop the wagon Clara," said Gabrielle. As they pulled alongside the straggly group, the two women recognized each other and seemed relieved they were friends rather than enemies. "Where are you headed," she asked?

"We were told to go toward St-Charles as the men seem to think it will be safe there for now," answered Lily." Could you give us a ride?"

"Certainly. Everyone get in the back of the wagon and keep low. Please hurry as we have a long way to go."

With 5 more people in the wagon, it was quite full. Clara hoped they would not meet any more groups of people on the road trying to escape as there was no more room and they would have to travel at a slower pace so the horse would not tire.

While driving, Clara thought back to the past five years she had lived at the St-Pierre farm. Gabrielle St-Pierre was a kind woman who believed in helping anyone needing assistance of any type. She had taken Clara and her brother Sean into her home when they had nowhere to go. She treated the brother and sister as her own children, allaying their concerns, teaching them a new language and helping them deal with the loss of their parents. How fortunate for the pair to have met the lawyer in Montreal who just happened to have a kind relative in St-Denis.

It was sad to think back to five years ago but sometimes the raw feelings of loss bubbled to the surface and tears of sadness would fill her eyes. It had all started as an adventure even though famine was the reason the Ryan family left Ireland. Clara, her brother Sean and her Mother and Father had boarded the ship leaving County Cork bound for British North America. They were to stop at Montreal and then take a steamboat to York in Upper Canada where her father was to receive a tract of land to homestead. It would be hard work for awhile but they would be able to grow their own food and eventually own their own land.

When the ship reached Quebec City many of the passengers were quite ill and some had died during the journey. The conditions on the ship had been deplorable with poor sanitary arrangements and food that was not really fit to eat. The ship was not allowed to go directly to Quebec as it was flying a flag indicating there was illness on board. They docked at an island called Grosse-Ile just up the river from Quebec. It was considered a quarantine spot to sort out passengers that were ill and to dispose of the bodies of the deceased. Anyone who seemed to be ill was not allowed back on the ship. All four members of the Ryan family were cleared to return to the ship and continue their voyage. The ship however was still filthy and contaminated and within a day; Mr. Ryan began to feel poorly.

When they arrived in Montreal, Clara's father was pale and refused to eat anything. While awaiting the steamboat west, his condition worsened and they were unable to continue on their way to Upper Canada. Hoping to recover they stayed at the shipping depot, which was really just a large unheated damp shed, spending part of their precious money on food for the children. Mrs. Ryan was very worried about her husband but tried to stay positive for the sake of the children. The next day Mrs. Ryan began to show similar symptoms, and two days later they both died of cholera leaving Sean and Clara orphans in a foreign country.

The children were taken by a policeman to a building that housed many people both old and young. Everyone spoke another language that neither Clara nor Sean had ever heard before. Some of the residents in the building seemed to spend their days yelling loudly, calling out the same words over and over or just pacing up and down the halls.

A stern nurse, who spoke a bit of English, showed them to a room and said, "According to the rules, you would not be allowed to stay together but since you only speak English we will allow it for a few days. Do not leave the room except to use the public toilet outside the door at the end of the hall."

The room was all white with 2 narrow beds, a small table with a wash basin and a water jug sitting on top. The small window looked out onto a field that had long grass and a few wildflowers blooming at spots. As it was June, the sun was high in the sky and Clara and Sean were unable to figure out what direction the window faced. Each bed had a thin grey blanket folded at the foot of the bed but there were no other bed linens on the stained mattress. The children sat on one bed beside each other not knowing what would happen to them now that they only had each other and neither of them was old enough to be on their own. They really were not even sure where they were except it was a foreign country where English was rarely spoken. Clara fell asleep leaning on Sean. He sat still allowing her to sleep. Although he was only twelve, he suddenly felt he had to become much older so he could protect Clara who was just ten.

The room was beginning to darken when the door opened and the same nurse entered carrying a tray with two bowls of food and two spoons. Clara suddenly woke up and sat up straight next to Sean. The nurse spoke in her accented English "Sit on your own beds and eat your supper. After you eat you should get ready to go to bed as it will be dark soon enough. We have no candles to spare for this room."

The children looked at the food in the bowls and were not sure what it was but it looked a bit like porridge. It tasted quite watery but it was slightly warm and as they were both hungry the bowls were quickly emptied. Their small suitcase containing all their clothes and possessions they had brought with them was at the end of the bed. Clara and Sean opened it and took out their night clothes but before they changed they decided to brave a trip to the toilet. They managed to get to the back door with no problem, but once outside they found a lineup to use the toilet. Some of the other residents just stared at them but a few others wanted to touch Clara's reddish coloured hair. Sean was very protective and pushed them away. When they reached the front of the line they both entered the building together as Sean did not want Clara to be alone. They quickly overcame their shyness with each other and completed their task and headed back to their room.

Once in bed they whispered to each other about what they thought would happen to them. Sean said "We will stay together no matter what anyone says. I will find a job and get some money so we can go to Upper Canada and get the land Father was to have. We have the papers for the land and a bit of money to buy some tools. We still have the boat tickets which maybe they will let us use. But we will always stay together."

The next morning a different nurse came to their room with another tray and two bowls. It looked like the same food as last night. "Good. You are dressed. Eat this and later a man is coming to see you. Stay in your room," she said. The children could see she really was afraid to be near them as she was likely worried they might be ill and she could catch it. They ate the watery porridge again but it did not seem as tasty as last night.

Clara and Sean stayed in their room occasionally looking outside at the bright sunshine but mostly sitting on their bed talking about how they would live in this new land. A few hours later a different nurse returned to their room accompanied by a tall man in a suit. The children were relieved when he spoke in English. "Hello. I am Mr. Drummond and I am the lawyer who will be looking after your welfare now that your parents are deceased. I need to know some details so we can find you a place to live. How old are you?"

Sean answered for them saying "I am almost thirteen and Clara is ten."

Mr. Drummond then asked "Why were your parents coming to Lower Canada? Do you speak any French? Do you have any relatives in British North America?"

Sean decided to tell him the whole story of the reason for leaving Ireland and the hope of starting a farm in Upper Canada. He chose not to show him the papers of the promise of land remembering his Father telling him to be careful who he told about their private matters. Mr. Drummond seemed kind in the way he asked and answered their questions, but you really never knew what others would do.

Mr. Drummond had been writing their answers in a notebook while Sean told his story. He closed his notebook and said "I have some ideas but I must contact other people about this. I will come back to see you in several days when I have an answer. In the meantime Nurse, I think these children should be allowed to take in some fresh air every day, the weather is nice and they are young enough to enjoying running around outside. But Clara and Sean, you must stay together while outside and do not talk to anyone or go anywhere with others. Of course not many here speak English so those rules should be easy for you to follow."

Nurse Looked crossly at Mr. Drummond but did not say anything. She just shook her head in disagreement.

A week later Mr. Drummond returned. He was accompanied by another man who was dressed in old rough clothing with an odd blue hat on his head. The two men spoke French. Both Clara and Sean were amazed. They had never met anyone who could speak two languages. Mr. Drummond turned to them and said "This is my sister's husband and they are willing to take you to their home and let you live with them. Clara you will have to work in the home with Mrs. St-Pierre taking care of children and cooking and Sean you will have to help Mr. St-Pierre with animals and the farm work. This is the best life for you and as you are both minor children. You will have to ride with Mr. St-Pierre for the next few days to get to your new home near St- Denis. He does not speak much English but he is kind and you will be safe with him. I will send a letter soon to see how you are doing. My sister will help you learn French. Now pack up you things and we will be off."

John Drummond left the room carrying their small suitcase. Clara and Sean followed him and Jacques St. Pierre walked behind them. They walked out of the building into the fresh air and sunlight toward a horse attached to a small cart with only two wheels. There was one seat at the front and a space at the back partially filled with straw. Mr. St-Pierre helped Clara climb into the back while Sean jumped in on his own. Mr. St-Pierre then climbed up to the front seat. Mr. Drummond put the small suitcase beside Clara. "Merci, Jacques. Au revoir. Your first French lesson, *merci* means thank you and *au revoir* means goodbye. Hello is *bonjour.* Those are always good words to know."

"Merci and Au revoir" repeated Clara and Sean. The words sound strange to them and awkward to say but they knew they had to try to learn French if they were to survive.

It was a very bumpy ride in the back of the cart but Sean and Clara sat close together and tried to think of all the nice things they had experienced in their short lives. However the past few weeks of turmoil seemed to override all the goodness. All the good times had included their parents and relatives. Soon Clara was quietly crying and Sean was being as brave as he could be but the big lump in his throat prevented him from saying anything to comfort Clara.

They rode along deserted paths surrounded by thick bush and tall trees. The sun was at their back and it did feel warm. Before long both Sean and Clara fell asleep. Suddenly the wagon stopped and the lack of motion startled them awake. Mr. St-Pierre jumped down from the wagon and spoke. "Come. We sleep *ici.*" He was pointing to what looked like a barn at the side of the road. There was a house farther away and a man was walking out the door towards the group. Sean hoped he was friendly.

Mr. St-Pierre and the farmer shook hands and began speaking to each other in French. The only word Sean and Clara caught was *bonjour.* It soon became obvious that the two men knew each other and they were all invited into the house. The house felt warm and smelled like baking bread. Mr. St-Pierre introduced Clara and Sean and they both nodded and managed to say, "Bonjour," and sat in the chairs Jacques pointed to. The farmer's wife was just putting dinner on the table and quickly put a large spoon in front of the children. There were three other children all younger than Clara already sitting at the table. They stared at both Clara and Sean but never said a word. Clara and Sean just looked down at their lap.

The farmer's wife brought over a large pot from the wood stove, carrying it with a towel wrapped around her hands. She then began to ladle the green liquid into all the bowls on the table. The children quickly grabbed a bowl and began to eat the green liquid. Jacques put a bowl in front of Clara and Sean and also put a large slice of bread beside the bowl. Using hand gestures he picked up his spoon and pretended to eat. Clara and Sean figured it must be soup but they had never seen green soup before. They each took a tentative taste. It was warm and had a lovely flavour to it. Also in the bottom of the bowl were what looked like beans? The brother and sister were soon eating heartily finishing all that was in their bowls. The fresh bread was also a treat as they had not had fresh bread since they left Ireland.

"C'est bon!" said Mr. St-Pierre. "Soupe aux, pois"

Sean wasn't sure what pois were but he figured it was either beans or peas as it was green.

Supper did not last long and soon the two men stood up from the table and motioned for the two to follow them.

"Merci," said Sean and Clara as they were leaving the kitchen. They hoped they said it right, and when the adults smiled they figured they had the right pronunciation.

They all walked to the barn. Jacques unhitched the horse and led it inside the barn to a stall. He tied it up to a post and then brought over a pail with water for the horse to drink. He retrieved some grain from the cart and gave it to the horse. It was still light out as it was summer time but Mr. St-Pierre gestured to the children that it was time for bed. He pointed to a spot where some straw was piled up indicating that was their bed for the night. He also pointed to what looked like an outhouse. Sean and Clara walked together to the outhouse and waited until each were finished. Sean whispered on the way back to the barn, "I think we should sleep in our clothes tonight and keep our shoes on."

"I don't think we will be safe in a barn," said Clara. "What if animals find us?"

"Don't worry, I will be beside you and keep you safe," said Sean. He had no idea how he would keep her safe if he had to, but he hoped Clara believed him.

It took awhile to get comfortable but eventually they both fell asleep. Clara awoke first to hear someone singing but the words made no sense. She quickly remembered where she was and it was Mr. St-Pierre singing as he was leading the horse out to the wagon.

"Wake up Sean. Mr. St-Pierre is leaving. We don't want him to leave without us."

The two were up in a flash and out standing beside the cart watching the horse being hitched to the cart.

"Bonjour, mes ami, venez." Jacques motioned for them to come closer and watch. He pointed out how to put the harnesses on the horse and where to hook them to the cart. Sean thought he might be able to do this soon by himself.

Jacques pointed to the house indicating they should go to the kitchen to get some food. Sean and Clara walked over to the house together and were greeted by the oldest daughter. She was almost eight so she was a big help around the house. She led them to the table where two bowls of what looked like porridge were waiting for them. The younger children were still at the table eating. The porridge was good and when they finished their new friend gestured for them to come with her. Sean and Clara both said "Merci. Au revoir!", as they left the house.

The farmer's wife handed them a bundle tied together and said, "Pour que vous mangiez quand vous aurez faim."

Clara and Sean said, "Merci." And hoped that was the right answer. They carried the bundle with them to the cart and showed it to Mr. St-Pierre.

He took the bundle and put it by his feet all the while laughing. "Ma soeur sait que les enfants ont toujours faim."

Again Sean and Clara had no idea what he was saying.

Mr. St-Pierre then said in a more serious voice, "Sean, viens t'assoir ici," as he patted the seat beside him. "Prends les renes!" He pointed to the horse and looked like he was passing the reins to Sean.

He then lifted his right hand and said "droit." He did the same with his left and said "gauche." He pointed ahead and spoke to the horse saying "Allez." The horse started moving forward and walked toward the path they were on yesterday. When they neared the farmhouse, He said, "Arrêtez."

Sean was amazed the horse understood what Mr. St-Pierre was saying. He figured out what each word meant and just hoped he could remember. While this driving lesson was taking place, Clara was standing behind them in the cart carefully listening so she too could drive the horse and cart someday.

The farmer, Jean and his wife, Marie and all their children were standing near the path as the horse stopped. Jacques spoke quickly in French, thanking them for their hospitality. What Clara and Sean did not know was that Jacques and Marie were brother and sister. After everyone saying "Merci" and "Au revoir," the group began the day long journey to St-Denis area.

It was a very long day with just a few stops to rest and water the horse and to take outhouse breaks. Sean had several chances to try driving the horse and cart and Mr. St-Pierre always said "bon travail," when he handed back the reins. Since he was smiling when he said it Sean figured he had done OK.

It was just starting to get dark when in the distance they spotted the faint outline of a house. Clara was tired of sitting and hoped Mr. St-Pierre might know someone else who would let them sleep for the night. Mr. St-Pierre announced with a smile and in English, "Home."

As the cart pulled closer to the house a women ran out of the house toward them. The cart stopped and Jacques jumped down and hugged the woman. "C'est Madame St-Pierre. And pointing to the children he said, "Sean et Clara."

Sean and Clara jumped down from the cart carrying their small suitcase and said "Bonjour." But before they knew what was happening they were enveloped in a big hug from Gabrielle St-Pierre.

"You must be so tired and hungry. Come inside and we will get something to eat. Where did you sleep last night? Did Jacques' sister make you sleep in the barn? She should have let you sleep in the house. You must be exhausted. Come with me you poor dears." said Mrs. St- Pierre.

Clara and Sean had not heard so much English for a long time, but she spoke so quickly there was no time to answer. They walked toward the small house that was plain on the outside but was warm and comforting on the inside. There was a lovely aroma of something good to eat. The two did not see any children in the house and Clara was sure Mr. Drummond had said there were children to take care of.

Clara asked," Where are your children?"

Sean gasped at the question but Mrs. St-Pierre smiled and said, “They are in bed as the twins are six months. You will meet them in the morning. Now there is left over chicken stew and bread to eat. Wash your hands in the bowl and come to the table.”

Sean and Clara sat down and devoured the stew. “This is delicious,” said Clara. “How do you say chicken stew in French?”

Gabrielle smiled and said “Ragoût du poulet. You can say: Would you like chicken stew Mr. St-Pierre? Just say Voulez-vous du ragoût de poulet, Monsieur St-Pierre? I think he is coming now.”

Jacques entered the house and Clara said to him, “Voulez-vous du ragoût du poulet, Monsieur St-Pierre?”

Jacques smiled, bowed to Clara and said “Oui, merci Mademoiselle!” They all laughed. Both Clara and Sean felt they were welcome in this home and maybe this would be a good place to live for awhile.

Clara was suddenly jolted from her memories when Gabrielle suddenly announced they were approaching St-Charles and asked Mrs. Bisset where she would like to be dropped off.

“Thank you. If you let us off in front of the church we will be fine. We can walk to where we are going. There is an outhouse at the church we can use before we walk and before you travel on.”

“Good idea,” said Gabrielle. “We still have a ways to go today. Clara you take the girls to the outhouse and I will stay with the wagon. We wish you all the best and be safe on your journey Lily.”

“Thank you so much and safe journey to you as well.”

With the small break over, the group climbed back in the wagon and continued their journey south hoping to arrive before dark.

TWO

'FAMILY ISN'T ALWAYS BLOOD. IT'S THE PEOPLE IN YOUR LIFE WHO WANT YOU AS THEIRS; THE ONES WHO ACCEPT YOU FOR WHO YOU ARE, THE ONES THAT WOULD DO ANYTHING TO SEE YOU SMILE AND WHO LOVE YOU NO MATTER WHAT.'

Author Unknown

John Drummond was quite worried. He was meeting with a friend after visiting the Governor, "The situation to the east of Montreal is intensifying. The Governor is concerned about a man known as Louis- Joseph Papineau," said John. "Papineau is a member of the legislature and wants to make Lower Canada a French Nation. He is the son of a seigneur and when his father died he inherited the seigneury. He is wealthy, privileged and has established himself as the leader of the Parti Canadien. His objective is to transfer the power of revenue control to the francophone population."

The two Lawyers continued to talk at length about the situation.

"But the population of Lower Canada is about four fifths French now and the Irish who are coming here also hate the English," stated John. "As well the Americans who are situated in the Eastern Townships still have a hate for the British who drove them out during the Revolutionary War. They dislike their autocratic ways."

"Yes I agree," replied Paul. "There is talk of the Patriots taking their cause directly to London and even though they have had a majority in the House of Assembly for many years; any reforms they propose are rarely accepted by the British Government. They want the same powers and privileges as the British Parliament. And if they do not get what they want, they are threatening to fight for independence and possible annexation to the United States."

"That would be disastrous, especially for our business in Montreal. We would have to decide whether to become English again or align ourselves with the French. I would hate to have to make that decision," said John.

The two men continued discussing the alarming thought of a disruption in their safe and comfortable lifestyle.

John Drummond had been born and educated in England but immigrated to North America after he became a lawyer. He was to work in Upper Canada with an uncle in a prestigious law firm in York, but as he was fluent in French the law firm sent him to Montreal to work with their associates.

John and his sister Gabrielle had lived a very privileged life in England. They had both attended prestigious schools and had travelled extensively through Europe. Both had learned French and were able to carry on a conversation socially and professionally. John's parents had not wanted him to leave for the colonies but he felt the social structure of Britain was very restrictive, and he was looking for a bit of adventure.

When both of his parents died within six months of each other due to cholera, he and Gabrielle inherited their estate. He travelled to England and discussed the choices they would have to make. Gabrielle was not keen to stay in London any longer and wanted to move to France. John convinced her that coming to live in Montreal was almost as good as living in Paris. She would be able to use her French and possibly even teach children. Gabrielle was sure the colonies were not anything like Paris, but she decided it would be nice to be near her brother. So John arranged to sell his Father's large estate and within a few months, the two sailed to British North America.

John owned a house in Montreal, so Gabrielle moved in and soon found she was meeting many new people. John was well known and respected in town so it was easy for her to be accepted into the elite social circle of his friends. Almost everyone spoke French, so soon Gabrielle was feeling confident speaking the language.

Several of her new friends would invite her to parties which were lovely, but Gabrielle was used to having more freedom than most young women. After she had been in Montreal for about six months, one of her friends, Justine Dumont, invited her to accompany her to her parents home north of Montreal. It would take a day to get there but she would be staying for several weeks. It sounded like a great adventure and she would be seeing a part of Lower Canada she had not seen before. Her friend Justine told her to pack some outdoor clothes as well as party clothes.

Gabrielle packed one of the trunks she brought from England, which seemed a bit absurd, but she might need all these outfits. The day to leave came and a covered carriage, pulled by two black horses, arrived at the Drummond home. The driver carried out her trunk and Gabrielle was relieved to see Justine had packed a trunk the same size. Justine and Gabrielle settled themselves in the carriage surrounded by a large basket of food and drink as well as umbrellas, gloves, shawls, blankets and other travelling items to keep them warm and amused on the trip.

"This is going to be so much fun," said Justine. "I hear there is going to be a meeting where some politicians will be speaking."

"What are they speaking about," asked Gabrielle?

"I am sure it will be something about the habitants not being treated fairly."

"Who or what are the habitants? I have not heard that term before."

Justine began the story of the habitants. "The French farmers in parts of Lower Canada are living a poor life. Those who live on farms owned by a Seigneur must pay rent on the land to the Seigneur. The land is poor and crops do not grow well. The animals are not fed well so are small in stature. The farm implements are not well made. The families have many children and there is not much food. The bread is black not white and meat is rare. They have to thin the pea soup down with water. Some have left their farms as they can't pay the rent. Have you not seen them begging on the streets of Montreal? As well, the Priest in the parish demands money from the farmers to pay for the upkeep of the church and to send money to the Bishop. The church is the social centre of each community and the parishioners think of it as theirs, but really it is not. They must even pay rent for a family pew."

"I did not know any of this," Gabrielle said in astonishment. "I did hear about some unrest but nothing this bad. We have to do something to help the habitant families."

"We may not be able to help as the French think of us as part of the problem and that is because we are part of the English party or Tories who are conservative business families and support the colonial government."

"How do you know all this and where did you find out all this information," asked Gabrielle?

"My older brother Emile works in the Governor's office and he tells me things. He never mentions any names as he is not supposed to tell anyone about what is happening. You have to promise not to tell anyone that I told you."

Both Gabrielle and Justine were concerned about those in Montreal who were poor and struggling to find food or a place to live.

They volunteered at an institution that tried to help the poor but it seemed like a losing battle sometimes. They often had to turn people away as they had no more soup or warm clothes to offer. Justine's parents did not like her working there but she was a strong minded person and went anyway. She just never told them she helped on a regular basis.

Gabrielle really did not have to report her activities to anyone and she had enough of her own money now to do as she pleased. She did mention to John occasionally what she was doing but he just cautioned her to be careful in what part of the city she walked.

They passed several hours looking at the landscape as the edge of the city disappeared, and the less inhabited countryside began. The land was still flat as they were close to the mighty St. Lawrence River. As they travelled farther, it was noticeable that the land became more rolling with large rounded hills dotting the horizon. Large areas of forest extended for miles. Gabrielle had never seen such large trees. In Britain the trees were much shorter and the trunks not nearly as thick.

"This land has not been set up as a seigneury so there are no farmers here. When we cross the next river you will see farms where wheat is grown. It is good farming land now. The seigneury once belonged to our family but due to money problems it now belongs to someone else. My father is still a commissioner for communication in the county. We have a house in St- Eustache but there is no bridge across the river so we live in a house on this side of the river." said Justine.

Justine's father was Louis Dumont and represented the seigneurial class not only at the local but also the colonial level. He felt because of his family background he had a role in the social and political leadership among the Seigneurs. He was tied to the British Colonial administration which handed out local leadership positions and controlled the small villages. He saw the new upstart bourgeoisie lawyers, doctors and local merchants with their nationalistic ideology and democratic notions as the enemy of the Seigneurs.

Gabrielle did not really understand the seigneury system completely but it seemed to her it sounded a bit like the feudal system in Britain that had caused so many peasants in Ireland and Scotland to leave the country or die of starvation. It also sounded as though the Dumont family were involved with both the French and English Authorities. She was also wise enough to realize that she should keep some of her thoughts to herself as she would be a guest in the Dumont house. She was surprised Justine was so aware of the social situation of so many residents in the city when she had been brought up in a privileged life style.

The carriage was now entering a small town surrounded on one side by wheat fields. The houses were small homes made of round logs with steep roofs and dormer windows in the upper story. The front of each house was very close to the road but behind the house there was a field that led down to the river. The log barns and out buildings were at the back but attached to the house. The road through the village was still as bumpy as the roads throughout the countryside, but a bit wider. There was a small store on the street in the midst of all the houses with a sign indicating it sold dry goods and farming supplies.

The road curved around a stand of tall evergreen trees and a larger house suddenly came into view. There was a gate that turned off the road to the left and followed a narrow path to the house. At either side of the house you could see the river behind it. Compared to the small homes in the village, this house looked very much like a mansion.

"We are here at last," said Justine. The two women were glad to finally reach their destination. It had taken the better part of the day and sitting on hard seats in the carriage travelling over bumpy roads was not something one wanted to do on a daily basis. They stepped down from the carriage and proceeded to the front door of the house but before they reached the door, it swung open and a young girl ran down the stairs and almost knocked Justine over.

"I am so glad you are here. We need some excitement as it is quite dull living out here. Tell me all about Montreal. Is this your friend? I can hardly wait to hear all your stories," the girl quickly said.

"Sophie where are your manners?" said a voice behind her. Mrs. Dumont had come out to meet Justine and Gabrielle and was appalled at her youngest daughter Sophie's behaviour. "Welcome home Justine and welcome to your guest. You must be Gabrielle. We are pleased you have come for a visit."

Gabrielle replied, "Thank you for inviting me and I am looking forward to this visit."

It seemed very formal to Gabrielle and she was hoping the whole visit would not be like this.

As they all entered the house and the first impression was a warm inviting home. Gabrielle hoped this was a good sign. The main hall off the entrance was as wide as some of the houses they had passed on the journey here. There were wide oak plank floors extending down the hall with at least six doors leading from the hallway. Along one side of the hall was a staircase curving up to the upper level. The craftsmanship in the design and finishing of the stairs and the railing was beautiful and reminded Gabrielle of many large English homes she had visited.

Mrs. Dumont took their cloaks and handed them to a young girl who had appeared from one of the doorways. The women then followed Justine's mother along the hall to the sitting room.

It was very formal with a number of upholstered chairs and sofas arranged in conversation groupings around the room. This room also had the wide plank floors but they were partially covered with multi coloured rugs. The room looked out toward the north and in the distance the river and the treed lot provided a spectacular view. Each window had floor to ceiling window coverings made from what looked like tapestry. These were open during the day but would provide a warm barrier to the cold winds in the winter.

"Please be comfortable and sit for awhile after your long journey," Mrs. Dumont said as she motioned to Justine and Gabrielle toward the chairs near the window. "I will have Camille bring us tea."

Gabrielle thanked her but was wishing she could go for a walk down to the river. They had been sitting for many hours and more sitting was the last thing she wanted, although the down filled chair cushions were much more comfortable than the carriage seats.

Sophie burst into the room and began asking a million questions and this time her mother let her continue. After the tea was served,

Justine suggested they be allowed to find their rooms and freshen up. Mrs. Dumont suddenly jumped up announcing "Please forgive me for not remembering you have travelled so far. Camille, please show the girls to their rooms and we will see you for dinner at 7 in the dining room."

Gabrielle and Justine followed Camille to the upstairs. The decor of this home was just as spectacular on this level as below. Gabrielle whispered to Justine, "You did not tell me we would be staying in a castle. I don't think I brought the right clothes for such formal living."

"Don't worry; Mother is just trying to make a good impression because you are from England. You will see tomorrow we can dress as we always do and do what we want. Our only requirement will be to be present for dinner each night, and we do dress somewhat formally for dinner as there are often guests Father invites. But the conversations are interesting and often about politics."

Gabrielle was shown the door to her room and once again as she entered she was taken aback with the quality of the furniture and the fabrics. The room had a warm glow from the rose and cream bed coverings and drapes. The dark wood of the furniture and wood work gave just the right contrast to make the room welcoming and cozy. She suddenly jumped as a door beside the bed opened and Justine jumped through it. "Isn't this the greatest? Our rooms are connected. We can visit all night if we want to. This used to be the nursery area of the house where my brother and I stayed when we were young. Of course Sophie does not have a nanny now and my Mother redid the rooms to make them adjoining. Our bathroom is just across the hall. Sophie is in a room down the hall and my parents' area is in another wing of the house so we have this area just for the girls while we are here."

"This is an amazing house Justine. I would almost think I was back in England at some manor house. Does Sophie have to sleep alone in this wing when no one is visiting? It might be a bit spooky."

"No, she has a room close to my parents where she stays when one of us is not home. It is a big house, but as Father is the councillor for the area he feels he must keep up appearances. Mother has done all the organizing for furniture and fabrics and she does have good taste. Originally this house belonged to the church and was used by higher ups in the church for meetings and to get out of the city. It was sold about twenty years ago as the parish needed money and the priests and bishops did not want to travel this far. My grandfather bought it and had it rebuilt to suit a family. It was more like a monastery than a home before as there was one big dining room, and living room and many monks like bedrooms. I will show you the part that used to be the chapel when we explore tomorrow. I guess we better get dressed for dinner. I am wearing that green floral dress I bought when we shopped together last month, so don't feel you have to get really dressed up."

"Thanks Justine. I was somewhat panicked about what I would wear tonight. I guess we should go down and bring up our trunks. Is there someone who might help us?"

"I think that has been done for us. Look in the closet."

Gabrielle crossed the room and opened a closet door and there she found all her clothes either hanging in the closet or neatly folded on a shelf. "Wow. Now I will be really spoiled when I go back to Montreal."

The rest of the evening was a blur of meeting Mr. Dumont and the other guests. Dinner was a multi course meal with soup, fresh vegetables, an entrée of pheasant and roasted potatoes and a custard dessert. After such a delightful meal accompanied by several wines, both Gabrielle and Justine excused themselves for the evening as the long journey and good food began to take its toll.

THREE

'MANY FRIENDS WILL WALK IN AND OUT OF YOUR LIFE, BUT ONLY TRUE FRIENDS WILL LEAVE FOOTPRINTS IN YOUR HEARTS.'

Eleanor Roosevelt

The sun was shining the next morning when Gabrielle awoke. She had slept soundly last night and was ready for a day of new discoveries. She quickly got out of bed, dressed and slipped across the hall to the bathroom. On her way back to her room she met Sophie running along the hall to meet her.

"Please may I go exploring with you and Justine today? I have waited so long for Justine to come and visit that I cannot bear to not spend time with her and with you too. If I stay here at home, Mother will make me do something boring, so please take me with you. You and Justine can tell her at breakfast that I will be going with you today. Where are we going anyway?"

Gabrielle could hardly stop laughing and suggested they see if Justine was awake so they could plan the day. They knocked on her door but there was no answer. Sophie announced, "We should just go in and see if she is sleeping." They opened the door and discovered the room was empty. "Justine must be down at breakfast already."

When the two arrived downstairs to the breakfast room, there was Justine having a conversation with her father.

"I hope you slept well," said Mr. Dumont standing up as they entered the room and pulling out a chair beside him for Gabrielle. "Now you must join us for a good breakfast."

Everyone sat down and helped themselves to breakfast from the warming dishes filled with eggs, sausage and potatoes. There was fresh bread and jam on the table along with tea or coffee. No one would be hungry this morning.

"Where is Mama?" asked Sophie. "Gabrielle and Justine have asked me to help them explore today. You would agree to that won't you Papa?" As Sophie stated this with authority to her father, she gave Gabrielle a pleading look.

"Yes we would love to have Sophie help us explore the grounds today wouldn't we Justine. We hope that meets with approval from the family." Gabrielle smiled. "Where is the best place to start Sophie?"

Sophie, who had just taken a mouth full of sausage, almost choked but managed a wide smile and indicated with her hand to wait a moment. She knew this would be one of the best days of the summer.

After breakfast, Gabrielle, Justine and Sophie gathered a shawl and straw hats and set off across the lawn toward the river. The grass was lush and very green as they walked along the stone path. Gabrielle noticed the several outbuildings at the back of the house and asked, "Sophie what are all these small buildings used for?"

"The first square one is the ice house where we keep the butter and cream. There is a hole to lower things into a trough containing water and it keeps everything cold. In winter the farmers bring ice from the river to put in the hole and it lasts all summer. The next one is where we keep the chickens. Sometimes I go with Mrs. Trembley to help collect the eggs, but the chickens are not always happy about us taking their eggs so they peck your hands." Sophie continued her tour moving from small building to building until all the buildings had been described.

The group were now at the river and looking across there was view of a large church along the banks. It looked as though there was also a small village situated around the church.

Justine commented that it was the village of St-Eustache where they owned a house but as there was no bridge across the river yet, they lived on this side. It took several days to travel up river to the closest bridge. "There are many people who live in this region who are not happy with my father as he is involved in a dispute with St-Eustache regarding a new bridge. Many of the people new to this area do not understand that the vote is decided by the Chateau Clique. They are the village merchants and professionals and Seigneurs. If a bridge is built, the residents will cross the river and possibly take their business elsewhere. The Clique always vote together and always side with the Tories."

"But do they not have elections to represent various factions in the government, and can they not change things," asked Gabrielle?

"It is hard as the people are split in their thinking. There are many Loyalists living in area and many came from the United States during the revolutionary war. They were still loyal to England when they arrived here, but now are not always happy with the path the Tories are taking. There are also many habitants and they have trouble dealing with the English and are speaking about wanting more control and power over their own dealings. There is also the church and a Curé or priest for each parish who exerts control over the people in the parish. And lastly there are the Seigneurs who appoint the men in the officer's corps and the militia and control things locally. There are too many people and too many levels of control. Each group is fighting for their own cause. It is just too bad that women are not allowed to vote. We could solve everything." Justine laughed at the mention of women voting, but in her heart she really felt women should be able to discuss issues and help make decisions that affected everyone.

Sophie had been listening to all this and although she wasn't quite sure what it all meant, she stated emphatically that she would make sure they could all vote someday. "Now let's go and explore the house before lunch. I am starting to get hungry."

Sophie took them around the side of the house to a stairway that led up to a tall door. It was locked, but Sophie picked up a rock beside the door and there was a very large key behind it. The key slowly turned and a loud click indicated the door could be opened. "This is the side door where the priests would enter the monastery when they were finished working in the fields. There used to be a large sink here for washing up but someone took it out. If we go that way there is a large room that used to be a dining hall but now just stores stuff. This way though leads to the chapel. I guess no one felt they should take it apart so it is still mostly the same as it has always been."

The women entered through a large door with a brass ring for a handle. Inside it was dark and dust motes could be seen dancing in the sunlight streaming through the coloured stained glass clearstory windows. The walls were all paneled in dark wood. There were a few plain wooden benches arranged in rows with short kneeling benches in front of each bench. At the front of the chapel all that remained of the altar was a short table. There were no crosses on the walls and all the vessels usually seen in a church had been taken away as well.

Gabrielle whispered "Why did the church decide to abandon this monastery, and why would they leave some things and take the rest? Have your parents ever thought about changing this part into something else or can you even do that to an old church?"

"The church was decommissioned or something like that so it is not really a church anymore so yes it can be changed, but my parents do not need the space and really do not know what to do with it so it just sits like this," replied Justine.

"The size of the rooms would make great school rooms or a place to do art work, but I guess not many people in the country have time for that. It just seems a shame to have so much space with no one using it. Justine, you could think up something to do with the space and bring people up here to work on whatever you decided it would be."

"Gabrielle, that sounds wonderful but very vague and quite an undertaking. Do you want to help me with whatever?"

"I see your point" laughed Gabrielle.

Suddenly a bell tolled making the two women jump. "That was Sophie. She has gone up to the tower to ring the bell to scare us. I did not notice she had disappeared as we were so involved here. I think she may be hungry as it is almost lunch time and she is trying to get our attention," said Justine.

Justine and Gabrielle walked back out of the chapel and found Sophie at the entrance with a big smile on her face. They both took her by the arm and half ran and walked back to the house for lunch.

After lunch the women sat inside and chatted with Mrs. Dumont about what was happening in Montreal, what the latest fashions were and about different food available in the markets. Justine and Gabrielle and Sophie took another walk around the property to see the animals and by then everyone decided it would be good just to rest for awhile.

Dinner tonight was to be special as several leaders from the area were joining Mr. Dumont and the family. Gabrielle was hoping that politics might be discussed and that the women would be allowed to at least listen.

Justine and Gabrielle consulted each other about what to wear to dinner as Justine had said several of the men attending tonight were single men who lived in the area and were quite influential in government affairs. "We have to look our best as one always needs to be ready to meet new people."

The women went downstairs to dinner as they entered the sitting room all six men stood up to acknowledge their entrance. Besides Mr. Dumont and Justine's brother Emile there was Mr. Deslauriers, Mr. Toupin, Mr. Dubeau, Mr. Paquet and Mr. St-Pierre. Justine and Gabrielle were offered a small glass of wine and they all sat while the conversation continued.

When dinner was announced, Justine and Gabrielle were seated across from each other and Mr. Paquet was seated next to Justine and Mr. St-Pierre was seated next to Gabrielle. The conversation was polite and somewhat stilted for awhile but as the evening progressed, conversations became more friendly and personal among the foursome.

Jacques St-Pierre turned to Gabrielle and asked "Where do you live in Montreal? Are you returning to England soon?'

"No I have left England for good and now live with my brother in Montreal. I do volunteer work helping new immigrants find homes and food so they can survive." She continued to tell him a bit about her past family life but was cautious not to reveal too much.

"How long will you be staying here at the Dumont's," asked Jacques?

"We are staying for two weeks and then Justine and I will go back to Montreal."

"Mr. Paquet and I are going to St-Eustache tomorrow by boat to look at some property. Would you and Justine like to join us? We will leave after breakfast and be back by late afternoon."

Joseph Paquet's head suddenly shot up and he looked at Jacques with a strange look on his face. Gabrielle caught the look and felt she should say no thank you. "We have plans tomorrow. Maybe we can go another time." There was a brief look of relief on Joseph's face.

After dinner the group, including the women, moved back into the sitting room where conversation turned to the dissatisfaction with the English Party and the colonial government. The French speaking farmers in Lower Canada shared a distrust of British power and were interested in changing how things were run. The English party in Lower Canada were of Scottish, English and American descent and defended the colonial government. At this time the colonial system and the concentration of power and wealth was in the hands of a few families in Upper and Lower Canada.

"Louis-Joseph Papineau wants us to become our own French Nation," stated Mr. Deslauriers, "and hopefully we will have the support of all the francophones in Montreal."

At this point Justine gave a look to Gabrielle that they should leave this discussion and Gabrielle nodded in agreement and both women excused themselves from the room with barely any notice from the men.

"Well that was certainly quite the discussion. I did not know things had gone this far. It seems these men are ready to fight for their rights," said Gabrielle. "On the other hand I think I would like to see Jacques again as he seems like a nice person, but not to go on a boat to look at property."

"Agreed. Joseph seems nice too. He asked me to go to a dance in town this weekend and I said yes. Now I have to tell my parents."

"That is wonderful Justine. I wonder if Jacques is planning on going. Maybe Joseph will tell him you two are going and he will get an idea to ask me."

The two women continued their talk about the evening on their way up to bed. They parted at their bedrooms and both went to bed with many thoughts of love and war running through their minds.

The next few days at the Dumont home passed quietly with the women, often accompanied by Sophie, taking leisurely walks around the property or sitting in the cool breezes by the river. One afternoon Jacques and Joseph drove their small cart up the driveway and saw Gabrielle and Justine sitting down at the river. They walked to meet them and joined them under the trees. The conversation was polite and formal for awhile until Jacques finally said, "Gabrielle. Will you accompany me to the community dance on Saturday night? Justine and Joseph are coming so the four of us can be together."

Gabrielle turned first to Justine to see if she had her family's approval to attend and when Justine smiled and nodded, she answered, "I would be pleased to accompany you. Where is this dance and what time should we be ready?"

Arrangements were finalized and the foursome began to walk toward the house. Mrs. Dumont was sitting on the porch and saw them and invited them to dinner that night. It all seemed to Gabrielle that the entire scene had been planned ahead by several parties but since she was happy about it, she made no comment. It was another delicious dinner with interesting conversation but very little politics discussed.

The community dance was a lively affair with fiddle music and singing and dancing. The local country foods were served at a buffet meal at midnight. It seemed that the whole town was there. Mr. and Mrs. Dumont and Sophie attended for a short time but left the party early much to Sophie's displeasure.

The next morning Sophie was waiting impatiently in the hall outside their bedrooms to get the full story on the dance. Justine and Gabrielle could barely get a mouthful of breakfast as Sophie was firing questions one after another and expecting immediate answers.

As was expected of the communities, everyone must go to church on Sunday morning. The priests allowed the local town folk to have Saturday night as a time for fun but all were expected to be at church the next day. Often the party continued on Sunday as residents were already at church. The priests in the local churches felt partying on Sunday was wrong as it was a holy day, and tried to exert this control on the people but often without success.

Gabrielle and Justine stayed at the church for a short time but after lunch retreated to the Dumont home. And to no one's surprise Joseph and Jacques accompanied them.

The next two weeks it seemed Mrs. Dumont had two extra guests at her home as Joseph and Jacques appeared everyday about dinner time. Gabrielle and Jacques quickly fell into a routine of walking around the property. They both told each other of their family life and their hopes and dreams.

"I have a farm near St-Denis along the Richelieu River and right now my brother is taking care of it. I am here near St-Eustache to purchase another farm for my brother Henri. I have a sister who is married and lives on a farm about a day away from St-Denis. The St-Denis farm belonged to my parents who have both died and the farm was left to my brother and me. We are lucky to have made enough money and have a few connections that we can buy another farm. I will return to St-Denis next week after the papers are signed." stated Jacques. "I would really like to see you again but it is so far to Montreal. When I return to St-Denis I will have to do the farm work again so I will not be able to visit here. I might try to convince my brother to let me get his farm started here for him and then I could stay around for awhile to get to know you better."

Gabrielle was somewhat surprised by Jacques' words. She knew she was beginning to fall in love with him but not quite ready to make such a life changing commitment in the next week. "I have to go back to Montreal in a few days and do not feel I can impose on the Dumonts too much longer. I do want to continue seeing you but I must go home and talk to my brother and tell him I think I have met the right person. Can you come to Montreal with Justine and I after you sign the papers for the farm? You can stay with us at my brother's house and then you can meet him."

It seemed complicated but the arrangements were all made and four days later Justine, Gabrielle and Jacques returned to Montreal. The trip seemed to go much faster this time. Gabrielle's brother John met Jacques and it seemed a friendship might just develop between the two men. John was concerned about Gabrielle marrying a farmer as she had spent most of her life living in large cities. He did like Jacques though and could see how much they loved each other.

brother to let me get his farm started here, [illegible] and then I'd still stay around for a while to get to know you better."

Gabrielle was somewhat surprised by Jacques' words. She knew she was beginning to fall in love with him but not quite ready to make such a life changing commitment in the next weeks. "I have to go back to Montreal in a few days and don't feel I can impose on the [illegible] [illegible] seeing you [illegible] [illegible] I think [illegible] [illegible] you sign the papers for the farm [illegible] my brother's house [illegible]."

It seemed [illegible] [illegible] days later [illegible] [illegible] [illegible] [illegible]

FOUR

'OUR LIVES ARE LIKE QUILTS. BITS AND PIECES, JOY AND SORROW, STITCHED TOGETHER WITH LOVE.'

Author unknown

In the few days Jacques spent with Gabrielle in Montreal, their love for each other grew and it wasn't long before they both felt marriage was the next step. One day when Justine was visiting and everyone was at the table finishing dinner, Gabrielle and Jacques announced they would like to be married. John was pleased but wished they would be living closer to Montreal.

"But we are not sure whether to get married here in Montreal or go to St-Denis where we will be living," said Jacques.

"I knew this was to be so I have sent a letter to my Mother," said Justine. "She would like to offer our home to you, so you and Jacques can be married there. You could be married this October when the trees are beautiful and it is not so hot. And you know Sophie will already be planning things."

Gabrielle was overwhelmed. "Oh Justine, your family is so wonderful. How will I ever be able to thank you enough? It is already August so you and I are going to be very busy with all this planning and packing."

John stood and proposed a toast." Here is to the best life together for my sister and my new friend about to be a brother. I will miss you being here in Montreal but know you are where you want to be. May you be happy, prosperous and most of all safe."

Jacques returned to St-Eustache a few days later, and Justine and Gabrielle went into high gear gathering things she would need for her new life on a farm, and of course finding the perfect yet practical outfit for her wedding. There were only a few guests to contact and by the last week of September all Gabrielle's belongings were packed in several trunks and ready to go with her to the Dumont's for the wedding.

She and Justine once again had help loading her things into a carriage and began the journey to the Dumont's home. John would remain in Montreal until a few days before the wedding and then join them.

This time arriving at the Dumont's was more like coming home. It was a joyous reunion with the family and of course Sophie was absolutely thrilled to have Gabrielle back. There was a lot of work to be done to organize food and decorations, but as it was a happy occasion it did not really seem like work.

It was two days until the wedding and it seemed as though, most things were ready for the big day but at breakfast Justine noticed her mother had not come downstairs and asked "Where is Mama?"

"She was still sleeping when I came down so I let her sleep as I know she has been working very hard these past few weeks. Sophie you run up and see if Mama is awake yet."

Sophie left the room and went upstairs but she returned immediately looking quite pale and with tears in her eyes. "Mama will not wake up even though I shook her."

In an instant everyone including the maid was running up to the bedroom. Mr. Dumont entered the room and came out giving instructions to everyone. "Call the Dr. Get some cool water as she is running a temperature. You girls are not allowed in the room or near her for the next while."

Gabrielle and Justine took Sophie, who was crying back down to the breakfast room and tried to calm her. "Is she going to die?"

"We certainly hope not. She may just have a cold." Justine assured Sophie but when she looked at Gabrielle, they both gave each other a nod as though they could read each other's minds. They were worried about cholera.

The rest of the day there were people coming and going delivering things for the wedding and taking things up to Mrs. Dumont. The Dr. eventually came and did not really know what she had but thought it was not cholera. Mrs. Dumont was now awake and resting in bed but was only drinking warm tea when she was forced to. She still had a slight fever so everyone was still quite worried about her.

That evening Justine moved Sophie's bed into her room so she would not have to sleep alone in her room. The three women sat on Justine's bed until it was almost midnight talking about everything that had happened. They tried to keep the conversation light for Sophie's sake but once she asleep, Justine and Gabrielle moved to the other room and expressed their fears to each other. "I am so afraid she will not get better," said Justine. "I do not know what I will do or what Sophie will do without her."

"We must stay positive about her recovery. We can postpone the wedding if it is absolutely necessary. Possibly we could find other places for guests to stay rather than here. Maybe my brother could stay with Joseph and if the hotel in town is ok the other guests could stay there. There really are only about five guests who do not live here." remarked Gabrielle. "We could set up a dormitory in the old monastery." They both laughed.

The next day Mrs. Dumont seemed a bit better and as she had started giving orders about what needed to be done, everyone figured she was getting better. Mr. Dumont would not let her out of bed and would definitely not let Justine, Sophie or Gabrielle visit her.

That evening as it was the night before the wedding, the dinner planned was scaled back to just the two families and Joseph. Mrs. Dumont was still not allowed out of bed and although she tried to say she was fine and could come to dinner, she did not protest when told she had to stay in bed and get her rest for tomorrow.

The party ended early and Gabrielle and Jacques took a stroll toward the river." I am so glad we will be going to your new farm for awhile after we are married. That way we can return here and visit with Mrs. Dumont while she recovers. No one seems to know what she has but thank goodness it doesn't seem to be really serious."

Jacques wrapped his arm around Gabrielle to keep her warm and replied, "Mrs. Dumont is a strong healthy woman and seems able to fight off any germs that have come her way. No one else seems to be ill so I think we escaped something serious. Tomorrow is our wedding day and I know it will be perfect. You can dream tonight about our new life together first in St- Eustache and later in St-Denis." Jacques drew Gabrielle close and kissed her. They both wanted to stay in the embrace forever but knew they had to get back to the house and since it was now October, the nights were getting colder.

Gabrielle awoke before dawn and suddenly realized this was her wedding day. She laid in bed thinking about all the preparations that were complete and the wonderful time it would be at her wedding party. She was also quite excited to become the wife of Jacques St-Pierre and begin a new life as a farmer's wife. Having a wedding in September was highly unusual in Lower Canada as most weddings took place in January or February. October was the height of the harvest season and every day without rain was a gift for the farmer. Jacques did not have any crops on his new farm yet and since only a few people were invited to the wedding they did not feel they would be inconveniencing too many people.

The door suddenly burst open and instantly Sophie was bouncing on the bed with Justine close behind. "I have just been to see Mother and she is so much better today. She promises to stay in bed until 10 and then will get ready for the wedding," Justine announced.

"Wonderful," said Gabrielle. "Now let's go and have some breakfast as I am starving. I think we should go down to the breakfast room wearing our dressing robes as it would be silly to get dressed and then have to dress again for the wedding."

Over breakfast all the wedding details of the location, the guests' arrival and the food were discussed and finalized until everyone was happy and sure the whole day would be perfect. It was time to go and dress in their wedding finery.

At precisely 11 o'clock on Monday, October 10th 1830, Gabrielle Drummond walked into the parlour of the Dumont home near St-Eustache to wed Jacques St-Pierre. The twelve guests were seated around the room. Jacques, Justine and Joseph stood at the front with the priest. Sophie was seated in the front row beside her mother and father. The entire room turned to watch as Gabrielle walked to the front holding onto her brother's arm.

Gabrielle had chosen a day dress to wear today. The dress had a scooped neckline with large pleats starting from the shoulder seams. The folds of fine cream coloured cotton crossed the bodice diagonally and ended at the V-shaped waistline. The fabric had rose coloured flowers printed in an overall floral pattern on the cream background. The skirt also had tiny gathers at the waist flowing to the floor giving it a very full skirt. The sleeves were fitted to just above the elbow and then flowed into a large puff until gathered at the cuff. The overall look was that of a summer breeze blowing through a garden. Gabrielle had pinned her hair up loosely with curls falling at the side and the back. She was a vision of beauty.

When Jacques first saw Gabrielle enter the room, he gasped. "She is so beautiful. How can I be so lucky?" he whispered to Joseph.

The wedding vows were spoken, the priest gave his blessing on the marriage and everyone cheered congratulating the happy couple. The newlyweds signed the marriage contract Jacques St-Pierre and Gabrielle Drummond as was the custom in this part of the country. The wedding party went outside to talk to their guests while the dinner was being set up in the dining room. The party was about to begin.

The wedding custom in Lower Canada had the bride and groom and the guests celebrating at the wedding venue. But then for three or four days everyone would travel by carriage or sleigh from house to house in the area. At each place the newlyweds would be asked to sing a song and then the partying would continue.

Since it was October, this did not happen for Jacques and Gabrielle. They would stay tonight at the Dumont home and then travel to Jacques' new farm. There was a house on the property that needed a bit of work that Jacques wanted to complete before Henri moved there. By late October they hoped to be in St-Denis and Henri would be at St-Eustache.

"This is the start of our new life together," whispered Gabrielle as she seated herself in the carriage next to Jacques. She had changed into suitable travelling clothes and they were surrounded by boxes and wooden crates of food, clothing and crates of other supplies that would be needed over the next month. Jacques just smiled as he put his arm around her.

Mrs. Dumont was standing at the end of the walkway next to the carriage. She looked much better today, but tiredness was quickly overtaking her. "We will see you in a month when you come back to gather all your things. We will have them all packed and ready to go but you must stay a few days before you leave."

"I will come from Montreal when you come back here so we can visit," Justine added. Gabrielle's brother stepped close to the carriage and spoke softly to his sister. "You must keep in touch with me both in St-Eustache and when you arrive in St-Denis. There is some trouble brewing in some villages and I want the two of you to be safe. I will possibly have information about what is happening."

Gabrielle promised they would and gave her brother a quick kiss goodbye. Everyone began waving and wishing them a wonderful trip as Jacques flicked the reins and the carriage left the property and headed north to cross the river.

FIVE

'FALL SEVEN TIMES, STAND UP EIGHT.'

Japanese Proverb

Sean and Clara were beginning to enjoy their new life in St-Denis. The farm was situated along the Richelieu River and ran south away from the river in a narrow strip. Jacques St-Pierre grew some wheat and hay. He had about a dozen cows but the number fluctuated with new calves being born and others being sold. The farm also had three horses, a flock of chickens and a number of pigs. Clara was never able to count all the pigs as the piglets ran around too fast and she could never be sure she was counting some twice. The farm was self sufficient with food for the animals and the family. Gabrielle also had a large vegetable garden giving the family fresh food in the summer and preserved food in the winter. There was also an orchard on the property with several varieties of apples.

Clara liked to get up early and sit with Gabrielle as she fed the babies. When Sean and Clara arrived at the St-Pierre farm, the twins were just six months old. The twins, Elodie and Julie, were not identical so it was easy to tell them apart. They were quite content and only cried when hungry. They were starting to notice things around them and were quite taken with Clara as she talked and sang to them whenever they were awake. Now that the girls were starting to eat food other than milk, Clara was a great help sharing the feeding duties with Gabrielle. One day while feeding the girls Gabrielle said "Clara, you can't keep calling me Mrs. St-Pierre all the time. You can call me Gabrielle or any name you wish. I know I am not your mother but you can call me Mama if you wish."

Clara was so touched by this moment tears welled up in her eyes. She truly loved Gabrielle but wasn't sure she was ready to call her mother. "What if I call you Mama as you are my French Mother?"

"I would be pleased if you called me Mama. When the girls are older it will be easy for them to understand as well."

Clara always felt this was a special day in her new life as she felt accepted into her new family. At that moment Elodie began blowing bubbles with her porridge and Clara found her face spattered in the gluey liquid. "You are part of the family now," laughed Gabrielle.

Clara's days were filled with indoor and outdoor work. She liked gathering vegetables and apples and also enjoyed helping cook some meals for the family. She did not like gathering eggs as chickens often pecked your hand. Gabrielle smiled. "My friend Justine has a sister who says the same thing about chickens." The eggs were a great thing to have though if you wanted to bake a cake or a pudding.

As the twins grew it was Clara who spent time watching them progress from crawling to walking. She read them stories and played games with them. She taught the girls many new words as they walked outside looking at the world around them. Clara did wonder though why she and Sean did not go to school.

One day she asked Gabrielle, "Mama why do I not have to go to school here? Will I get in trouble for not attending school?"

"Oh Clara I should have told you before. We do not have a school here in our village. Many children never learn to read or write and only know what their parents tell them. They should go to school but the local authorities do not feel it is necessary. Most children grow up to be farmers and farmers wives just like their parents. When I was young I went to school and continued learning for many years. I can tell you have gone to a school as well as you already know how to read. I will ask my brother to find us some books and send them to us so you can continue to learn subjects like Mathematics and English and French. I will help you with the work. Then when the girls are older you can teach them. You can ask Sean if he wants to have some books to learn new things as well."

Clara was excited about the new books that would arrive from Montreal. When she asked Sean, he shrugged and muttered," I don't have time for book learning. Jacques is teaching me everything I need to know and anyway, I am teaching him more English and he is teaching me French."

Sean's life was good but busy as well. There was a lot of work to do on the farm and some seasons were busier than others. Sean and Clara had arrived midsummer when everything was growing at peak speed. Sean learned to cut hay and stack it in the barn. He was quite good at driving the horse and wagon now. He could milk six cows without his hands getting tired and in almost the same time as Jacques. He had accepted Jacques' invitation to call him by his first name and within a few months the two of them worked as a team almost reading each other's minds. His favourite job was walking behind the horses with a plow. One day Jacques was watching at the edge of the field. "You are one of the best plowmen in the township. Those furrows are nice and straight and just the right depth for the wheat seeds."

"I had a good teacher," smiled Sean. "Besides this horse could plow the field by herself she's done it so many times."

When Sean and Jacques worked together repairing equipment, Jacques took the time to explain what he was doing and why. Sean was careful to listen and enjoyed it when he was given a chance to do the repair with Jacques watching. Only once did Jacques get angry and yell at Sean. Sean had left the door to the pigsty unhooked and the pigs pushed the gate open and escaped to the garden. Jacques had warned him to always hook the wire to shut the gate when he went into the pen, but Sean forgot. It took great effort to round up the pigs and get them back into the pen. Then Jacques made Sean go to the house and tell Gabrielle why her garden was a bit of a mess. Gabrielle quietly thought it was funny but made Sean carry all the water into the house for laundry and then go and repair the mess in the garden. Sean always remembered after that. That night at dinner Jacques asked Sean, "Do you think you will become a pig farmer when you have your own place?" Everyone laughed. "No pigs on my farm," said Sean.

Life continued in a predictable routine on the little farm. Occasionally several men from neighbouring farms would stop by to talk to Jacques. Jacques never indicated to Sean that he should leave them alone, so he stayed and listened carefully. They all spoke French and spoke so quickly that Sean could not understand every word so did not really pick up the gist of the conversation. After they left, Sean asked, "I understood a few words but I am not sure what they were discussing. What does Patriot mean and are the men angry at the British or just the Governor?"

Sean and Jacques continued cleaning out the stalls and putting new bedding down for the horses. Jacques began explaining the reason for the anger in Lower Canada. "The habitants who farm here in the Richelieu Valley are beginning to be angry at their treatment, not only by the local authorities and the priests, but by the government in Montreal. My friend George was elected to the Assembly representing us from this area, but everything the members of the Assembly suggest or ask for is always turned down by the legislative council. They follow the orders of the Governor. He is in charge of giving the province money for roads or improvements to buildings or schools to teach the children. He takes his orders from the King who has no idea what life is like here and really doesn't even care. Many of us are beginning to form groups who will fight together if we have to so improvements can be made. We call ourselves Patriots and you can tell who we are by our clothes. You have seen me wear my big grey coat and red striped scarf around my waist. I also sometimes wear a blue hat. That is the dress of a Patriot. When you are a bit older I hope you will join us as a Patriot. There are some farmers who are Loyalists in this area and believe the King is doing the right thing, but they are not in the majority and often find trouble following them."

"But I am Irish and came from Britain. Am I considered a Loyalist?"

"You are part of my family now so you don't need to worry unless you think the King did the right thing by letting your family starve in Ireland. Gabrielle is also from Britain originally but feels the King and his friends in high places here are not really helping the habitants in Lower Canada. People around St-Denis know Gabrielle and know what she stands for so she is safe and so are you and Clara. You should try and speak French whenever you are around others and you should have no problems."

"I see. I think I am getting better at French. What kind of trouble happens to the Loyalists?"

"Often at night some Patriots have gone to Loyalist houses and demanded money from them or destroyed some properties or have shaved off the tails and manes of their horses. The horse then has no way of swatting away flies and bugs so goes crazy and can't work. It is mean. It started as a way of humiliating a couple who married but were mismatched as one being a lot older than the other. They called it charivari. If they paid money and gave the group refreshments it was ok. If not the public humiliation continued. Now though some groups are targeting some local authorities who may not have the best interest of the habitant in mind. I do not like to get involved with these young men and you would be wise to not go with them either. They often have too much to drink and their actions can get out of control. Just before you arrived, they ended up burning a farmer's barn because he did not give them as much money as they wanted. Now let's get this load of manure down to the river to dump it before dark."

The Habitants of Lower Canada were in the habit of dumping the manure from their animals in the river. This was a practise they had always followed. No one had told them that if they spread it on the land it would help fertilize their crops. As a result their crops were small with lower yields. No fertilizer and no crop rotation would lead to huge problems in the next few years for the habitants.

One day in late summer, a traveller in a carriage stopped by the St-Pierre farm. He had come from Montreal and was on his way to

Quebec City. The road past the farm was the only road along the Richelieu River. In summer if it was dry, the road was dusty with ruts which made for a bumpy ride; but in rain and snow the road became a muddy slippery mess with holes filling up with water. The soil was heavy clay that stuck to everything that touched it. Boots often had an extra few pounds added to them as the clay stuck to the bottom. Today was a dry day so there was only dust to deal with.

The gentleman in the carriage was well dressed and very polite in asking if this was the home of the Jacques St-Pierre. Gabrielle assured him it was and invited him into the house. He was carrying a large package wrapped in brown paper and sat it on the floor at the door. He also had a letter which he handed to Gabrielle. "This actually has your name on the envelope and not your husbands," he stated with surprise.

"It must be from my brother in Montreal," she said and took the letter from him. Gabrielle wanted to open it immediately but reluctantly laid it on the table as she made tea for Mr. Gagnon. "Do you know my brother John Drummond?"

"No Madame I do not. I only met him when I picked up the parcel at his office."

Mr. Gagnon was not a great conversationalist so the next twenty minutes trying to engage him in any kind of talk was difficult. Gabrielle was almost pleased when he announced, "I must be on my way as I am expected at Sorel by tonight so I can catch the morning ferry across the river. Thank you for the tea and I hope this parcel is what you wanted." And he was out the door and back to his carriage as quick as lightning.

"I was hoping to find out some news from Montreal but that did not happen. Maybe my brother has sent interesting news. These must be the books we asked for. Clara you open the package while I read the letter."

Dearest Gabrielle

I hope you are all well at the farm. I am well but am beginning to worry about the state of health of the city of Montreal. As you may or may not know Mr.

Papineau has been stirring things up. He feels he is the leader of the French. He is a newly made aristocrat and a proud but stubborn man. He is an eloquent speaker and is very believable to the public. About eighty percent of the population of Lower Canada is French so he has a willing audience. He is constantly asking the government for more of the share and government reform for Lower Canada. He is very much a thorn in the side of the council as there is talk of Papineau as leader of the French Party or the Papineau Party as it is now being called.

The council though had other ideas and George Moffatt, who is my boss here in Montreal, decided that as this was a British Colony, the authority of the British Government must be restored once and for all. We are to have an election in Montreal in the new year and much is being written in the papers about how the council works here in favor of the elite. Two reporters in particular support Papineau and I am afraid for their welfare if they continue this way. I will keep you informed as to what happens. Are the farmers in your area in favor of Papineau or do they know what is happening? Keep your ears to the ground for any indication of trouble.

There are still ships coming into port carrying people ill with cholera. It is really terrible and many friends have left for their country homes. It was a miracle that Sean and Clara did not pick up cholera while on that dreadful ship. They may have been lucky they were at the beginning of the outbreak. I hope they are doing fine and I am pleased to hear they wanted the books I can always send more if you need them.

Justine has left the city and is living at home with her parents. She is fine and wishes you were closer for visits. I suspect she and Joseph will be engaged soon.

I am considering leaving the city within the next year if the situation continues to deteriorate. I will of course let you know where I am going. Maybe back to York.

Keep safe and all my best to the whole family.
Your Loving Brother John

~

After reading the letter from John, Gabrielle became very quiet. With tears in her eyes and a lump in her throat, she said to Clara, "I really do miss talking to my brother. Like you Clara he is the only one left from my original family. I know I have Jacques and all of the rest of you and I love everyone dearly but a brother or sister is special. I am worried about where he will go and how far away he will be if he goes to York. What if the situation here continues to worsen? Where will be safe? I need to write him a letter and ask if he knows the safest place for us to go if we have to. I always said John was the one who worried about things so the rest of us did not have to. Now listen to me. I am doing it too."

Gabrielle looked over at Clara and saw the tears in her eyes. "But you must not worry about this. Where ever we go, you and Sean will always come with us. Now tell me what books my brother has sent to us? Which one will we start with?" Just then the babies started crying as they were waking from a nap. School would have to start tomorrow.

Later that night Gabrielle showed the letter to Jacques and added, "I will write to John and ask him if he knows anyone in the Richelieu Valley where we might go if we have to leave here. I do not want to stay here with the children if there is going to be fighting."

"That might be a good idea, but I don't think this dissatisfaction will come to fighting. The government do not want to bring troops here to stop the speeches and arguments. And the habitants are no match for the British troops. We have very few guns and no experience for fighting. Hopefully Papineau and his friends will tone down their speeches and not continue to rile up the habitants as they have been."

Life continued as it had for the past few years on the St-Pierre farm. Winter arrived in early November with very cold temperatures and heavy snow seemed to fall every other day. Jacques hitched his horse to the sleigh but it was tough going for the horses to travel through the deep snow. The family stayed indoors except to go out to fetch water from the well and to feed the animals. They had enough food for the winter to keep them going as Gabrielle and Clara had preserved beans and beets in crockery pots. There were barrels of apples stored in the cellar along with potatoes and turnips. There would be some meat as well during the winter when Jacques and Sean slaughtered an animal as needed.

Christmas was quiet at the farm as the snow was now waist deep and no one travelled anywhere. Gabrielle and Jacques decided it was smarter to skip midnight mass on Christmas Eve as they did not want to get stranded in a snow bank with the children. Clara has made a stuffed toy for each girl. She used some fabric from a dress that she had grown out of and stuffed it with a worn out towel. The girls loved it and soon it became their constant companion. Clara had also stitched a quote she found in one of the books and surrounded it with hearts for Gabrielle and Jacques. Sean had repaired a broken shovel that Jacques said was worthless. When Jacques saw it he was almost speechless but quickly added "I have another pile of worthless things that you are welcome to fix if you want to."

Gabrielle and Jacques had given Sean a sharp knife in a sheath that he could use on the farm. For Clara, Gabrielle discovered a comb in her things that had belonged to her mother and thought Clara might like this to hold her hair back. Clara was thrilled and felt very honored and very grown up. There were small practical gifts of clothing for the girls that Gabrielle knew they needed. Despite the weather, it was a happy time as there were special treats of food only eaten at Christmas. Christmas songs were sung as Jacques accompanied them on his fiddle and Sean attempted to play the spoons. It had been many years since Clara and Sean had remembered a Christmas as happy as this one.

1832 ended on a happy note for the family, but in the valley there was anger, discontent, calls for reform, poverty, and hardships. Men were worried about rebellion and women were worried about having enough food to feed their children. The men in government were all trying to exert their authority and power and control while Britain was attempting to control the country from across an ocean. The next few years would certainly be interesting times.

Spring finally did arrive in the Richelieu Valley but it was early May before the farmers could plant their crops. The heavy snow of the previous winter had left the fields wet and muddy. Several times Jacques had attempted to try plowing the fields but the horse became stuck in the mud and the walking plow was useless. When some of the fields on higher ground did dry up enough to get on the land, the clay had turned as hard as rock and the plow seemed to bounce off the soil instead of cutting through it.

The flies and mosquitoes were thick this spring bothering both the horses and the men. One evening when Sean and Jacques came into the house for dinner, Sean's one eye was swollen shut and he had large red welts on his face and neck. "What happened to you," asked Gabrielle?

"The bugs are biting anything that is out there," replied Jacques. "I have been bitten so many times they don't seem to bother me anymore, but Sean is fresh food for these beasts. Can you make a poultice with oatmeal for him to put on the spots? It will help take the itch out. I have never seen so many bugs out there. I hope they end soon or they will be eating the crops."

June arrived and with it came more agony for the farmers of Lower Canada. The crops were planted late that year and by midsummer the hay was still too short to cut. Only some of the wheat had formed a head and the wheat flies and caterpillars were eating it as fast as it formed. The kitchen gardens were struggling as well with most of the vegetables being devoured by pests. The animals were suffering because of lack of food and the results ranged from little milk from the cattle to not much wool to shear from the sheep.

Most of the farmers still did not practise rotating their crops as the new English immigrants were doing. They also did not fertilize their fields so the nutrients in the soil were depleted giving poor crops. Farmers are always at the mercy of the weather and 1833 there was a recurring cycle of floods and droughts and in parts of Lower Canada below Quebec City and the harvest was a complete failure. Some people had enough food to live on until the next harvest, some would be starving by spring and some were already starving. Many abandoned their farms and moved to other parts of Lower Canada just to survive. To make matters worse cholera returned killing many. This dreadful life continued for the Habitants for the next three years and crept down from Quebec to the Richelieu Valley and toward Montreal. It was a cycle of crop failure, illness and starvation.

Jacques and Gabrielle were by no means wealthy farmers but Jacques had watched some of the new English Immigrants and in discussions had learned about crop rotation. He still hung on to some of the old habitant methods but his crops did better for a few years and he was able to store away some grain and hay for the animals. Gabrielle preserved as much food as she could so they were not about to starve for a few years.

One day in the fall of 1834 a young boy stopped in at their farm. Jacques was just coming from the barn to the house when he saw him standing beside the house.

"Can I help you," asked Jacques?

"Could you spare some food?"

"Yes come with me to the house. How far have you walked today and what is your name?"

"My Name is Louis. I lived farther down the river but my family have all died from the sickness going around. I have walked for three days but no one has any food to spare. I could work on your farm if you need any help."

Jacques was not sure if he should take Louis into the house as his family had likely died of cholera. There were the twins and Sean and Clara to think about and now Gabrielle was pregnant as well.

"Sit here by the well. Wash up a bit and I will bring some food to you."

Jacques went inside to tell Gabrielle about the boy.

"We must feed him and he could help you and Sean with the harvest if there is one this year."

"I would feel better if I fixed up a spot in the barn for him to stay for awhile until we get to know him better and to make sure he does not get ill," said Jacques.

Gabrielle had fixed a plate of food for Louis while they were talking and sent it out with Jacques. She then went and found an extra blanket for him to take to the barn. Clara and Sean quietly looked on as all this was happening. They were remembering sleeping in the barn at Jacques' sister's house and coming here to stay after their parents had died.

Jacques watched as Louis quickly ate the food. He decided to wait until Louis finished before asking him any more questions as he could see how hungry Louis was.

Louis thanked Jacques several times for the food and did not seem surprised that he would have to sleep in the barn. He accepted the blanket and walked with Jacques where he was directed to the hay loft that was to be his bed for the night.

The next morning when Jacques went out to fetch some water from the well, there was Louis sitting beside the pump waiting for his work orders for the day.

Jacques went back inside brought him out some bread and coffee and began asking Louis what he knew about farming. It looked like he had a new farm hand and maybe a new member of the family.

Louis was a hard worker but remained quiet around Jacques and Sean. As they worked Jacques and Sean often discussed what they were doing, how to accomplish the job in the best way and sometimes what was happening around the countryside.

Jacques was shovelling some grain into the granary and said, "My brother near St-Eustache was speaking to Joseph, who is a friend, awhile back and he heard that Papineau had written some resolutions that they want the British government to look at and change some of the ways they govern Lower Canada. It lists all our complaints and apparently Papineau has collected a large number of signatures agreeing with it. Of course the British government as well as the Governor in Quebec disagree. The Assembly passed the resolutions but the Governor was so angry he ended the parliament so now nothing is getting done. Now the English communities are organizing military units to preserve their connections to Britain. Some of the Patriots and friends of Papineau are calling for us to be a separate French Nation."

"Does that mean we are going to have to fight the British," asked Sean?

"I sure hope not as we do not know nearly as much about fighting as the British do. There are meeting and gatherings in the valley where the Patriots are talking and planning but I'm not sure how organized they are. I may go to visit a friend tomorrow to see what he knows. You and Louis will be in charge of the farm tomorrow. Do you think you both are able to do the work without me?"

Before Sean could answer, Louis said, "I know we can do it. Sean knows lots and I have been watching both of you. I helped my Papa run our farm before the crops failed. You don't need to worry about us."

"For sure Jacques," replied Sean. He felt comfortable being around Louis and this would be the first time the two of them would have a chance to work just by themselves.

Louis still stayed in the barn at night, and he had moved some things around in an unused horse stall to create a room for himself. Gabrielle had said he could move into the house but he liked his private space. He might change his mind when it got cold, but for now he was happy. He wasn't sure that fighting the British was a good idea, but he did think some changes needed to happen to help out the habitants in the valley. Right now he was feeling really happy. He thought Sean was a good friend and tomorrow they would work together, and he knew Jacques liked him and trusted him enough to leave him alone for the day. He still missed his parents and his old life but he felt he had been lucky to find the St-Pierre farm.

Louis was lying in his bed, trying to go to sleep that night, but his mind was racing. He was thinking about how he really could not defend himself if he was somehow left alone and there was trouble. Finally it came to him. He would go back to his family farm and see if his father's gun was still in the barn. He had often seen it there when working in the barn but never had the courage to ask his father to show him how to use it. If he could find it and bring it here Jacques would likely help him learn to shoot. Now he would just have to find the right time to return to the family home.

SIX

'FAMILY MEANS NO ONE GETS LEFT BEHIND OR FORGOTTEN.'

George Bernard Shaw

"Let's go girls. We have to get dressed this morning so we can help with chores around the house," Clara said as she tried to convince the twins they could dress themselves. "Let's name the pieces we put on. I will say a word and you have to find that piece of clothing and put it on." Sometimes Julie and Elodie who were almost three years old became silly together and it was hard work to get them to do anything. Clara knew Gabrielle was going to have the baby before the end of the year so she really tried to help as much as she could. Today Jacques would not be there so she must remind Sean or Louis to bring in water from the well. It would be a busy day. When the girls were finally dressed, Clara took them down to get their breakfast.

"Gabrielle. Are you all right?"

Gabrielle was lying on the day bed by the stove. "I am fine but I think we may have a new baby by the end of the day. My labour started just after Jacques left so he does not know. It was too late to send one of the boys after him. You and I will have to do this but we could send for Mrs. Simard who lives a few miles down the road. She has delivered lots of babies."

"I will find Sean and send him. Louis does not know her." Clara sat the girls at the table and gave them some bread to eat while she went to find Sean.

Sean was soon on his way down the road as fast as he dared. He had hitched the horse to the wagon so the neighbour could ride back with him. He was glad that Jacques had just taken a horse and left the wagon. This was not turning out to be the day he had planned.

By the time Sean returned home, Clara had the girls playing with their dolls and Gabrielle had moved up to the bedroom. He was amazed that Clara had prepared some food for meals and had lots of water boiling on the stove. Mrs. Simard had followed him to the farm in her own wagon accompanied by her husband as it might be late by the time the baby was born. Apparently one never knew how long it would take. "Is there anything you need like water or more wood for the stove Clara," asked Sean.

"No. Louis has been great bringing things in all morning. You need to have some lunch and take some for Louis as well. He didn't ask for any the last time he was in."

Mrs. Simard went up to see Gabrielle and her husband followed Sean to the barn. The rest of the afternoon dragged slowly in the house. Clara could hear some moans from the upstairs bedroom every so often and as dinner time approached the frequency and intensity increased. Fortunately it was a warm fall day so Clara and the girls spent most of the afternoon outside playing in the leaves. They made leaf houses, big piles to jump in and gathered the best coloured ones to take inside. Clara asked Sean to watch the girls outside for a few minutes while she went in to prepare dinner.

As she entered the kitchen, Mrs. Simard rushed downstairs. "There is a new baby girl in the family. She is fine but very tiny so we need lots of warm blankets to keep her warm. Gabrielle is fine, just tired. I will stay for awhile to make sure they are fine, but we must not leave too late."

Clara was thrilled and quickly ran upstairs with blankets to see Gabrielle and the baby. She had never seen such a tiny baby before and was amazed at how she was perfect despite being so small. "Do you have a name for her?"

"Jacques and I have thought of a few but I think we will wait until he gets back to actually pick a name. Could you bring me a cup of tea and a small piece of bread please Clara and thank you for being so good with the girls and for taking care of the house today? Sean and Louis took care of the farm all day. The three of you are quite a team."

Clara went back downstairs to make some tea bursting with pride. She was quite happy living here with the St-Pierre's. After taking food up to Gabrielle, she hurried outside to tell Julie and Elodie and Sean and Louis they had a new sister. She and the girls danced a little dance and then went inside for dinner. It was a cold dinner of leftovers but tonight the five of them and Mr. and Mrs. Simard didn't seem to mind as everyone was happy.

The Simards left for their home down the road, Clara prepared the girls for bedtime and the boys went off to the barn to settle the animals in for the night.

Before putting the girls in their beds, Clara took Julie and Elodie in to see the baby. They were speechless and just stared at their new sister. "Doll," asked Elodie?

"No a baby, said Gabrielle. "Now you and Julie will have to be the big sisters."

"Like Clara," replied Julie.

After kisses from their Mother and being allowed to softly touch the baby's arm, the girls trundled off to bed. Tonight was a good night and hopefully the girls would continue their love for their new sister.

Clara was up early the next morning as she had to do everything in the house for the next few days. Gabrielle was up as well but she sat in a chair and answered Clara's questions about where things were and how to make certain foods. Shortly after lunch Jacques returned from visiting his friend. Clara and the girls were outside playing and when they saw him, they rushed over and started saying "Baby, baby."

Jacques wasn't quite sure if he understood them and looked at Clara.

"Yes. They are right. There is a new baby in the house. A nice surprise for you."

Before Clara could add more, Jacques was up the steps two at a time and inside the house. There he found Gabrielle rocking the baby. "I thought the baby wasn't due until December. Is everyone good? Is it a boy or a girl? I am so sorry I wasn't here."

"We have a new daughter and she came early. She is very little but Mrs. Simard who came to help thinks she will be fine. She has a loud cry and she seems hungry. You had been gone about a half hour when I realized the baby was coming. You would be so proud of Clara, Sean and Louis. They took control of everything and we all survived quite nicely. Now we must decide which name we will choose as we can't keep calling her baby."

"Let's call her Marie after your Mother and after Clara's Mother."

"I like that name. Go and tell Clara and the girls to come in so we can tell them. I think the boys are at the barn. There seems to be a great camaraderie between the boys these past few days."

The next few days were very busy for everyone. Clara kept the girls busy and helped Gabrielle with housework. There was a lot more laundry to do now. Little Marie was a hungry baby and cried loudly about every two or three hour. Whenever the crying started Julie and Elodie covered their ears and ran to another room. Fortunately when the baby cried in the night, the girls did not wake up. During the day both Gabrielle and Clara were gathering the last of the ripened vegetable and preserving and storing them for winter.

"We do not have as much stored as last year and we have one more mouth to feed this winter," remarked Gabrielle while loading apples into a barrel. "I hope we have a better year next summer. No one has any extra to sell this year either."

Jacques and Sean and Louis were working at getting the last of the harvest cut and into the barn for winter. Sean was grinding some grain into course flour to use for making bread. It was a hard job but it had to be done. The local mill had closed as not many farmers had enough grain to take to the mill to be ground. Louis was stripping the kernels from the plant and putting them in the grinder for Sean. Every so often they would trade jobs but it was a slow process. The end product was not the fine white flour Gabrielle used to make bread in previous years, but it would have to do. The bread she baked now came out a dirty gray colour and was much heavier than before. It still tasted like bread though so no one was complaining.

While Louis was taking his turn at the grinder, he turned to Jacques and asked. "Did you find out any new information from your friend the other day?"

Jacques did not answer right away but then slowly began to tell the boys what he found out.

"My friend told me that many of the habitants who now call themselves Patriots are very distressed about the way some francophones, who are part of a group, are trying to control the politics of the area. There was some violence at the polls where an election was taking place at St-Andrews which is an English settlement to the west. The English side thought they had won and a fight broke out which brought in reinforcements from both sides. After a lengthy standoff of several days, the English side finally conceded, but there are hard feelings on both sides. Everyone knows who their enemy is now and they all remember who did what. There is a group in St-Eustache called the Constitutionalists who are the ruling bureaucrats and enjoy the position of privilege. They are French but they feel superior to the habitants and want to keep them out of any position of power. No one is very organized at this point but there are bad feelings and talk of forming groups to help the minorities in the province. It does not help that so many crops have failed this year. Many farmers are leaving their farms and walking to Montreal. Also cholera has returned and it is very bad in Montreal. We just have to stick together here and hope next year is better. But you must be careful what you say to neighbours as you never know what side they are on."

Both boys were amazed at what Jacques had told them. They did not fully understand the political structure, but trusted Jacques that he would know what to do if trouble ever came to St-Denis.

The winter came early that year and by December the snow drifts had filled in the roads and often reached to roof of the house. Digging out of the house was a ritual each morning and digging to get into the barn followed. Jacques taught the boys to take hot water from the stove in the kitchen and pour some down the pipes in the well to unfreeze it so they could get water for the house and the animals. Louis had moved into the house when Jacques and Gabrielle insisted it was too cold to stay in the barn.

Clara had unraveled some wool from an old sweater and had knit a sweater and hat for the baby. She had even knit stockings for her to wear at night and all day. Julie and Elodie were wearing coats inside the house made from several pieces of clothing they had outgrown. It was a good thing for them to grow, but it meant being very creative keeping them clothed. Most of their day was spent close to the wood burning stove in the kitchen. At night the twin girls always slept together, but lately they had been coming into Clara's room and crawling into her bed and cuddling up close. Clara didn't mind as the three of them created more heat than one person could. Clara taught the girls how to put their clothes close to the bed so they could grab them in the morning and put them in the bed to warm them up. The tricky part was trying to get dressed in bed. Socks and stockings were always the hardest part. Everyone was usually laughing and in a good mood by the time they were dressed and raced down to the warm kitchen for breakfast.

There were some worrying things happening on the farm though this winter as well. One morning Louis and Sean came in from the barn and announced," One of the calves is dead this morning. It was in the pen with the other calves. It looks like it froze to death."

Louis continued, "We dragged it out but just left it outside the pen as we weren't sure what to do with it. You don't think it had something else do you Jacques?"

"You boys eat your breakfast and then come back out to the barn. I will go out now and take a look." Jacques gave a bewildered and worried look to Gabrielle but said nothing. He just finished his coffee, rose from the table, walked to the door, bundled up and went outside.

In the barn Jacques inspected the calf. It had seemed healthy the day before. He poked the animal and it was not quite frozen solid which meant it had died very early in the morning. The big question now was whether it should be thrown outside waiting to be buried in the spring, or could it be ground up and used for animal feed. There was no way he would take a chance and use it to feed his family, but if it truly had just frozen to death then it could be added to the feed for the pigs.

Sean and Louis appeared in the barn door and watched Jacques as he tried to pry open the mouth of the dead animal. Louis jumped right in and helped Jacques. Sean though remained at the door and looked on. He had not seen a dead animal before and wasn't sure he wanted to be close to it. After a few minutes, Jacques decided to dispose of the animal and not take any chances. He didn't want to lose any of the pigs this winter either. "Let's carry the carcass out to the manure pile for now. We can't do any digging now. We need to check the calves carefully over the next few days to make sure none of them seem sick. I should probably separate them but then they would freeze to death so it's best they stay together in this pen."

The bitterly cold winter continued. Christmas and New Year's joy was scarce and there was little visiting during the usually festive season. The only way to travel was by horse and sleigh but the heavy snows made it difficult for the horses to plough their way through. Everyone in the Richelieu Valley seemed to hunkering down in their homes hoping to have enough food to eat and wood for heating until spring arrived.

An early spring was not to be though. Cold rain continued on through May keeping the farmers off the fields. Only the bugs seemed to flourish. Mosquitoes were biting anything and everyone. Worms were spinning their nests in the trees and bushes and eating the leaves as fast as they emerged. The farmers were very worried about another year of poor crops or worse.

Unfortunately the habitants in Lower Canada would have to endure this repeating cycle well into 1837. Many farmers gave up and walked away hoping to find work in either Quebec City or Montreal. Both cities were also experiencing a poor economy as well as overpopulation. Many people were living on the street begging for food to keep them alive. Cholera had returned and claimed a record number of lives. Life was not good for the residents of Lower Canada.

When the calendar finally said it was summer, it was still rainy and not overly warm. One day that looked like the sun might stay out all day, Gabrielle announced, "Girls today we are packing a picnic and going to a meeting at Mrs. Simard's home. The women in the valley are meeting to talk about how we can help our farms survive. I have made our lunch so Clara, find some sweaters for you and the girls and we will be off in the wagon. Sean is bringing it to the house for us."

Clara was totally surprised. "Are the other mothers bringing their children?"

"Yes. The older girls will help and play with the younger ones, so Clara you can sit in the meeting to find out all the things we need to know. I think you are old enough to be included in the planning."

Clara was pleased that Gabrielle thought she was old enough but a bit worried she wouldn't understand the language enough to be of any help.

"I know the French may be hard to understand as sometimes the women speak very fast, but don't worry, I will help you with the language. You are getting very good at speaking French though and I rarely have to translate to English for you anymore.

It wasn't long before the five were all packed and in the wagon and on the road to Mrs. Simard's home.

The ride took about forty minutes and Clara was surprised to see so many wagons and carriages in the yard when they arrived. Clara lifted the girls from the wagon and very quickly both girls took a hand and almost crushed Clara as they walked toward the house. "Girls, you don't need to be afraid as everyone here is a friend. One of the older girls is going to play some games with you. Mama and I will be in the house talking. I will come out in a bit to see if you are having fun. I have our lunch with me so we will all eat together." The girls reluctantly let go of Clara's hands and tried to look brave as she left them with the other small children and their leaders in the yard.

As soon as Gabrielle entered the house carrying Marie, all the mothers made a big fuss over the young baby. Mrs. Simard who was now holding Marie looked very pleased as Gabrielle told the story. "We are all so thankful that Mrs. Simard was able to come and help with the birth as Jacques was away. She stayed late into the evening to make sure we were all right." Baby Marie seemed to know she was the centre of attention and just smiled at everyone. Gabrielle took Marie in her arms so the meeting could start and she and Clara found chairs near the door.

The women began their meeting by relating the fact that the Assembly in Quebec had passed a bill taking the vote away from the few women who had the right to vote "Previously only women who owned property were allowed to vote and those women mostly included widows who had inherited the property from their husbands." said Mrs. Simard. "Papineau thinks it is scandalous and indecent to see women at voting stations."

This statement created a small fuss but they quickly went on to the real matter at hand as to how they could help their farms during this time of crisis. There were not many suggestions other than to make sure as neighbours everyone kept in touch and helped each other. They came to an agreement that if anyone had clothing their children had outgrown and no further need for it, they could be dropped off at the church to be made available for others.

Clara slipped out the door to check on the girls to see them running around playing a game with the others. They were hanging on to each other's hand, but they were laughing and having fun. She returned to the meeting before they could see her so as not to destroy the happy moment.

At lunch time everyone took their food basket outside and sat under a tree to enjoy lunch. The talk quickly turned to other matters in the home regarding meal ideas, what to do with squash and how to get mud stains out of all the clothes.

Gabrielle also mentioned the return of cholera. "How can we keep our children and ourselves safe from this disease? It is very contagious and so many people have it especially in Montreal."

Several women offered suggestions they had heard about but nothing was very practical or proven. The social aspect of this meeting was probably as beneficial as the ideas put forth. By mid afternoon the process of collecting tired children and belongings began, and the women started their journey home. The motion of the wagon bumping over the rough road was enough to put Julie and Elodie to sleep in the back of the wagon. After Marie was nursed, she too fell asleep in Gabrielle's arms and Clara had a chance to practise her driving skills.

When the horse and wagon pulled into the yard in the late afternoon, both Clara and Gabrielle knew something was wrong. Sean was sitting on the steps by the back door, and Jacques was in the process of harnessing the other horse to take it somewhere.

"What has happened and where are you going," asked Gabrielle?

"Louis has disappeared and we think he has gone back to his family farm. Sean noticed he was gone when he first went to the barn this morning. He must have left at daybreak."

The girls were still sleeping in the back of the wagon so Clara left them there and came to sit beside Sean. "Was he angry with us for some reason?"

"Not that I know of," replied Sean. "He was talking last week about learning to shoot a gun and how he could take care of any British soldier who came around here. But I don't know where he would go to get a gun unless he thinks he can find the one his father used to have. Maybe he knows where it was stored."

"That's why we think he has gone back to his old home to try and find it," Jacques added. "I doubt if it is still there as someone likely took it by now. We just can't leave him out there. It's at least a two day walk and then back again. I should have picked up on what he was saying and let him try with my gun. If I leave now, I should be able to catch him by noon tomorrow."

Gabrielle put her hand on Jacques arm and calmly said, "Jacques. Louis is a strong brave young man and he has lots of outdoor sense. He will be fine. You should pack some food and leave very early tomorrow. You will likely catch him before tomorrow night. Now let's get these sleeping children in the house and prepare dinner."

Sean and Clara went to the wagon and woke up the girls and took them inside. The nap, the outdoor playing and fresh air had reenergized the pair and even though the mood inside was quite somber the girls were full of energy and just wanted to run. It was still light out so Sean and Clara took them outside again for a game of tag.

Jacques and Gabrielle both began to speak.

"You go first Jacques."

"I was so worried about Louis being gone and I guess I felt guilty, that I didn't think straight when I decided to go find him tonight. I just wish he felt he could come to me if he was worried."

"He is still new here and as much as we think we treat him like family, he may not feel that way yet. In time it will work out, but maybe we have to try and talk to him about what his family was like. He lost everything he knew. You can go tomorrow to find him but maybe you have to go with him to his farm and look for the gun even if you know it is gone. One last trip there might be good for him especially if he is not alone."

"You are right Gabrielle. I will go tomorrow, and I promise not to be angry with him."

It was a long night and neither Jacque nor Gabrielle slept well. Gabrielle kept thinking about things that could happen to Louis while he was on his own over night. Jacque kept thinking about what he should have done to make Louis feel more welcome. Finally at five a.m. Jacques was up and dressed and making some breakfast and packing some food for the trip.

"I will just go out and see if everything is ok in the barn and then I will be off. Sean will have to do the chores by himself today and tomorrow, but I know he can do it. I am taking the gun with me so don't worry. We may even get in a bit of target practise before we return."

"Travel safely and hurry back."

Jacques travelled all day stopping only a few times to water his horse. About six p.m. he figured he was nearing the place where he thought Louis had lived. There was no one in site but he could see a dilapidated house and barn off the road just up ahead. He slowed the horse and turned onto a dirt laneway. The growing year had been so bad that even the weeds were not surviving along the lane. Jacques dismounted from his horse and led it along. He noticed some recent footprints in the dirt and certainly hoped they were Louis'.

"Louis. Are you here? It's Jacques." The last thing he wanted to do was to scare him especially if he had found the gun.

A young man stepped out from behind the house and when he saw Jacques, he started running toward him.

The two embraced in a hug and then stepped back.

"Are you mad at me? I really didn't mean for you to come and find me. I would have been ok going back to your home by myself. Maybe you don't want me to come back as I have caused a lot of trouble," Louis almost whispered.

Jacques could see there were tears in his eyes that Louis was trying to ignore. "You are part of our family so of course I needed to come. I just wish you had told me you wanted to learn to shoot a gun. I can teach you. Let's sit here and eat some food Gabrielle sent. We can't have any left by the time we get home or she'll think we don't like her cooking. Before dark you can show me around here and we'll see if we can find that gun."

After eating some dinner, Jacques and Louis walked to the barn and entered the lower part. Jacques looked up at the structure hoping it was safe. Louis went right to the back corner behind the pen where pigs might have been kept. He moved around some of the rotted straw and to his surprise, there was the gun.

"I knew it would be here," he exclaimed in an excited voice. "This is where my father always kept it. I found it one day when I was cleaning out this pen. I never saw my father ever shoot it but I'm sure he did as we often had rabbit for dinner."

He picked up the gun and walked out of the barn, followed by Jacques. They both looked at the gun, wiping off spots of dirt. Louis then handed the gun to Jacques and said, "What do you think? Is it any good?"

Jacques looked at the gun, checked to see if it was loaded which it was not, tried the moving parts to make sure they weren't rusted shut and declared," I think we can get this gun in working order with a bit of sanding and oiling. Would you like to show me anywhere else around here before we figure out where to sleep tonight?"

"No. I looked around a bit before you came. I don't really want to go in the house as it won't be the same without my family being there. I would just as soon get on with my new life."

"That's alright by me. Should we bunk here tonight, or ride a bit and find a friendly farmer on the road?"

"Let's start back tonight. I will show you a farm where I stayed on my way to your place when I first came."

Jacques agreed and the two climbed up on the horse's back and started down the road. Louis was carrying the gun carefully across his lap.

Life at the St. Pierre farm continued on with the routine chores being completed each day. The girls were now growing more independent and could help Gabrielle and Clara with some simple tasks. They were almost five now but felt much more grown up. Baby Marie still needed lots of attention and there were now four people to attend to her. Julie and Elodie were always happy to play games with Marie.

Jacques was devoting a bit of time now to show Sean and Louis how to shoot a gun. They had worked on Louis's gun and it actually now worked. When the boys had any extra time they would take the gun to the woods and try to shoot lumps of mud from a tree branch. Jacques was always relieved to see them return with no blood streaming from a body part.

There was one growing concern that always remained on the adult's minds though. There was more talk now among the local farmers about their frustration with the British trying to keep the habitants from participating in governing their own affairs.

Jacques had been at a meeting in St-Charles recently and had heard several new complaints. "Apparently Papineau has written ninety-two demands that the assembly here have passed and he wants to take them to London for the British parliament to pass. It would give the habitants more control over how our government is run. There are more French than English here yet the group who really govern us are mostly English and wealthy. There is talk of organizing a group to fight if we have to. But for now we will just watch. I suggest we do not get involved in any talk with others and really only speak French when you are with others."

"Maybe I should send that letter to my brother to see if he is planning to leave Montreal and where he is going to go," Gabrielle added. "I never did get it written before. And I will ask him if he has friends around the country where we might be safe if we have to leave here."

"Send him a letter and ask, but I am sure we will be safe here for awhile."

Clara and Sean looked at each other and once again the strange feeling of being alone returned. They both knew what it was like to be hungry and not knowing where you would live, but they had hoped they would never feel like this again.

SEVEN

'NOTHING IS MORE POWERFUL THAN AN IDEA WHO'S TIME HAS COME.'

Victor Hugo

It was a rainy dull day in April and the mood of the city matched the weather. John Drummond was sitting at his office desk in his home in Montreal. While sipping a glass of scotch, he reflected on the funeral he had just attended. Horatio Gates could be described as a very enterprising man. He had come to Montreal thirty years earlier from the United States and opened up the immense export business with the west. It seemed he had contacts everywhere and had influenced his friends to invest in his new bank. He had been appointed to many positions of authority and power that had helped him amass a large personal fortune. Now his death had thrown a veil of mourning over the city. The funeral was like reading a list of the elite of Montreal as it was so well attended by the wealthy and powerful.

But behind the sadness of his death another ill wind was blowing toward the city. Papineau had taken his 92 Resolutions of grievances to London to present to Parliament and was awaiting an answer. Papineau and his Patriot politicians were demanding more power for the elected Assembly and wanted the same privileges and immunities as the British Parliament. There were also veiled threats of Lower Canada wanting independence.

The by-election over two years ago was still on everyone's mind. Many still recalled and discussed the fight that broke out between a crowd and British soldiers resulting in the death of three francophones.

The population of Montreal was half British and dominated the commerce in the city. There was a great division in the thinking and the politics between the French and the English. Just north of Montreal in the County of Two Mountains, the French were by far the majority of farmers tilling the rich agricultural land. Recently though many English-speaking settlers began arriving in the area from the United States and within ten years immigrants from the British Isles joined them. This changed the cultural fabric of the area. Politics recalled from home countries played a part in how men would vote in local elections thus creating tension in the area.

John thought of Gabrielle's friend Justine and her family in St-Eustache. Recently a bridge had been completed at St-Therese that linked St- Eustache with Montreal. Now it was a village very popular with many from Montreal and the area.

John had recently talked with Justine and she and Joseph were to be married in the summer, so she had moved back to her family's home in St- Eustache.

John began to think of his sister Gabrielle and her family. He knew she was in a hot spot as well in the Richelieu Valley. He would write her a letter as soon as he had made his decision about moving his job to York from Montreal. Possibly his boss George Moffatt would know someone offering refuge to loyalist families if they had to flee their area. He knew that Gabrielle might be considered more of a Patriot now, but her English ways might just help her if need be. He knew Clara and Sean would be looked at as Loyalists from Ireland.

George Moffatt was the leading partner in a prestigious law firm in Montreal. He was involved in the fur trade, had been an officer in the War of 1812 and in his foresight had established a branch of his law firm at York in Upper Canada. He was also involved in business in Sherbrooke, east of where Gabrielle lived. George had invited John to relocate to his firm in York, which was now called Toronto, as he needed someone who spoke both languages to liaise between Montreal and Toronto. John had not decided but as the troubling events in Lower Canada loomed on the horizon; the new location began to look appealing. He would decide by tomorrow. One more night to sleep on it. John refilled his glass and looked out the window at the sunset over the river and thought about what life in York might be like.

Amazingly, he slept well that night even though he dreamt about a lot of places. First he was back in England, then on the ship coming to Canada for the first time. Later he was in Toronto and then in Montreal living in his present home with his sister. When he awoke at 7 he remembered most of the dreams but did feel quite refreshed. He also knew the answer to the decision regarding his job. After breakfast he sat down and started a letter to his sister.

Dear Gabrielle and family

Thank you for your most recent letter. I have been quite worried about you and Jacques and your family. I have inquired about places to go and be safe and my friends have been most helpful in suggesting spots. They all seem to have friends of friends who live in the townships in Lower Canada and are willing to help keep Loyalists safe. The one sticking point is they are all Loyalists and want to help other Loyalists. So you will have to practise your English. The best direction to go would be south toward the American border. You can always cross there easily and there are many loyalists living there.

I know that you and Jacques are living in a true French part of the country but are not fully committed to the rebels cause so be careful what you say when out in public. Clara and Sean are old enough to understand this as well and I hope they have not forgotten all their English. The younger girls will be fine, though knowing you Gabrielle; I bet you have been teaching them English.

I have included on the last page a list of names and addresses of safe places. I have also included some directions as to how to find these places as best I could. I suggest you have a small case of things you want to have with you such as crucial documents and extra essential clothing for the children. Keep it ready so you can leave in a moment's notice.

I must tell you my other news. George Moffatt, the owner of our firm, has offered me a job in Upper Canada. He needs someone to liaise between Montreal and York. York by the way is now the city of Toronto. As I am bilingual, I seem to be the perfect fit. I have after much thought decided to take the job and I will be moving to Toronto before winter. As soon as I arrive at the office this morning I will be giving Mr. Moffatt my decision.

I will be sad to leave Montreal as it has been a wonderful city to live in especially if you know the right people and have money to enjoy the benefits. But lately it has become a different city. Earlier this year a group of radical English started a club called the Doric Club. They are a paramilitary group who are very much opposed to the Patriot Party. They feel they must defend the British population in Lower Canada and will go to almost any extreme to carry out their mandate. They also dislike the Société des Fils de la Liberté. There are reported skirmishes in the city at night. There are also rumours of the Governor bringing in more British troops to keep control in Montreal and to the North. It is not the pleasant town where you and I lived when we first came after our parents died.

Keep your ears to the rumour mill and have safe travels if you have to leave. Please let me know where you are. You can always send a letter to the office in Montreal. The address is on the letterhead.

All my love
John Drummond

~

John slipped the letter into the envelope along with some paper money he had at his home. He knew times were tight for farmers and hoped Jacques would not be offended. It was sealed and set on the table by the door so John could take it to the office this morning and send it by courier to St- Denis.

Even though John would be leaving Montreal, he had already decided he would not sell his house. He could have the staff close most of it and they could stay in the staff quarters. There would be people living in the home to protect it and allow him to use it when he came to Montreal on business. He also secretly hoped to return to Montreal sometime and maybe Gabrielle or her children would also.

John had many friends in town, and one very good female friend but a relationship had never developed. He would certainly miss Helene when in York, but wondered if they could keep the friendship going from a distance. John had met Helene several years ago at a party held at a friend's home. She was tall, classically educated and wore glasses. She lived in a large home with her parents and helped with several charities in the city. For several months they continued to meet each other at gatherings in the city. Over time if John was attending an event where bringing a guest was acceptable, he always asked Helene to accompany him. They often would meet for dinner on a weekend and catch up on the latest social news in the city. John was beginning to feel they could possibly become a couple but there were several obstacles in the way. Helene was an only child and took care of her elderly parents. Both parents had some health issues and so caring for them seemed to be her mission in life. There was no chance she could ever move away while they were still living. So John was resigned to remain good friends for now.

John was a partner in a prestigious law firm in Montreal. By the standards of the day he was in the elite group of Montreal well-to-do. He had access to many of the powerful and wealthy men in Montreal. His social life consisted of theatre events and gatherings of the best known people in the city. This was the group that made most of the decisions for all of Lower Canada. He owned a large home in the safe and exclusive part of town and had invested in several businesses that helped his estate grow. His one regret was never marrying and or having a family. Gabrielle was his only living relative and of course her children were his nieces and nephews, but he rarely saw them because of distance. At the moment the heirs to his considerable estate were Gabrielle and her children including Sean and Clara. Louis had been included to receive a set sum as part of his inheritance as well. The three older children were certainly lucky to have found homes with Gabrielle and Jacques who treated them so well. It had been arranged by John several years earlier to complete the paper work so Gabrielle and Jacques could legally adopt Sean and Clara. Louis was already the age of majority so he could not be legally adopted, but he was certainly part of the family.

Now, as John walked to the office, he thought of all the concerns that were floating around waiting to be settled. The turbulent times were likely going to become worse for everyone and there were no certainties in business or politics right now. First he must talk to Mr. Moffatt and settle the task of moving to Toronto.

He placed his letter to Gabrielle on the desk and hoped someone going that direction could get it to St-Denis as soon as possible.

His meeting with Mr. Moffatt went well and his boss was pleased that a competent lawyer would soon be in Toronto to handle the business between there and Montreal.

"There have been rumblings in Toronto, John, of a group not being happy with the way the Tories are running Upper Canada.

One man in particular by the name of Mackenzie seems to be writing hostile information, and since he is the editor of a newspaper he has easy access to publishing it. He sounds similar to Papineau. Let's hope they don't meet and conspire against all of us."

"I have heard some of the stories, but they do not seem well organized as a group. The Family Compact in Upper Canada is strong and has the power to control just about everything there including an uprising. We will have to keep our eyes on that situation."

The two men continued to talk business and finalized all the details regarding the job in Toronto. It was decided that John would leave before winter arrived in Montreal and be nicely settled in by Christmas. "I am sending letters of introduction to several of my friends in Toronto," George said. "There will be no need for you to spend the holidays alone once you are there. You can take advantage of the holiday season to get to know the right people in Toronto which will help us in our business. I do believe one of my friends has a home he has made available for sale to the right person."

"Thank you sir. That will certainly make my move easier." But secretly he thought finding his own house and establishing his own friendships might be more to his liking.

The next few weeks flew by with all the details that John was arranging. Finally at the end of October all his files, household goods and personal belongings were packed and on their way to Toronto. John would be travelling separately by steamship the next day.

He arrived at the docks early and boarded the steamship *Lady of the Lake.* He was travelling first class so he had a small room with armchairs, a table and a bench that likely turned into a bed. A gentleman in uniform immediately entered his room to help stow his cases and bring him refreshments upon request. He was comfortably ensconced in his room drinking coffee when the whistle blew indicating the ship was about to leave port. As it sailed out of the harbour, the brick warehouses of the dock area disappeared behind him. The tall hills of the city came into view as they passed the island. John felt a bit nostalgic about leaving the city as life had been good in Montreal while he was here. Now it was on to a new life hopefully as good as his time in Montreal and with not too much restlessness or revolution.

The ship was now sailing west where the river narrowed and the land on either side was quite flat. There was what looked like Native villages along the shore with people fishing. By mid day they had passed the flatness and were into a channel with rocky shores and islands in the river. The shoreline was covered in tall trees and there was no sign of any inhabitants. As it was fall the trees were showing their many shades of reds and golds that reflected in the blue water. John counted five deer along the shore drinking from the water. The scenery was quite beautiful but with a wildness to it. Suddenly the rocks and hills gave way to larger islands and peninsulas in the distance and civilization reappeared. The sun was just setting when the ship arrived in Kingston and stopped to let passengers off as well as pick up those heading further west.

After leaving Kingston, the shoreline grew farther away and the ship entered Lake Ontario. They followed along the north shore of the lake but only the occasional fire burning on the shore could be seen. To the south the view was only the blackness of the lake. John enjoyed his dinner in his room and went for a short walk along the corridor of the ship to stretch his legs before bed. When he returned to his room, the bench had been turned into a bed ready for the overnight trip to Toronto. Even though it was a short narrow bed, the sound of lapping water against the hull of the ship, put John to sleep.

Suddenly there was knocking at the door of his cabin, and the sound of a whistle blowing. John awoke to daylight and the voice of his butler announcing they would be docking in Toronto within the next hour. He had slept through the entire night. He quickly dressed and tried to look as presentable as possible even though he was not expecting anyone to meet him. When he returned from finding a bathroom, the bed in his room had disappeared and breakfast was set out on the table. As they sailed into the east end of Toronto, warehouses and brick buildings came into view. It was as if he had not left the port of Montreal as it looked the same. There were no hills in the background though and only one church spire on the horizon.

The shipped docked and his butler for the trip advised him that a carriage was waiting to take him to a hotel in the city. John thanked him for making his trip comfortable and walked down the gang plank toward a waiting carriage. After the rocking of the ship, it was difficult to walk on dry land without listing to one side or the other, but John made it to the carriage. The ride to the hotel was a very different experience. The roads in Toronto were mostly mud with large logs barely covered by the soil. The result was a very bumpy ride. Fortunately it was sunny and dry on this fall day, but when it rained the roads would be almost impassable. John had heard the city called 'Muddy York' before it became Toronto. He hoped it stayed dry for a long time, but knew that was most unlikely.

He arrived at the hotel and was settled in by noon. After changing clothes and dressing as a lawyer should, he began the short walk to his new place of work. The Moffatt law office was in the heart of the city and located in a fairly new two story brick building on the main north–south road that started at the waterfront. It was surrounded by other similar building; all well kept giving an impression of prosperity.

Upon arriving, he was greeted warmly and shown to an office where four well dressed men were seated around a table. It appeared to be a meeting and John hoped he was not interrupting it as he did not want to start off on the wrong foot.

To his surprise, they all stood and introduced themselves. "We have been waiting for you to arrive. We hope your trip was good and you are settled at the hotel. I am George Macauly and these are your new colleagues William Duncan, Allan Jones and Robert Sullivan. We are pleased that you are here."

"John Drummond. It is a pleasure to meet you all and I am looking forward to working with you here in Toronto."

There were handshakes all round and as they were seated, George said. "I thought today we would just fill you in generally on our business here and how we work with the government as they are our biggest clients."

The rest of the afternoon passed quickly and although John was feeling somewhat overloaded with information, he was excited about the new location and business he would be doing. There would be several late nights reading the files he had been given and becoming familiar with who's who in Toronto.

The next few weeks followed a busy schedule. John would go to the office, meet with the partners in the firm, sit in on meetings with clients and one of the other lawyers, go home in the evening and read about things happening in Toronto and Upper Canada that involved the law firm. It was almost always after midnight when exhausted, he fell into bed each night.

At the beginning of December, Robert Sullivan stopped by John's office at the end of the day. "John. My wife has planned a dinner party for Saturday evening and we would love if you could join us. There will be about twenty or so there. It's sort of a pre Christmas party. Come about six. The dress is not formal but I and the other men will be wearing suits. Of course the women will be wearing their finest holiday outfit. I will leave my address and directions with our assistant."

"Thank you Robert, but I was going to catch up on some reading this weekend."

"We will not take no for answer John. Besides, you need to meet some people other than the lawyers here at the office. I have a friend coming who wants to sell his home and it may be just what you are looking for. I understand you have been looking for a place but haven't found the right one yet. You must be getting tired of living at the hotel by now."

"Well I am tired of the hotel room and I am still looking. Yes I would love to join you on Saturday evening. Thank you Robert. I look forward to meeting your wife."

On the way home that evening John began to get a bit excited about doing something other than reading files all weekend. He had looked at several homes for sale but most of them were too large, too old, or not in the best location. This might be the start of a new adventure for him.

Saturday evening arrived and with it was the first snow of the season. John had hired a carriage to avoid being soaked by the wet snow. The Sullivan home was quite palatial and with candles burning in the front windows it had a magical glow to it. A Christmas tree that stood at least ten feet tall was centered in the front hall. The branches were almost invisible as they were covered with beautiful decorations. There must have been a hundred candles sitting on the branches ready to be lit on Christmas Eve. Past the front hall John glimpsed more elaborate decoration in the parlour and beyond. Even back in England he had never seen such Christmas splendour.

The party was attended by all the lawyers from his office plus many more people he did not know. There were men in uniform with long lines of medals adorning their jackets, as well as gentleman in religious garb that would equal that worn by an Archbishop. John just hoped he would be able to remember the names after being introduced.

At dinner he was seated between Mr. and Mrs. Samuel Jarvis. After polite conversation, Jarvis turned to John and got right to the point. "I understand you need a house. I have a lovely cottage for sale just off King Street near Yonge Street. We had it built six years ago but now it is too small for our family. We have moved to a larger house off Richmond Street so we are ready to sell it. Why don't you come for lunch tomorrow after church and we can visit it later in the afternoon."

John felt he had no option but to accept the luncheon invitation and a preview of the cottage. He just hoped if he did not like the house there would be an opportunity to refuse the offer to buy it. "Thank you Samuel, I would like to look at the home. I have not decided yet but there are two that I have previewed that might work for me. It never hurts to compare several. Having lunch would be lovely."

As the evening continued on John met a number of new people including Reverend John Strachan, the Anglican bishop of Toronto. Many of the men at this party were the elite of Upper Canada who held the power and the purse strings for the province. They were part of the Family Compact that John had heard about before he came to Toronto.

The Family Compact was a small group of conservative families who dominated both business and government in Upper Canada.

They favoured British traditions and supported the idea of keeping government in the hands of an appointed legislature and executive council. John figured they were similar to the Chateau Clique who tried to control Lower Canada.

At the end of the evening John was exhausted but invigorated having been introduced to so many new people. He just hoped he remembered all the men's names the next time he met them.

The following morning John attended the service at St. James Church. It was the oldest parish church in Upper Canada having been established almost forty years earlier. It was now a stone structure replacing the old wooden structure. Thankfully John found a seat beside the Jarvis family as many of the box pews had name plaques on the doors belonging to other families. One would not make a good impression if you sat in someone's reserved spot.

After church and a delightful lunch at the Jarvis home, John and Samuel left the house and took a carriage to view the cottage. It was a white wooden house with a beautiful front porch on the front. Around the base of the porch were red bricks with matching brick pillars. It looked as though it was just a single story but upon further investigation, John learned it was two stories at the back. The front door led to a large foyer with high ceilings. Dark mahogany panelling continued along a hallway opening to a large formal sitting room on one side and a formal dining room on the other. At the end of the hall a door opened to the kitchen painted entirely in white with white tiles on the floor and on the wall behind the sink. There were numerous doors in the kitchen leading to somewhere. John thought he could get totally lost in the back of the house. One door led to a butler's pantry while another went to the upper floor. The third door led to the back garden with another going to a storage area and cistern. Upstairs there were three bedrooms and a bathroom with an indoor toilet of sorts, and washing facilities. This house was quite modern by today's standards. After looking at all the rooms inside, John and Samuel went to the back garden. It was quite large with lovely shade trees and many colourful plantings. At the back corner was a small building.

"What is this building for," asked John?

"That is where the servants live and also where the laundry is done."

"Oh, I don't think I need servants. How many servants would live there?"

"Only the gardener, his wife who was our cook, and the boy who takes care of the horses live here. There is a stable at the back behind the trees. The butler and housekeeper live in the upper level. There is a back stairs from the storage room leading to the upstairs apartment."

John hadn't realized there was a third floor. "I don't know if I need a house this large as it will only be me living here."

"I must sell this house as we do not need two houses to care for. Our new house is much larger and more costly to keep. And I do not need the worry of two houses." Samuel quoted him the price of the house and added, "I am asking less than the going price for houses in the area. I do want someone here who can keep the staff as well. Think about it John and let me know."

"I will think about it. Let me do some discussing with my bank and I will let you know by the end of the week." John was beginning to like the style and location of the house and after really looking at it; it did not seem too big after all. He knew he would like to have a housekeeper and a butler here in Toronto, and someone to care for the grounds would be nice as well. This was worth considering.

The two men returned to the new Jarvis home where John thanked Mrs. Jarvis for lunch and began his walk through the snowy streets back to the hotel. He had a lot to think about.

Work at the office began to slow a bit as Christmas was approaching so John had time to think about which house he would purchase. After much thought and several discussions with his banker, John called Samuel Jarvis one day. "Good day Samuel. I think I may have good news for you today. I have decided your cottage would be the perfect house for me and I am willing to purchase it for the price you quoted me."

"That really is good news. I think you will be happy there. Will you be keeping the staff on as well?"

"Yes I think that will be a good idea. If possible I would like to move in a week before Christmas. I do not want to spend Christmas in the hotel. I have some furniture stored here in Toronto that can be delivered. I will draw up the papers and bring them to your office tomorrow."

"That will be fine. Thank you John. I will see you tomorrow at three."

John felt a weight being lifted off his shoulders, as not having a permanent place to live had been bothering him. Now he could be totally settled by the new year.

The rest of the week was a blur of signing papers, organizing deliveries of furniture, meeting the staff and actually moving in with just five days until Christmas. He had received an invitation to the Sullivan house for Christmas day so now he had to go out and do a bit of shopping for gifts for their children.

The new year was a little more than a week away, and everything seemed to be falling into place. He had not received a letter from Gabrielle so he hoped all was good news in St-Denis. He had been so busy with his new position in Toronto he had not paid much attention to the political details of Lower Canada. He did hear trouble was still brewing in Montreal but really hoped it would all be solved and life would be better in Lower Canada.

Little did he know that 1837 would be a year of unrest, revolution and reform for both Upper and Lower Canada. The country would never be the same.

EIGHT

'WHEN IT IS DARK ENOUGH, YOU CAN SEE THE STARS.'

Ralph Waldo Emerson

Gabrielle decided she must take the time and write to John to let him know what was happening in the Richelieu Valley. Once again Christmas had been sparse. The gifts for the children and the family were only the necessities needed to survive. There was no special dinner. They did have roast goose but the goose was quite small and barely enough for the family of eight. There were potatoes with very thin gravy and small carrots. Instead of pie there was an apple dessert with no pie crust. The drizzle of maple syrup over the top seemed like such a luxury. Even though Christmas dinner was not at all like other years, the family were happy to be warm and felt blessed to be together. The day was spent singing and playing games around the fire which was the real treat. Gabrielle did not want to tell John all the bad news so she put off writing the letter. But now she must reply and at least tell him his letter and list of places to escape had arrived.

Gabrielle still had some money from her parent's estate but there were no provisions to buy as the growing season had been so poor. Also she and Jacques felt they needed to keep some money in case they had to leave and start over. Jacques had originally suggested that Gabrielle, Clara and the three girls leave and travel to the St-Eustache area and stay with his brother on the farm, but he heard lately that the area just to the south was becoming a hot bed of trouble. Being close to Montreal, it had the attention of the government and there was talk of troops being sent there to control the Patriots. His sister lived near St-Hilaire and Jacques knew it was also an area of conflict, so it was not wise to go there either. John had sent names and addresses of friends in the Eastern Townships but that might be a last resort. It really was a wait and see situation. Gabrielle sat at the table one evening thinking of all the scenarios that might play out as she began her letter to John.

My dearest brother

A belated Merry Christmas. We hope you are settling in and did not spend the holiday by yourself. Your new position in the law firm sounds quite exciting. It is strange to think that as different as the two areas are, similar conflicts exist between the people and the government. The higher ups in England are the common factor so maybe they are to blame for this upheaval.

We enjoyed a quiet and plain Christmas this year. The crops again have been poor so the harvest yielded very small amounts of produce. We have lost a few animals to sickness and often there is not enough hay or grain to adequately feed the rest. Even though we do have some money to purchase extra, there is none to purchase.

You would be so proud of Sean and Clara. Sean, now an adult really, is such a help to Jacques. On several occasions he has taken care of the farm while Jacques has had to be away. Louis has also proven to be a great help as well. I sometimes have to laugh as I see the three of them walking around the farm. The two boys are as tall as Jacques and have picked up his farmer walk.

Clara is quite grown up now and is excellent with the girls. I don't know how I would manage without her. Both Sean and Clara are now completely fluent in French and Clara has taught the girls an amazing amount of English though they do speak more French than English. We are quite the interesting family of eight. I do think about the life we had growing up and how different Clara and Sean's life is. I worry that they are missing out on so much being here in the country. I know Sean is happy and Clara seems happy and I guess her life with her parents on a farm in Upper Canada would have been the same as here.

Thank you for sending the list of friends we could stay with if need be. We thought about going to either Jacques' brother's farm near St-Eustache or his sisters's near St-Hilaire, but have decided against those areas. We will keeping listening to the rumours going around about trouble, and as you suggested, we are ready to leave at a moment's notice.

I am sorry to send you this letter with what seems like mostly bad news. I hope its arrival is not too delayed, but the post is rather unreliable these days. You must write and tell me about where you are living. Are you buying a house or are you still in the hotel? If you move, you need to send me an address, unless it is all right to keep sending this to your office.

Thank you for all your help
Love, Gabrielle

~

PART II

FIGHT OR FLIGHT

NINE

'THE GOVERNMENT THAT ROBS PETER TO PAY PAUL CAN ALWAYS DEPEND ON THE SUPPORT OF PAUL.'

George Bernard Shaw

The folks in Upper Canada liked to read the news from their newspapers. As early as 1824 the opinions of usually the editor were available for all to read. In the Niagara region a Scotsman, William Lyon Mackenzie, published a paper, the *Colonial Advocate,* freely expressing his opinions about how he thought the province should be run. After a few months his paper became so popular throughout the province that Mackenzie moved to York and began to report on the debates of the Assembly. He continued criticizing members of the Family Compact, but went even further inventing falsehoods about some families. This led to a group of men, whose names had appeared in his paper, to break into his office and destroy his printing press. Mackenzie filed a civil suit against them and won, so was able to purchase a new press and continue publishing all paid for by the Family Compact.

Andrew Hunt sat in his office chatting with his partner about the grain business. He was a second generation Loyalist who had been born in Upper Canada and had inherited the business his father had established.

"I am worried about these people who seem to want reform in the province. As it stands now it is getting harder to sell our grain because of government rules and American competition. What line are the reformers going to take?"

"Well Andrew," replied Robert, "they seem to want the common folk, not just members of the elite here in York, to be given government appointments. In this past election the reformers dominated and have a majority in the Assembly but still have very little power. William Lyon Mackenzie, who was elected in York County, has written a number of anti-government resolutions that he wants taken to London. I also heard that he feels closer relations should be established with Lower Canada and the opponents of their administration."

"It is just too bad that any ideas proposed about reform always have to go to London for approval and of course the answer is always either no or wait and see."

Robert then changed the conversation and commented "We will have to keep in touch with all our farmers to make sure they keep their production of grain at its maximum."

"Yes. Next week we shall make some visits. Let's hope this session of the Assembly is productive and actually accomplishes something. So many of the sessions end up spending time discussing bills, but nothing is ever passed. They often can't even figure out how to get the money to pay the elected members let alone pay for any new building in the province."

As it turned out, within a year the assembly was dissolved upon the death of King George IV. The next year would see a new King, a new British Prime Minister and a new Governor in the colonies. When a new election was called to elect members of the Assembly in Upper Canada, the voters swung right back to their old ways and elected a conservative Assembly. Despite their majority, they had no real leader and no plan for governing. Once again the reformers, sitting as a minority party, continued their fight for reform and occasionally were encouraged by positive reports from London.

Andrew and Robert set off early Monday morning and headed north of Toronto. "How far are we going today Robert?"

Andrew pulled his horse closer to Robert and said, "We should go north as far as we can along the Humber River today, and then work our way back south the rest of the week. I want to visit Bolton Mills today where a fellow named George Bolton runs a grist mill. He and his brother built it recently and I want to see how many farmers are bringing in grain to be milled. We can find a place to stay near there. Tomorrow I would like to travel from Bolton to Lloydtown where there is another mill along a branch of the Holland River. The mill in Lloydtown is said to work night and day producing as much as a hundred barrels of flour each day. We need to know these men and some of the farmers and see if we can encourage them to let us sell some of their grain outside the province."

Robert was the son of a Loyalist farmer who ran a successful mixed farm to the east of Toronto. His grandparents arrived from Upper New York State in the late 1700's and settled along the north shore of Lake Ontario near Kingston. They had been able to acquire a large tract of land bordering the lake. As a child Robert enjoyed living in the country near the lake. There was always lots of work to do but there was also time for fun in the lake during the summer months. His father wanted Robert to stay on the farm and eventually take it over just as he had done, but Robert had an interest in the buying and selling of products produced by farmers. He convinced his father he should go to University to study science. He said he could help more if he knew more about how plants grew efficiently. After graduating from University of Toronto in plant science, he was lured away from farming and began working in the grain business. His father was not happy about him leaving farming but hoped some day he would return.

It was late afternoon when the two riders approached the village of Bolton Mills. They rode straight to the mill and introduced themselves to George Bolton.

After introductions, Andrew said, "Mr. Bolton, how much grain do you think comes in every day to be ground into flour?"

George replied, "The first year we opened there was a steady stream of farmers coming in sometimes with three or four bags on the wagon and often a boy carrying more on his shoulder, But lately the numbers have gone down. The river isn't as strong as it was either. They say the trees are being cut down for clearing the land and that may be the reason. Anyway we have about twenty bags of grain to grind most days."

Robert nodded his head and then added, "Do you think the farmers would ever consider selling some of their grain rather than grinding it into flour?"

"No one has any extra right now. They need the flour at home. The farmers are just surviving out here. The government doesn't make it easy for them either. They don't want to spend any money on roads or help build bridges for the villages. There still are no schools though there is enough work to keep all children at home helping with the farm."

Robert and Andrew nodded in agreement and decided it might be best not to get involved in this discussion and instead Andrew asked, "Is there a hotel in the village where we can stay for the night?"

"No hotel but Mrs. McGuire at the end of the village road takes in visitors. She is a good cook so you'll be wanting to eat dinner with her for sure. It's the big wood two story house with a porch. Only one like it in town."

"Thank you George for your time today. We always like to hear how the farmers are doing."

As they led their horses down the road to the rooming house, Robert said," I guess there will be no business from this area of the province."

They found Mrs. McGuire's' house and knocked on the door. As the door opened and a women in her forties smiled and said hello, a delicious smell of roasting meat and baking bread drifted out onto the porch. "How can I help you gentlemen tonight?"

Robert answered, "We wondered if you might have room for the two us to stay one night. We are travelling around York County to visit grist mills. George Bolton gave us your name."

"Oh, George is always sending me guests. Yes I do have two rooms. Will you be wanting dinner? The cost includes your meals. There is an extra cost for boarding your horse for the night."

Andrew quickly answered "That is fine and we can pay you now. Whatever you are cooking smells so delicious we will for sure be staying for dinner."

Mrs. McGuire chuckled and said, "You can pay me later. We have a barn out back where you can tie up your horses. My son Henry is out there now and will help you get them settled and fed."

The two men walked down the porch steps and led their horses around the back. "Let's do this fast as the smell of that dinner is making me very hungry."

After unsaddling and getting water for the horses, Mrs. McGuire's' son Henry said he would feed them and put them in a stall for the night. Robert and Andrew quickly went back to the house to wash up for supper.

Mrs. McGuire met them in the front hall. "Your rooms are the two first doors on the right at the top of the stairs. Washroom is last door on the left, and the outhouse is back by the stables. There are towels and a hanger in your room to dry the towels. Dinner is in ten minutes here in the dining room. You can pay me at dinner time."

Together Robert and Andrew both thanked her and headed upstairs and within the ten minute time frame were back in the dining room ready for dinner. "Mrs. McGuire, it smells delicious in here. We are looking forward to dinner. It has been a long day with just cold meat on bread for lunch many hours ago." Andrew said to their host as she brought in plates filled with what looked like roast beef. She was followed by a young girl carrying bowls of potatoes and carrots. There was gravy and bread already on the table. "Are we your only guests tonight?"

"Yes. This week has not been busy. My son and my sister's girl and I will join you since we do not have a full table tonight."

"That would be enjoyable," said Robert. "We might have to ask you some questions about the area around Bolton Mills."

Mrs. McGuire did not answer but continued serving the plates for everyone at the table. As everyone began eating, the room grew quiet until Mrs. McGuire asked, "What brings you men to our village to see Mr. Bolton? I figure you must be from Toronto as your clothes are not from the general store."

Andrew smiled, "We are here to see if we can help the farmers around here sell their grain overseas and to the United States. We understand most just have it ground to flour for home use, but if they ever had more than they need, we could set them up with buyers."

Henry joined the conversation suddenly saying, "The crops have not been good here for the past couple of seasons so right now that won't likely happen. Farmers here won't do any selling that involves the government in Toronto." Henry then continued in the same vein as Mr. Bolton had about how nothing was being done to help the rural people of Upper Canada.

Robert spoke up when Henry stopped to take another bite of dinner, "Andrew and I do not work for the government. We own a grain trading company that helps find buyers for grain products. The buyers pay us for the deal as well as paying the farmers for their grain. The government does not really get involved in these kinds of deals. We are far more efficient than the men in the Assembly in Toronto."

Henry nodded in agreement to the last comment, but did not add anything else. He just kept eating. Mrs. McGuire began clearing the table and then brought in a large pie that looked like apple. "Now I'm sure you gentlemen would like pie tonight," she said as she cut the pie into six large pieces.

Robert and Andrew both answered at the same time. "We certainly do."

The conversation continued as the group ate their pie and drank their tea, but it only centered on topics like the weather and the growth in the communities.

The light in the room was beginning to fade and Robert announced," That was a delicious dinner. Thank you so much. We have an early start tomorrow as we want to get to Lloydtown by early afternoon."

"Breakfast will be ready by 6:30 so you can be on your way early. If you want me to I can pack you some roast beef sandwiches to take for your lunch," said Mrs. McGuire.

Andrew said, "That would be much appreciated. Maybe we can settle up with you tonight if that makes it easier. And don't forget to include lunch in that bill."

Mrs. McGuire left the dining room and returned and offered a piece of paper with numbers on it listing the cost of the room, meals for both he and Robert and board for the horses. "I hope this is satisfactory and that you are happy with all we have to offer."

As he paid the bill, Andrew commented, "This is a very friendly place to stay and your cooking is delicious. Thank you."

Robert and Andrew went out to the barn to check on the horses and then returned to the house and went to bed.

Breakfast the next morning was plentiful and delicious. The roast beef sandwiches for lunch were thick fresh slices of bread loaded with beef and mustard wrapped in a piece of cloth. If they hadn't just finished eating, Andrew would have been tempted to eat one immediately rather than wait for lunch.

They saddled up their horses, said goodbye to the McGuire family and headed east toward Lloydtown. The day was clear and bright and was cool now but would likely be quite warm by mid day. They travelled east along a branch of the river until they came to a village that was really only three houses. At this point they turned north toward Lloydtown.

Along the way they chatted about whether they would find any farmers willing to sell their grain through their brokerage. Robert added, "I have heard that there are some farmers that are friends of Mackenzie. Apparently he has made trips up here from Toronto organizing public meetings to show the government that the people wanted reform."

"Is the rumour true that Mackenzie is in contact with Papineau in Lower Canada?"

"I have heard that same rumour, but don't know if it is true. I can't imagine they would ever agree on anything. How does Mackenzie get away with all this nonsense being a member of the Upper Canada Assembly and mayor of Toronto?"

"Well he has been thrown out of the assembly several times, but he always seems to get re-elected. Maybe it's because the assembly really doesn't do much as it's all controlled by the elite after all."

Robert laughed. "Now you are starting to sound like a reformer."

They stopped about noon to take a rest and eat the delicious lunch Mrs. McGuire had packed for them. She had included two slices of apple cake as well. They rode for about another hour when the village of Lloydtown came into site. They rode right to the mill in town and met the owner Jesse Lloyd.

Robert mentioned "You must have been the founder of this town as it is named after you."

Jesse laughed and said, "I came here from Pennsylvania, bought some land and started the grist mill. Now we have a saw mill and a woolen mill plus several other industries. It is a good location as we have the river, good soil, and people who work hard. Now if we could only get a government that cared about the farmers, we might have schools and bridges to make getting places easier."

Robert and Andrew didn't laugh but just nodded. This was the same story they were hearing at every stop. They continued talking to Jesse telling him what they were looking for and asking about farmers who might be interested.

Jesse replied, "There might be as the mill is now running all day and night producing flour as fast as we can grind it. I will ask around, but right now people are getting riled up about the government in Toronto. We are having a meeting tonight to talk about what we can do to change things for the better. You are more than welcome to attend. We are about to start training meetings where we practise with weapons."

Both Robert and Andrew were amazed what they were being told. Robert quickly added, "We probably will not attend as we have to leave later this afternoon to head back to Toronto." We hope to get to Richmond Hill before dark tonight."

Andrew did not look at Robert as he knew this was not the original plan, but realized being from Toronto, they might not be welcome. "We will leave our name and contacts with you and you can pass on this information to any interested farmers.

They left their names and addresses with Jesse Lloyd and walked their horses to the south end of town. There would be plenty of time while riding to talk about what they just heard.

As the two partners headed their horses to the east away from the village, Robert started the conversation. "I think if we had stayed and attended that meeting tonight, we might have feared for our lives. If they found out we were from Toronto, they might have assumed we were part of the Family Compact. There seems to be a real hate in these parts for what they represent. I have no intention of going as far as Richmond Hill tonight but instead we shall go as far as Newmarket. There is a mill there and a good hotel where we can stay. Possibly we can talk to someone tomorrow about our offer to farmers. Apparently the village has two mills, a distillery and a tannery. During the war of 1812, American soldiers came this far north trying to take over the country. I have a friend who has stayed at the North American Hotel and says it is quite nice."

"Sounds like a good plan. I think this part of York County is the riding Mackenzie represents in the Assembly. Maybe he will be staying at the hotel tonight," Andrew joked. "The reformers are really trying to get the farmers on board, and with poorer crops the past few years, the time may be right for trouble. Looking at these roads we are travelling, the farmers may have a point about no money being spent in the rural areas to help improve their lives. Also with poor crops, there may not be enough grain to sell and thus no need for grain brokerages. We may have to rethink our strategies."

"You may very well be right on all counts. It can't be much further to Newmarket. My body is tired of riding this horse. Next time we will bring a carriage. I heard a rumour that they were thinking of building a rail line up Yonge Street."

They were just crossing the road called Yonge Street which really was more of a trail. It started at the lake south of Toronto and continued north as a way of reaching rivers and lakes that connected to the trappers and lumberjacks that worked in the north. The actual village of Newmarket was centred around the mill pond a bit to the east. Finally about dinner time the two arrived at the hotel.

Andrew spoke first when he saw the three story building. "I did not think there would be a hotel of this size in such a small village." This looks quite promising for a good meal and a good night's sleep."

"There must be a stable around the back where we can board the horses. Let's go there first."

They followed a trail around the back, thankful that the weather had been dry as otherwise it would be a muddy pond. After securing a spot for their horses to be watered, fed and safe for the night, they returned to the front veranda of the hotel. As they entered, a poster caught Andrew's eye and he walked over to read it.

"Robert you must look at this."

Robert strolled over somewhat annoyed as he just wanted to check in and have dinner while sitting in a comfortable chair. The poster promoted a meeting to take place in August at this hotel. The speaker was to be none other than William Lyon Mackenzie promoting his reform platform. Farmers throughout the county were invited to come and be part of this reform movement.

"Well now we know what not to say to people around here. I think listening would be a good strategy tonight."

The two returned to the check in desk, were given their room keys and advised by the clerk that dinner was served in the dining room until 7. The lounge was open until 10 but no alcoholic beverages were allowed, and breakfast was served from 6 to 7. There was to be no loud noises in the rooms after 10 and friends were not permitted in the rooms of guests.

Andrew and Robert quietly said thank you, mentioned that they would be having dinner after they washed up and changed in their rooms. As they began walking up the stairs, Robert whispered, "I forgot to tell you that this town was settled by Quakers who came here so they wouldn't have to fight in the American Revolution."

Andrew just looked at him and said, "I guess there will be no party tonight."

The partners had an uneventful but delicious dinner and then decided to walk around the village before dark they passed a pub and on their return decided to go in and have a drink and possibly chat or listen to the locals.

They ordered whisky and sat at a table for four over to the side of the room. There were only three or four other tables occupied in the room. Two men who were sitting close by got up and came over and asked if they could join their table.

"Certainly," answered Robert. Introductions were made with Robert and Andrew only saying they worked at a grain brokerage out of Toronto.

"We saw a poster at the hotel saying Mackenzie is coming here to speak in August," remarked Andrew.

The older of the two men quickly replied, "Yes most of us are looking forward to hearing what he has to say. The big shots in Toronto who run this country sit in their offices doing nothing but talk. They go home to warm comfortable homes at night. Their children can go to school, the roads are better than ours. If they need land for their sons to build homes, it is given to them for nothing. Life here in the small villages is not like that."

Robert remarked, "It is often like that for many in Toronto who live in the poorer areas as well. Many have recently arrived from Europe with nothing but the clothes they are wearing and many end up begging on the streets. It is only good for a select few."

"That is so correct." The younger man with the long hair stood up from the table and spoke to the room. "We must all go to this meeting and we must arm ourselves to fight these people who take everything for themselves."

"Sit down boy. You don't want to be causing trouble."

Robert felt he had to defuse the situation a bit and changed the direction of the talks, "I hear that the farmers in Lower Canada are angry about the way they are being treated by their assembly as well. What do you hear about this reformer Papineau? Is he going to join with Mackenzie?"

Silas, the older man, said, "I have heard a bit about him. He apparently is holding meetings too in the country villages getting the farmers on side. I heard they have some guns but not enough. Here, some have guns but many do not as a lot of the farmers around here are Quakers who are peace loving and don't believe in fighting. They don't like the way we are being treated, but don't want to fight either. I hear from my sources that there could be maybe 700 farmers planning to come to this meeting here in August. That would be something."

"The hotel will be full that night," said Andrew. Speaking of hotels, we need to get back there as we have a long journey home tomorrow."

The foursome left the hotel and went their different directions. Back at the hotel, Robert quietly said, "We have a lot to talk about tomorrow on the ride home. First thing in the morning though, we will go to the mill to get a feeling on the grain situation from the owner."

The next morning the two partners left the hotel and walked their horses to the mill. It was just at the end of the street near a mill pond that had been created by damming up the river. There was lots of noise and work taking place at the mill. Several farmers were bringing in their grain to be ground for flour. In fact there were five or six wagons lined up waiting their turn. Andrew and Robert took the opportunity to go over to the group of men and find out more about the grain situation in this area. One of the farmers said he hoped to have excess grain this September but you never knew until harvest time. The others were worried their crops would be poor again this year as they had the past two years so were not interested in selling any extra they did have. They painted a bleak picture of farming in 1837. One spoke up and said, "If the reformers succeed in overtaking the government, we could be better off but it's a bit of a long shot as I see it."

The older farmer in the group quickly answered, "Well we can't count on Mackenzie winning points for us as we are not organized nor have the gun power to take on any trained militia. I wouldn't bet on being any better off next year if I were a betting man."

The others laughed and Robert and Andrew left to meet with the owner. They were only meeting him out of politeness after hearing the stories from farmers in Newmarket. They now felt there would be no new grain contracts with farmers in York County this year. Reform was on the minds of the rural farmers and possibly taking up arms in a civil war to protest the aristocracy of Upper Canada who only showed contempt toward the hard working people.

The others lingered and Robert and Andrew left to meet with the owner. They were only meeting him out of politeness after hearing the stories from farmers in Newmarket. They knew that there would be no new grain contracts with farmers in York County this year. Reform was on the minds of [illegible] all farmers and possibly taking up arms [illegible] until war [illegible] to protest the [illegible] of Upper Canada who only showed contempt towards the hard-working [illegible].

TEN

'I BELIEVE THAT THE MOMENT HAS COME TO MELT DOWN OUR TIN PLATES AND TIN SPOONS AND FORGE THEM INTO BULLETS.'

Wolfred Nelson

The summer of 1837 was a strange time. The weather was either extremely hot and dry with no rain for weeks, or without warning torrential rains with strong winds blowing from the north gave a feel that summer was over. The rains often lasted for days flooding the fields and turning roads and paths to muddy ponds.

On the St-Pierre farm, Gabrielle and Clara were trying to preserve all produce they could to feed the family the next winter.

Today they were canning the green beans in crocks with vinegar. "Clara I think we need to talk a bit about what you and I and the girls are going to do if the British do invade our area. Jacques says there is a meeting in St-Charles in a few weeks to talk about what is going to happen here in Lower Canada. He says Papineau and of course our own Patriot Wolfred Nelson, will be speaking. They are expecting thousands of people to attend."

"Are you going with Jacques? I can stay with the girls here at the house. Are Sean and Louis going as well?"

"That's a lot of questions Clara. I think we will all go as a family," said Gabrielle. We will take our lunch with us. As it will be October we will have to dress warmly. It is not too far for us to go. It will be quite a sight to see, and we will get to see the great Papineau speak."

"You sound like you are in favour of this uprising. I am not sure whether I want to be a Patriot or a Loyalist. Even though the British did not treat us very kindly back in Ireland, I still feel a bit of loyalty to them. Is that wrong to think like that?"

"No Clara you are not wrong. I myself do not agree to the violence that is often happening here in the valley because someone is hired to do the work for the British. But the government in Montreal do not treat anyone not associated with the men in power very well. There have been arrests in Montreal just because of words being said. I also still feel some loyalty to the British as that is where I grew up. John and I and our parents had a good life in England but we were from a privileged family and did not really know how others were living. But what I really worry about is where we will go if we have to leave here. John sent me a letter with names of friends in the townships where we could find safety if we had to. It would be a hard journey especially for the little ones. I asked you to pack a small bag of a few extra things to take in an emergency. I have a bag packed for us to take if we have to. This week I am going to bury some things in the yard that we can't take. When we come back we can dig them up. If you have anything you want saved, let me know."

Clara was almost in shock when Gabrielle finished. She could think of nothing to ask, or say so she quietly whispered, "Alright I will think about it."

Clara continued all day with preserving the vegetables for the winter. Apples had to be put into barrels. The potatoes and squash were put in the root cellar and covered with straw. The carrots remained in the ground as long as possible and then they went to the root cellar as well. Beans were put into salt and vinegar and then put into crocks and kept on a shelf in the cellar. The pumpkins were usually kept under straw as well but this summer the flowers never developed so there were no pumpkins to store. It was hard work but when all the produce was picked and preserved, the root cellar looked very organized and gave you a good feeling. Clara was worried though as she looked around thinking, there was not as much food stored as in the past. What if they had to leave? Would they be able to take some with them? Would any be left when they came back?

She also thought about whether she had anything she wanted to bury in the yard. She really didn't have anything of value but she thought Sean might still have the papers from their parents. She didn't know if the papers for the land would still be worth anything but she would talk to Sean about it. It was sad to think that after their life had been turned upside down when they arrived in this country, it might all happen again. Clara remembered that Gabrielle said they might have to leave in a hurry, but she never mentioned whether Jacques or Sean or Louis would be coming with them. Would they have to stay and fight? What if something happened to Sean and she never saw him again? Just that thought made Clara feel ill. She wiped the tears from her eyes and left the root cellar and went back into the house to ask Gabrielle some more questions.

The next day was the first sunny day in about a week and Clara took advantage of it. She decided to walk to the orchard and see if Sean and Louis were finished picking the apples. Sean was sitting on the ground eating an apple.

"Where is Louis?"

"He's taking the cart full of apples up to the house." Are you here checking up on us to make sure we are working?"

"No. It is such a nice day I thought I would walk out here to talk to you. I have a lot of questions for you. Gabrielle was talking the other day about how we might have to leave in a hurry if the British came through here. I have to have a case packed ready to go at a moment's notice. Did Jacques tell you the same thing?"

"No, not about leaving. He did say the British might come through here and we would have to defend the area. Jacques has been helping Louis and me learn how to shoot a gun. Louis has his own gun and Jacques had an extra one so he gave it to me. I'm getting pretty good at hitting tree branches and lumps of earth but I don't think I could really shoot at a person or an animal. So I hope it doesn't happen."

"Sean, you can't stay here and fight off the British. You might get killed."

"I know, but I really don't think I have any choice. My place here is to help Jacques. We are part of this family now so I have to defend our home. We also have to stand up to the people in Montreal as they are not treating the farmers fairly. Don't worry as I know Jacques will not let anything happen to us."

"Sean I do worry. You are all I have left of our Ryan family. I just hate that all this fighting is going on and we may have to run away again. Do you have those papers that Father gave you? They could be worth something. Maybe we should find a box and bury them in the back yard. Gabrielle said she is burying some valuable things in case we have to leave. She said we will dig them up when we come back."

"I asked Jacques about those papers about a year ago. He read them and apparently there was a date they had to be used by. So he said they were worthless. He even asked a friend in town about them and they said the same thing."

"Oh. I was thinking that you and I could go to Upper Canada and get some land and start our own farm. But if we don't have the papers for the land, I guess we can't do that."

"Clara. We have no money or equipment to start a farm. It would be too hard for you and me to ever do that. But it doesn't really matter as we will not be getting land given to us. I know this is a hard time as you don't know what will happen next. But we are older now. I really like working with Jacques and I know you like doing things with Gabrielle and you love the girls. So we just have to be ready for anything that happens and try and stay happy."

"You are right Sean. But I still don't think you should fight. How will you know where we have gone if we leave and you stay?"

"I think Gabrielle and Jacques have a plan all worked out, so we don't have to worry. Just do as you're told and don't ask so many questions."

Louis was coming down the path with the cart for the last load of apples. Clara stood up and started back to the house. "I guess I have more apples to put in the root cellar, so I better get back to work."

As Clara began putting more apples in barrels and crates she began to think about the past year. The Patriots decided to boycott the textile industry to make a point about their treatment by the English. It was decided at meetings, by the men who attended, that their clothes would not be made of foreign fabric imported from Britain. Many of the farmers raised sheep and grew flax so wool and linen was available once they were processed. She and Gabrielle had washed, cleaned, carded, combed and then spun the wool into yarn. It was a long process but the councillors reminded them this was the way to help the rebellion effort. The yarn then had to be knitted into sweaters, hats and other clothing.

The councillors also felt the Patriots and their families should dress in humble toile fabric rather than imported cloth. To make the fabric, flax had to be pulled up by the roots and beaten to remove the seeds. The stalks were then soaked in the pond or laid on a grassy field to let the dew rot them. Then they had to dry before a process of scutching took place. Much of this process was done by the men or boys in the family. Scutching removed the broken woody parts followed by combing and then the fibres were spun into yarn and woven into cloth. It was a lengthy process and it often took months before the fabric was ready to sew into clothing. The fabric was often rough and scratchy and stiff once it was made into a dress or shirt. Clara did not really like it and wished for the soft fabrics she sewed with before all this rebellion talk started. She also remembered how it was almost a competition between some of the ladies in the Valley to see who could produce the finest cloth. Gabrielle was very good at it but Mrs. Simard always seemed to produce the finest. She sometimes used plants to dye it a different colour. Gabrielle said her seven daughters must help her do the other chores.

Life was changing for the women in the Richelieu Valley as well. At first when there were meetings about the rebellion held in various towns, only the men would go. Sean and Louis went sometimes if Jacques didn't need them to do some farm work. At first women did not embrace the Patriot cause with enthusiasm, but lately they had started to attend the meetings. Often they were held in a field and it was more like a big picnic. Women did not always feel welcome though, as some men thought it was indecent and scandalous for women to be involved in political business. However Papineau was in favour of women attending as he felt if they were involved they would support their husbands and help with the cause. Clara chuckled to herself thinking about how she often didn't even listen after awhile as it all seemed quite boring.

Her thoughts were interrupted and she was startled as the door to the cellar opened. "Oh. You frightened me."

"We brought the last load of apples. We will help you pack them and then this job will be done for the season," said Sean.

The conversation turned to how many apples were in the barrels. Their guesses ranged from hundreds to thousands. It made the work go faster thinking of things other than the rebellion.

One evening several days later, the adults were sitting in the kitchen drinking their tea. The younger girls were all tucked in bed and this was a time when important farming ideas and problems were discussed and sometimes solved. Jacques and Gabrielle had very different parenting styles than most farmers living in the valley as they welcomed questions and suggestions from Sean and Clara and Louis. Tonight Clara asked "Jacques why are the farmers cutting off the tails and manes of their horses? Today I saw a horse running along the road acting as if it was crazy. No one was with it and it did not have any harness or reins on it so it could not have just run off."

After a few moments of silence, Jacques answered. "In most communities a prominent person is chosen to be the local leader of the area. He becomes the Captain of the militia and is in charge of the annual muster at the end of June. They all show up in front of the church, count how many are present so they can send in a report to the local government. It ends with three cheers to the King and then everyone goes to the tavern to drink. The Captains have very limited powers from the legislature and often these positions are granted as a way of recognizing loyalty to the legislature. It is often just ceremonial with deep historical roots. The captain usually has a maypole erected in front of his home to honour the position. The maypole is usually just a stripped pine tree with the evergreen left on the top but again there is quite a ritual when it is erected. Lately though many of the Patriots feel these captains should resign their post as we do not want to be governed by the British. If we are going to have our own government, then no one should be taking orders from the British."

"Jacques I have not heard you speak so strongly about the reform before," Gabrielle said in a very surprised voice.

"Well we are all getting tired of not being recognized and almost being tred on by the British. I hope it doesn't come to fighting but I am afraid it will. Anyway, as I was saying some local Patriots have taken it upon themselves to convince any Captain who does not want to resign his post to do so by using some old tactics. There has been some intimidation going on at night especially near St-Eustache. They have cut down maypoles, threatened to burn houses and as you saw Clara, they cut off the tails and shaved manes of their horses. The poor horse is maddened by insects and is no good to do any work. Often it just has to be shot. There is one poor Captain who they tied up in a chair in his house and threatened to shoot him in front of his wife and children. That is going a bit too far by my thinking. Also in some counties where there are many immigrants from Scotland and Ireland who want no part of this fight, the Patriots are forcing them to become part of the rebel group under the threat of having their barns or houses burnt. Several have been."

Sean added, "That must be happening here too if Clara saw a horse like that."

"We are fairly safe here as most farmers think the same way, but yes there are a few men threatening anyone who does not conform." Here in St- Denis we are lucky as this is the home of Nelson, and he is able to keep most on a sane path. There are men stationed at the river to watch for any troops coming from Montreal or Quebec. If that happens we might have a days notice if we are lucky."

"On that happy note I think we should all turn in for the night," Gabrielle said as she cleared the cups from the table. "There will be more work tomorrow."

"Speaking of work," Jacques added, you all did a great job of picking all the apples and storing them in the cellar. The apples are small this year but it was a fair crop considering the weather."

Several days later a rider stopped by the farm with a letter for Jacques. He was quite surprised as he rarely received any mail. He walked to the house to read it with Gabrielle.

"Gabrielle we have a letter from my brother in St-Eustache. Do you have time to sit with me and read it?"

"Of course I do," she said as she hurried over to the kitchen table. She sat down beside Jacques and read it together.

Dear Gabrielle and Jacques

I am writing to let you know what is happening here in our area. As you know most of us are angry as to how the British are treating the French. There are many more French speaking habitants here in our area than there are English speakers. Sorry Gabrielle, I do not mean you of course. They go against any of our requests and will not spend any money for roads or our own French schools or bridges to cross the rivers. Of course Papineau did not get his resolutions approved from Britain, so the feeling here is the only way to get any change is by force. The farmers are gathering and practising to fight the British. The Assembly in Montreal think we are not really a threat so have started sending troops toward your valley. They think you guys are the threat. Any farmer who does not want to be part of this is being given a rough time, often at gunpoint until they agree to fight. We have tried to reform things peacefully but that has not worked so I think a revolution will happen.

I have talked to Marie and Jean in St-Hilaire and Jean tells me things are quite tense where he is. He says that troops are often seen at Fort Chambly along your river. He says if you decide to leave St-Denis do not go toward the river or toward Montreal. They are gathering people up and taking them to jail in Montreal if they suspect you are French. Marie has left the farm and taken the children to her parents place near Napierville, so Jean is there with just the hired hand. I talked to Joseph the other day and he said Justine has gone with her mother and Sophie to Montreal to stay with Mrs. Dumont's elderly mother. I guess they feel it is safer there but I am not sure it is. I guess parts of the city are safe.

Gabrielle, you must be happy your brother is no longer living in Montreal. Though I hear the Mayor of Toronto is complaining about how the British are treating the people of Upper Canada and they are English speaking. Someone told me he is starting to talk about fighting as well.

I will sign off for now and remember to stay safe and listen to the rumours about where the troops are going. Let me know if you leave and where you end up.

Stay safe mes Amis
Henri

~

"Well that is quite the letter. He is almost telling us we should leave now before fighting breaks out," said Jacques. "I think though that after the big meeting next week in St-Charles we will have a clearer picture of what will happen. I don't like the part about troops being sent to the valley though."

"I really do not want to leave our farm here or leave you behind," replied Gabrielle. "If we go I want us to all go together, but I know that will not happen. I was thinking if we had to leave I would try to get as far as Marie and Jean's farm for the first day, but now I am not sure we should go that way as it is so close to the river. We will have to rethink our original plan. But for now we should not tell the girls including Clara as I know she really worries about this. You should probably talk to Sean and Louis about what will happen. By the way I know they have been doing practise shooting in the field. Are they getting to be good shots?"

"They will be just fine so do not worry. I need to get back to work. See you later."

ELEVEN

'WAR IS WHEN THE GOVERNMENT TELLS YOU WHO THE BAD GUY IS. REVOLUTION IS WHEN YOU DECIDE THAT FOR YOURSELF.'

Benjamin Franklin

Fall arrived early in the valley. By mid October there had been several hard frosts killing any late vegetables remaining in the gardens. The trees along the roads displayed their brilliant reds and golds, defying the unrest felt by the farmers. Over the past summer there had been rallies held in several counties around Lower Canada in defiance of the government. The protest movement was growing and finally the largest rally so far was being organized for the six counties in the Richelieu Valley at St-Charles. Revolutionary ideas were being spread, encouraging the Patriots to join and fight for equality. The leader of the Patriote Party, Joseph Papineau was to speak to the public.

"Gabrielle, are you sure you want to take the girls to this rally," asked Jacques? "It is rumoured that five thousand people may attend. It will be cold to just sit on the ground and listen."

"Clara and I have no intention of missing this historical event. We will bundle up the girls and there will a place for them to run around as other children will be there too. Lily is going and bringing her young ones. We will only go the morning of the second day rather than for both days. You want to go too don't you?"

"Of course I do, but it may not be comfortable or even safe for women."

"Gabrielle and I have the whole trip planned out with food and warm clothing and even a plan to leave in a hurry if we have to," added Clara.

"Fine then. You just need to be careful and try to watch the girls all the time. There will likely be an unsavoury element there as well." Jacques walked out of the kitchen to the barn as he knew he would not win this argument.

Two day later everything needed for the trip was packed in boxes and loaded onto the wagon for the short ride to St-Charles. Sean and Louis rode the horses beside the wagon.

Clara was amazed at the traffic. "I did not think this many people would be on the road going to this rally. Where have they all come from?"

"Word has been spreading all summer, so I am not surprised," replied Jacques. "Mr. Papineau has a large reputation."

As they approached the field outside of St-Charles, the traffic was a solid line of wagons waiting to go into the field. Finally Jacques found a spot midway between the entrance and the stage to park the wagon. The horses remained hitched and tethered to the wagon in case a hasty retreat was required. There was no sign of any speakers at the front yet, but a group of young men were lined up near the front and appeared to be taking an oath of allegiance to an older man in front.

"There are still more wagons coming in, but this does not look anywhere like five thousand to me," remarked Gabrielle. "They may have been very optimistic when planning this."

"You may be right," said Jacques. "The boys and I are going over to speak to some other farmers up by the stage to see if we can find out what is happening."

Just then, Lily Bisset came over to their wagon with her children who instantly began playing games with Gabrielle's three girls. The women all sat together and the conversation turned to the events of the day and the well being of neighbours.

After at least an hour, Jacques returned and reported what he had heard. "The organizers are disappointed as only about half the number expected has arrived, but the speakers are going to start any time now. Gather up the children and maybe feed them lunch during the speeches as some of the organizers do not think women and children should be here."

The speeches began and every time a statement was made regarding defeating the British, a roar went up from the crowd. Papineau spoke of regaining the right to elect judges and militia officers from their own parishes as way to political reform. But for some of the more radicals in the party, he had not gone far enough. Several from the valley called for armed insurrection rather than speeches. Just as things were becoming serious, a loud crack of thunder was heard and the dark clouds that had been gathering opened up and a drenching rain began. The speeches continued, but many families gathered up their belongings and began leaving the field which was quickly becoming a sea of mud.

It was a long cold wet ride home that afternoon to the safety of the farmhouse. Dry clothing, a warm fire and hot soup revived the worried family somewhat. That evening after the children went to bed, the adults gathered around the kitchen table to talk about what they had heard today.

"I am not sure that this will just disappear without a fight," said Jacques. "Papineau did not seem as keen to fight as the rest of the speakers, but I think the others may out vote him if it comes to that. Papineau did declare that the six counties in the valley were now independent so I think the British Militia have us in their sites."

"Nelson was adamant that we just start fighting the government, I was so surprised when he said that," Gabrielle added. "Who was the doctor from Napierville that said we must send lead to our enemies not speeches?"

"I think it was Dr. Côté," Sean replied. "What are we to do now? Do we leave before anything happens or do we stay and fight?"

"Stay and fight," said Louis very loudly. He then realized he had almost yelled that statement as everyone was looking at him but not saying anything. "I know you may think I am wrong, but my whole family died because the government did not care about how we were surviving here in the valley. Someday I want to have a family and live on our old farm. I have learned so much about farming that I know I could be a good farmer like you are Jacques. I cannot let the memory of my family just disappear by running away from the changes that need to be made. The British do not care about the French and they never have cared. They are trying to force us to become English by getting rid of our language and our culture. We must fight."

The rest of the family were speechless as they had never heard Louis say so much and be so passionate about his heritage.

"You are right Louis. Your history and the memory of your parents are very important. But you must realize that the British are very strong and have a lot more guns than we do." Jacques continued even though Louis tried to interrupt. "I too am French and know that what the British are trying to do is all about keeping more land away from France. I am not willing to risk my life for political power. I also do not want to lose this farm after all we have put into it, but if I am alive I can always rebuild. If I am dead there is no future for those left behind." Jacques looked over at Gabrielle and saw the look on her face. It was a look of hopelessness.

"Louis if you feel you have to fight, we hope you will not be angry at us if we do not fight. We know you are doing what you think is right, but so are we." Sean continued. "We are all part of the St-Pierre family and we all respect each other and their thinking. I would like to take over this farm when Jacques gets too old to work anymore and would be thrilled if we were almost neighbours." Sean looked over at Jacques and smiled.

The last comment broke the tension in the room and the conversation continued at a friendlier manner. By the end of the evening, a plan was made if the inevitable happened, and everyone knew the part they would play.

Unbeknownst to the St-Pierre family and the rest of the valley, the path Lower Canada was about to take would change all their lives forever.

On the same day as the rally in St-Charles, a warning was heard in the streets of Montreal. The President of the Bank of Montreal spoke to at least four thousand people regarding the government's feelings about the steps the Patriots were suggesting. He stated that they had a right to meet and discuss and petition if they felt wronged, but if the laws were ignored or overstepped, their behaviour would not be tolerated.

The Bishop of Montreal, who had sided with the Patriots in the past, wrote a letter issuing a warning to them and condemning their actions. He warned against revolution as the guilty and the innocent would all be considered the enemy. He reminded them that every revolution was as he called it *'a bloodthirsty act.'* By the time the Patriots heard the warning by a person they thought of as a supporter, it was too late.

The next few weeks were tense as every time Jacques met a neighbour, he came home with upsetting news. As he walked into the house one afternoon, Gabrielle looked at him and said "What have you heard now?"

"The rumour is that there have been street fights between the English and French clubs in Montreal almost every night. The authorities are starting to lose their patience. The Militia are on guard all the time and arrests have been made. The Governor has also sent several troops out of the city toward Two Mountains and south of Montreal."

Clara was sitting in the chair by the window sewing while listening to this news. "Are the Patriots fighting in those areas? Have people from both side been arrested?"

"The Patriots are fighting but they are very disorganized. They do not have a strategy, but have lots of bravado as they fight for survival. They seem to be winning at this moment, but many local leaders have been arrested. No English have been arrested but some have been held hostage and harassed by the Patriots. The English have been snooping around some villages and giving names of leaders to the militia."

Two days later Jacques, Louis and Sean came in for lunch and Jacques announced, "The governor has issued warrants for the arrest of the Patriot leaders including Papineau and Nelson and several others. They have been charged with high treason. Apparently a Patriot force attacked the Montreal Volunteer Cavalry near Longueuil and some were killed. So now the British are on the lookout for the leaders. Since Nelson is from this area, I am sure they will be looking around St-Denis. It's November so the river will be frozen soon. It is easier for them to come up the river with their canon if it is frozen. Of course there are Patriot lookouts everywhere."

Gabrielle spoke quietly and slowly. "I guess it is time to put our plan into action."

"Likely sometime in the next week," answered Jacques

No one spoke during lunch but everyone was having the same conversation in their head about the situation. "Where will we end up? What if I have to shoot someone? Will we be safe anywhere? What will the British do to us if they catch us? Will we ever see the whole family together again?" And of course there were no answers at this time.

The next five days were very busy. Anything of value was buried near the barn in what everyone hoped was a safe spot. Sean piled straw and manure on top of the digging spot to make it inconspicuous. Gabrielle dried some meats that would be easy to carry along with some other portable foods. Everyone had a small sack packed ready to take, except for the men. They were preparing their guns and stowing ammunition in small sacks that they would carry in their pockets. The harnesses for the horses were kept on the wagon so they could hitch up the horse quickly in an emergency. The family was as prepared as they possibly could be and ready to escape in moments when necessary.

There were Patriots on watch in the woods looking out for any British that might be in the area trying to find Nelson and Papineau.

Several were spotted but as they were travelling in small groups, the Patriots were able to chase them off.

At the end of the week, as the family were sitting at the dinner table, Jacques announced. "Gabrielle, I think you and Clara and the girls should leave tomorrow morning and head toward St-Hyacinthe. You have the name of a friend where you can stay one night. It is a long way for a day, but you will be away from the river where the British will be travelling. Do not stop to give anyone a ride unless you know them and do not go out of your way to take someone to a different place. I know it sounds harsh but it could be a matter of life or death."

Everyone just kept eating while staring at their plate of food.

Clara went to bed early as she knew tomorrow would be a long day. Earlier she met Sean out by the well and began to talk to him. "I know that you are staying to fight with Jacques and Louis, and even though I think that is stupid, I understand why you are doing it. I just hope that we can meet somewhere after this is over, or when you decide to not to fight anymore."

"I will always keep fighting as long as I have to, you know that. When we beat the British and the fighting is over, I will be back here at the farm. You can return and we can continue living here. So you know where you can find me."

"I will come and find you and I just hope you will be here. I would really like to go to school when this is all over and become a teacher. Gabrielle says I have almost finished enough school work to be able to go to a school for teachers, in English of course. Maybe there will be one in Montreal."

It suddenly became quiet and neither Sean nor Clara could think of anything else to say, but neither wanted to leave and go inside. Clara walked over to Sean and gave him a huge hug and to her surprise, he hugged her back.

"Good bye Sean. Be safe and I hope we will be together again," Clara murmured softly. Clara then walked into the house with tears streaming down her face.

TWELVE

'THE WORLD MAKES WAY FOR THE MAN WHO KNOWS WHERE HE IS GOING.'

Ralph Waldo Emerson

Clara and Gabrielle planned to leave right after an early breakfast the next morning, but as often happen, plans can change.

Very early the next morning a rider passed the St-Pierre farm and stopped to alert the family.

"The British have been spotted coming from the north and should be here in St-Denis about mid morning. They have about three hundred soldiers in their company. Also there are many troops now south of Montreal and are headed north toward St-Charles. Patriots are gathering at the stone house in the village as soon as possible."

Jacques sprung into action, awakening the family and sending Louis out to the barn to ready the wagon and saddle the horses. Sean appeared downstairs and was told to help Louis and get the guns ready. By this time there were several neighbours standing at the farm lane all talking at once and reporting the news they had heard.

Gabrielle was shouting instructions to Clara and gathering the packages of food to take with them. It looked like an army of ants scrambling to gather their supplies ahead of a torrential rain storm. Everyone was running in different directions but doing the job at hand.

Clara brought the wagon to the house and Gabrielle loaded the supplies and the children. Jacques and Sean came over to the wagon and quick goodbyes were said. Hugs and kisses exchanged. The wagon then set off down the road, no one knowing if they would ever see each other again.

Jacques returned to the house and gathered up the belongings he wanted to take. "Sean. If you have anything you need now is the time to get it as we may not be back for awhile. Meet me outside in five minutes. I am going to get Louis."

"I will." Sean went to his room and picked up a warmer coat and hat, took one last look and went outside to meet up with Louis and Jacques. He was fond of this house and all the good memories that had been made here. Jacques and Gabrielle had welcomed him and Clara into their home. They had adopted them into their family and now it all could end. This was not anything like the plan he envisioned for himself or Clara. What if he never saw Clara again? What if something terrible happened to Gabrielle and Clara and the girls while they were travelling? What if he discovered he was not as brave as he thought? Sean straightened himself up, spoke to himself saying. "Smarten up. You are a man now and you must do your duty. You can do this. Clara and the others are afraid but brave as well. You can do this."

He walked tall as he left the house but there was an ache in his heart and the tears were close to filling his eyes. By the time he found Jacques and Louis, he had regained his composure and was able to begin this next chapter in his life.

The three men walked into the village of St-Denis and arrived at the large stone farmhouse. Many men had already arrived, some walking, some on horseback.

Inside the house, both Nelson and Papineau were talking to local leaders. Nelson then spoke to the whole group. “The British were planning a two prong attack from the south and the north focusing their attack on St. Charles, but due to rain and snow, the group from the north had to stop and rest for a day. They have a large canon which is getting stuck in the mud so it is slowing them down. They will be cold and exhausted when they arrive. They have more guns than we do and more soldiers, but as we know they are coming, we have the advantage. Some of you go into the woods behind the house and start firing once you see them close to the house. We are safe inside so keep the windows and doors covered. The walls are almost a foot thick.”

“I must also tell you that we have a British officer captive here. He arrived at my home several nights ago not dressed in uniform. He said he was a civilian going to St-Charles. After he warmed up by the fire, I asked to see his papers and discovered he was a British Lieutenant. I did not tie him up but had two Patriots guard him all night. Today we are putting him in a cart and sending him to St-Charles. I do believe he is spying on us, and I did see a note on his paper about the ammunition being given to the British Militia. So be careful about strangers in the area.”

Suddenly the church bells in the village began to ring. This was the warning that the British were in site. Everyone took to their stations and very shortly gunfire could be heard.

~

After Gabrielle and Clara left Mrs. Bissett at the church, they climbed back in the wagon and started their journey on the road heading out of St- Charles. Gabrielle was driving the wagon now so Clara could take a break. She was relieved to be riding as she could feel the tightness in her shoulders and arms from holding the reins while driving.

“Clara, we have to find the road to St-Hyacinthe that goes off to the left. It is called the mountain road and there may or may not be a sign. The road that goes straight goes to St-Hilaire but it is too close to the river and there may be militia there. Also," added Gabrielle, "Jacques' brother said the family has already left the farm in St-Hilaire because of possible trouble so we must go to the south east instead. John said he has a friend in St- Hyacinthe that will let us stay on our way. We may have to sleep on the floor but we will be ok for a night. Their names are Mr. and Mrs. Hawley and they are originally from Montreal but moved to the townships where it is more English. So while we are there we must speak English. The girls may not know enough but speak to them in English or whisper to them in French. It will be fine for one night."

"The girls will be fine as they may be so shy they may not speak at all. I see a road up ahead that may be the one we are looking for. At least I think it is a road and not just a farm lane."

"Oh yes," replied Gabrielle. "I do remember this corner. This is the road we take."

The sun behind them was getting closer and closer to the horizon and soon it would be dark. The family had stopped only twice to change drivers and take needed bathroom breaks. They were starting to see farmhouse lights along the road and hoped it meant they were getting close to St-Hyacinthe. Ten minutes later they were approaching the edge of the village. Gabrielle had instructions to turn at the small store on the corner across from the church.

"This looks like the place we turn to get to The Hawley's house. It's a good thing there is only one church in town." The followed a narrow road until they came to a house with a fence around the front with a gate leading to the front door. "This looks pretty fancy. I hope they won't be appalled by the way we are dressed."

Gabrielle pulled the wagon alongside the fence and stepped down to the ground. "I will go to the door and introduce myself. Wait here until I come back out."

Clara hoped they would be able to stay as she was really tired of sitting on the hard seat, and the girls were starting to complain about being crowded in the back. "Listen to me girls. When you are introduced to Mr. and Mrs. Hawley, you must answer in English. You will say Hello Mr. and Mrs. Hawley." The girls repeated the words and just in time as the front door opened and out came Gabrielle.

Gabrielle was followed by a nicely dressed woman about the same age. "Girls, this is Mrs. Hawley who has kindly agreed to let us stay here tonight. These are my girls Mrs. Hawley, Clara, Elodie and Julie, and Marie.

"Hello girls. I am pleased to meet you and glad that you are staying with us tonight."

Just as they had practised minutes before, the three youngest girls said together, "Hello Mrs. Hawley." The pronunciation was almost perfect. Clara then added, "Hello Mrs. Hawley. Thank you so much for having us tonight."

"Let's get you all into the house and washed up. It is almost dinner time and I bet you are starving," said Mrs. Hawley as she helped Marie down from the wagon. "I knew you would be coming but was not sure when, so I have beds rolled up for you in the extra rooms at the back of the house. Gabrielle, you can take the horse and wagon down the lane past the fence and turn the horse loose into the field. There are oats or hay in the barn as well."

"Thank you Mrs. Hawley. We did bring food for the horse with us."

"Please use some of ours and save yours as you don't know how long your journey may be."

Dinner that night was plain but delicious after a long day on the road. It was even better when someone else had cooked it for you. It turned out the rooms Mrs. Hawley had set up for their night, were the part of the house that would have been designated as the servant's quarters. It was clean and dry and quite nicely appointed. The girls quickly snuggled into their beds after Mrs. Hawley had insisted they have a bubble bath in the large metal tub out in the back kitchen.

After the girls were asleep, Clara, Gabrielle and Mrs. Hawley sat in the parlour and chatted. Gabrielle was curious so she asked, "How did you know my brother in Montreal?"

Mrs. Hawley chuckled and said, "I was a secretary at the law office where he worked. My husband was one of the young lawyers just like your brother and we were just starting out. Money was tight and the law firm needed someone who could type and file. Fortunately I knew how to do that, so they gave me the job. It was quite rare for the firm to hire a woman especially as I was married. We got to know your brother quite well and became good friends. Several years ago we decided to leave Montreal and moved here to the townships as life there was not as safe or friendly if you were English. My husband set up a small law firm here and travels around the township if he is needed. Life here is a slower pace and more friendly. Now please tell me what is happening where you live and how far away are you planning to travel? Is your husband involved in any of the fighting?"

Gabrielle told Mrs. Hawley why they left in such a hurry and what was happening. "We are planning on going to the border and cross into the United States. Apparently there is quite a community of French now living there, so we can stay there. Hopefully when it is safe we can return and continue our life as farmers. We just hope Jacques and Sean and Louis are safe."

"You have had quite a journey today. You may stay here several days if you wish before you journey on. Where are you going next?"

"We are planning on travelling to a friend's house near Granby where we will rest for two days. They are parents of a good friend when I lived in Montreal. It is not as far tomorrow so I think we should keep moving away from the river. I do thank you for your offer and of course for your hospitality tonight."

Mrs. Hawley looked over at Clara and saw a big yawn escape. "I think we all should retire as I am sure you will want a fairly early start after we all have a big breakfast. I have kept you talking way too long."

~

Jacques and Sean were assigned to the second floor at the back of the stone house to shoot at any British coming close to the house. Louis went with a friend into the woods on the north side of the house to stop the British from advancing. "I wish Louis was here with us, "said Sean. "How will we ever find him again?"

"Don't worry Sean, Louis is a good shot and he can take care of himself. All the men out there are covering for each other. You are a good shot too so just take a deep breath and aim well if you have to."

Sean noticed two men dressed like habitants come out of one of the bedrooms and head down the stairs to the back of the house. They were carrying guns but were watching carefully to make sure they did not encounter anyone rather than focusing on the activity outside. "Did you see those two men going downstairs Jacques? They looked suspicious."

"No I didn't notice them. How were they dressed?'

"Just like us."

"Everyone has a job to do so who knows what their job is?"

Sean decided they were not likely spies and maybe his imagination was working overtime, so he sat at the window watching for the British.

At the front of the house several men were putting Lieutenant Weir into the cart and decided they needed to tie him to the side and prevent him from escaping on the journey to St-Charles. Many of the Patriots did not realize what was happening and in the confusion several shots were fired. Lieutenant Weir tried to jump from the cart but the strap tying him became caught in the wheel and one of the guards stabbed him in the neck. Men were yelling and dogs were barking. The horses bolted dragging the poor man behind the cart and the men at the scene began attacking the unfortunate Lieutenant with their clubs and pitch forks yelling "British Officer. Finish him off."

The rebellion had begun.

The British fired cannons at the stone house but they just bounced off the thick walls. Church bells were ringing to alert the village. From the windows of the stone house Sean and Jacques could see a steady stream of fugitives, mostly women and children and a few men heading south away from St- Denis.

The Patriots out in the woods were protected by the trees, houses and trenches that had been dug behind the house. They were able to surround the British who were left out in the open. Realizing this, the British quickly retreated back toward the river and North. The battle had ended after just six hours.

At the end of the day the Patriots were celebrating their victory. The talk was of the fifteen hundred habitants fighting off the three hundred British. In reality there had only been half that number of habitants with about twelve dead and wounded. The mood was upbeat despite the losses and knowing that their families were safely out of the town. What the Patriots did not know was another troop of British soldiers approaching from the north met up with the ones leaving St-Denis. They were regrouping and awaiting orders to attack when the soldiers from the south met up with them.

That evening Nelson met with the Patriots to discuss what had happened. He was annoyed that Lieutenant Weir had been killed. He also wanted to know where Papineau was.

Nelson would later discover that in the midst of the fighting Papineau and another leader had dressed as habitants and left the village with the women and children and were headed to the United States.

The Patriots victory was marred by rumours of defection of their leader Papineau.

Jacques and Sean found Louis sitting by a campfire near the stone house. "Let's all go back to the farm tonight and stay there. We will be safe and tomorrow we will find out what the next step is."

The ride home was quiet and at dinner there was no talk of victory. Sean and Louis both had a grim look on their face. This was not as exciting as many had expected. War may seem glorious, but right now, farming seemed like a better choice of lifestyle.

~

Gabrielle awoke early. She had slept well considering their situation. As soon as she heard Marie stirring, she decided it was time to get up and get ready for another day of unending bumpy roads.

"Everybody get up and dressed for the day. It will be cold again, so put on warm clothes. We must hurry and have breakfast so we can be on our way."

"Why can't we just stay here? Mrs. Hawley seems to like us and said we could," asked Julie.

"We must keep going as we are still too close to where the fighting is. Besides, we have plans to meet Papa and Sean and Louis near the border."

Everyone nodded in agreement and once dressed followed Clara down to the kitchen. Mrs. Hawley and her helper were busily cooking and putting food on the table for their breakfast.

"Good morning ladies. I hope you all have a good appetite as we have made you a large breakfast to eat before you leave," Mrs. Hawley said in her welcoming voice.

The three young girls did not quite understand all the English words, but with some hand motions they realized they were to sit at the table.

Breakfast was eaten and a thank you was said and the family of five were in the wagon and on their way.

Even though it was somewhat out of the way, Gabrielle decided to travel further east than was necessary. "We will be away from the river where there may be troops," she told Clara. "Jacques told me that Patriot groups often hide out in the woods but you can see smoke from their campfires. They will not harm us, and we will know it is not the British.

Today there were more groups of people on the road coming from St- Charles and from the west. Many were women and children walking or riding in wagons as they were. Gabrielle felt bad, but she stuck to Jacques statement not to give rides to anyone they did not know. Those walking did not ask either. It seemed everyone was afraid of each other as no one knew who the enemy might be.

When they came to the crossroads that led east to Granby or west to Fort Chambly, Gabrielle turned left and said to Clara, "It seems most people are going the other way. I am sure Jacques said Chambly is where there is a large group of British soldiers stationed. It may be easier to travel along the river but it is also easier for the soldiers."

They followed the road east until they were in an area with no houses or others on the road. Gabrielle could see smoke in the distance but it felt safer to stop here for a rest and change drivers. There was also a small lake beside the road with a sloping bank. Clara helped her unhitch the horse and take it down to the edge for a drink. They had to break the thin ice at the edge to get water for the horse. After bathroom breaks and a snack of delicious cinnamon buns from Mrs. Hawley, they began again with Clara driving the horse. It was cold enough to freeze the shallow water but the ground was only slightly frozen. There were still ruts in the road but at least they would not get stuck.

It was a monotonous day of riding with only one small village and lots of forests. As they passed through the village there was not a single person in sight. Clara did notice the movement of curtains in the windows as they passed several houses. People were in their homes but keeping watch.

By late afternoon the weary travelers came to the village of Granby. Like most small villages in this part of the country, the house had steep roofs to allow the snow to slide off in the winter. The barns were attached to the side or back of the house and led to fields that stretched away from the road. In the centre of the village there always seemed to be a church, unless it was a very small village. They found the house they were looking for almost at the other end of the village, and once again Gabrielle went to the door while the others waited in the wagon.

A woman about the age of Gabrielle answered the door. Gabrielle introduced herself, and mentioned she was a friend of Justine Dumont.

"Oh hello. I am Sheila Kelly, Justine's friend. My parents and I moved here to Granby a year ago as Montreal was changing with more violence and disruptions. Justine wrote to me and said you would possibly be stopping here. Do you have the children with you? You must bring them inside. We have a field and a barn at the back where you can put your horse for the night."

Gabrielle went back to the wagon and asked Clara to take the children inside while she dealt with the horse.

Clara introduced the girls to Sheila and to Mr. and Mrs. Kelly as well. Clara recognized the name Kelly as being Irish and Mrs.

Kelly spoke just as she remembered her mother talking. She felt she shouldn't ask that question just now. Maybe later.

Gabrielle returned to the house and was glad to accept the offer to sit in front of the fireplace for awhile. It was becoming much colder out tonight and the sky looked like it could snow.

Mrs. Kelly asked the first question almost the instant Gabrielle sat down. "Is there fighting in your area yet? We do not always hear about what's happening. We do know that the British Militia is gathering at Fort Chambly, but no one is saying where they will go next."

"The British did arrive outside St-Denis just before we left two days ago, but they came from the north. We have not heard what happened. My husband, Clara's brother Sean and our step son Louis stayed there to hold off the British. We hope they are safe."

Sheila quickly added, "We are pleased you are staying with us. Justine has told me so much about you. We worked together as volunteers in Montreal." She then turned to Clara and asked, "Clara I understand you were born in Ireland and came to Canada to settle here. Justine told me about your arrival here and how your parents died of cholera. I am so sorry for your loss. As you probably can tell by my parents' accent, they too were born in Ireland, and so was I. Where in Ireland did you live?"

"We lived in County Cork where we had a farm, but once the potato crop failed we had to leave as there was no food. I do miss the green hills and fields, but here we have good food to eat. Sean and I were very lucky to find such kind people as Jacques and Gabrielle who took us in."

Gabrielle quickly added, "Clara is such a help with the girls, I am not sure how I would cope without her. She is teaching the girls English and how to read and write."

"I hope you will be staying more than just one night with us, "Mrs. Kelly said. "I would love to get to know these lovely girls better. Tomorrow I was planning on making cookies to get ready for Christmas. Would you girls like to help me?"

"Oh yes," exclaimed Elodie and Julie at the same time. Marie just smiled.

That night the twins shared a big bed in a room all decorated in blue. Clara had a bed all to herself in the same room. Marie slept in another big bed with her Mom in a different room. This was a real treat for them and Elodie announced, "We all could be princesses."

The next day was one of the best days in a long time. There was no work to do on the farm and the girls and Clara helped Mrs. Kelly make cookies. Sheila and Gabrielle took the opportunity to sit in the other room and discuss the political issues happening in the country without having the girls hear about more problems. Sheila was able to give Gabrielle information about the unrest in Upper Canada, especially in Toronto.

"John told me about some of the problems but seemed to think they were not as serious as here."

"You are right. It is mostly one man trying to stir up trouble among the farmers. I guess they are not happy with how their government is treating them either. John is likely not involved much unless his law firm gets involved."

"He seems to know quite a number of people in the government as the head of his law firm there is well connected."

Sheila changed the subject. "Are you really going to go to the United States? Do you know anyone there? Is it easy to cross the border? How long will you stay? Forever? Sorry. That's a lot of questions."

Gabrielle laughed and then became quite serious. "I do not have many answers. Jacques and I decided it would be safer there as around St-Denis the men are all Patriots and hate the British. They think they can fight and win. I personally do not think that. The British are well organized and have more money. Many Patriots only have old guns that often do not work. Many only have clubs and pitch forks to fight with. I do agree with their reason for fighting, but it is very scary. I worry about Jacques and the boys. What if something happens to them? Maybe we can go back, but I am not a farmer and do not know enough to run a farm. Jacques has several friends living just south of the border who have already left rather than stay and fight. There is a small town in Vermont called Swanton and that is where we are headed. It will take us at least four more days to get there. Apparently crossing the border is easy if there are no British stopping or looking for people. We are just women so it should not be a problem. It is really hard on the little ones. They are being so good sitting in that wretched wagon all day. They hardly complain, but they must be tired of sitting. I know I am."

"Gabrielle you know you can always come back here and stay with us if you need to. We have lots of room and Mother loves the girls being here."

"Thank you Sheila. That is a comfort to know we have a friend if needed."

The girls enjoyed another night pretending to be princesses, and in the morning helped gather up their things to load in the wagon. Mrs. Kelly walked out to the wagon with the girls holding their little hands and Julie was carrying a large package containing lunch. Everyone knew that in that package were freshly baked cookies.

~

The day after the victory at St-Denis, Jacques, Sean and Louis fell back into their daily routine at the farm. The stalls were cleaned and the animals fed and watered. Jacques decided to haul a water trough away from the barn and fill it with water. With the current temperature, he knew it would soon be frozen but at least the cows could lick the ice. He also carried several forks full of hay and some grain out past the barn and put it against a fence.

When Sean saw him doing this, he asked why? "Aren't you worried wild animals and rodents will just eat this and it will be lost?"

"The sad truth Sean is the animals may need it if we aren't here to feed them. If we leave again to fight the British, I will let the animals loose to go where they want to. If we lose the next battle I think all our building will be burnt. The British are famous for fighting, winning and destroying property when they leave an area."

"Will we be fighting again soon?"

"I am afraid so. Someone said the group at St-Denis did not travel too far north again and another group have now joined them.

Some of our men have been following them from the woods and have reported back. Also another report from the south said a large group were leaving Fort Chambly and wanted to move north before the river froze as the ferry would still be running both as a way to cross the river and also as a means of retreat if needed. By the feel of it, I don't think it will be long before the river is frozen."

The rest of the day was filled with jobs that might never be done again. That evening as soon as the three men finished dinner, they blew out the candles and sat in the dark before taking shifts watching for approaching militia.

The British soldiers had returned to Fort Chambly waiting for a break in the weather. They had attempted to travel north marching in the dark to surprise the Patriots, but it had been rainy and cold and the roads were washed-out in spots sinking their cannons into the mud. The horses floundered in the mud often overturning their supply wagons. Several days later the troops began their march again. This time they were rested and well fed and in good spirits. At night as they marched they noticed off in the distance near the river and in the woods fires burning. The Patriots were watching them and sending warning messages ahead to their friends. Gun shots often came from those areas as well. As the troops marched north, many of the bridges were broken and road blocks had been set up with fallen trees. The British knew the Patriots were close, but marched confidently toward St-Charles.

The next morning Jacques awoke to loud knocking on his door. The person entered and called that the British would be attacking St-Charles soon. The three men were up and dressed in their warmest clothes in no time and had stuffed their pockets with food to eat on the walk. "We will not be taking the horse but we need to go to the barn and turn all the animals loose. Grab you guns and we will be off shortly."

When they left the farm, no one looked back even though all three wanted to. They decided not to follow the main road from St-Denis to St-Charles but instead took a back way through the fields. It was actually a shorter distance and this way they had no chance of meeting up with British troops.

They reached the village and quickly followed the other Patriots into a makeshift fortress built as a defence in the field. Shortly after, the British troops entered the village from the south, but not a Patriot was in sight. When the officer sent a prisoner to ask permission to pass through the village, the British troops from the north arrived and confusion began. Gunfire erupted, the village was surrounded and most of the occupied houses were burned. Within two hours, the battle at St-Charles was over. The Patriots had suffered great losses. Fifty-six men were dead; Jacques and Sean were now prisoners along with twenty-five others locked in the church at St-Charles. Louis was not one of them. They were held there for two days. The British General then forced his prisoners to march for three days and nights in the cold and snow toward Montreal.

Sporadic fighting erupted along the Richelieu River over the next few weeks with the casualties being innocent habitants. Many women and children were left homeless as houses and out buildings were looted and burned.

Once the prisoners arrived in Montreal, Sean and Jacques were herded into a jail cell with many others. Every day more prisoners arrived. It soon became impossible to lie down. No one talked much but Sean and Jacques did whisper to each other. The room was very cold and damp, their clothes had never dried out from the march and the food was never hot and certainly not as tasty as Gabrielle's cooking. Jacque's biggest worry was not being able to contact Gabrielle or Clara. Sean asked one day, "Do you think we will hang for being a Patriot?"

"There are getting to be too many prisoners here for that to happen, but we won't know until they tell us."

Neither of them mentioned to each other about Louis, but both worried he had been killed at St-Charles.

~

Clara and Gabrielle were always nervous about going on to the next place John had arranged for them to stay. The Kelly's had been so welcoming and friendly and Clara had enjoyed being able to speak

English without having to think about every word. "I hope our next stay is as nice as the Kelly's."

Gabrielle quickly added, "I hope so too but we never know until we get there. It is so cold out today, and I hope if it snows it won't be much as the wagon will not go through much snow. We just have to keep going and hope for small amounts of snow."

"How far are we going today?" asked Clara.

"I hope we can get to Clarenceville. It is not as far as our second day but it is still a fair distance. If we are welcome we can stay two days as then it is only two days to the border."

This morning was somewhat different from other mornings. There were a lot more women and children on the road heading south. Some were in wagons, but most were walking. No one looked at any one else and no one asked for a ride. They were all moving south with a single purpose. When Gabrielle and Clara stopped to give the children a break today, someone always stayed with the wagon and horse.

By mid afternoon it was a steady stream of habitants entering the town. The home they were looking for was a large two story house on the main street with a shed and then a barn attached to the back. Gabrielle knocked on the door and after what seemed like a long time, a stern looking woman answered the door.

"Yes. What do you want?"

"Hello, I am Gabrielle Drummond. My brother John sent me a note saying you might be able to let us stay for a night on our way to Vermont."

"Oh yes I did get a note. We are not in the habit of taking in strangers as my husband and I are alone here and one never knows about country people. Are those all your children in the wagon?"

Yes they are. I am originally English but have lived in this area for about fifteen years. I assure you we are law abiding citizens and we do have our own food with us."

"Since we do know your brother, we will let you stay. You will have to put your horse and wagon at the back as I do not want it seen in front of my house. You may stay in the shed at the back of the house. There are some old beds out there for you to use. There is a stove you may light for heat and cooking. There is also an old privy at the back you may use. Now please do not bother us anymore tonight."

Gabrielle barely had time to say thank you before the door shut and the locks on the inside were bolted.

"We are able to stay here tonight but we are out in the back shed and not to bother those in the house. Tonight will be very different from the past two nights."

Clara added, "I could see she did not look pleased to see us. We will just try to make the best of it and think of it as an adventure."

The back shed turned out to be what was used as a summer kitchen. The family would have moved the cooking stove from the kitchen out to the shed and cooked there. This helped keep the house cool in the summer. The walls were not insulated and in fact daylight could be seen between the boards. There were spots that looked like large chew holes made by some sort of animal intent on getting in. Gabrielle hoped they were not in the shed tonight. It was quite dusty inside and smelled musty and what was likely the odour of dead mice. She shivered just thinking about trying to sleep tonight.

"Clara, bring in the food in the box and we can make a cold supper. I will get a large stone to put on top of it tonight to keep four legged creatures out." The food box was actually made of tin so her plan should work.

Clara decided she had to get the girls involved in the dinner plan as at the moment they were huddled together sitting on an old chair looking like they had lost their best friend. "Elodie bring in a blanket from the wagon and spread it on top of that chest. We will use that as a table to make dinner. Julie you go and bring in the bed roll from the wagon and put it on the chair for now. Marie, I will need your help to gather our cases from the wagon." Everyone now had a job and the mood seemed a bit happier, but not much.

Gabrielle was able to start a fire in the stove and the illusion of a fire helped a bit, but it was really only warm when you stood very close to the stove.

Dinner was cold stew and bread that Mrs. Kelly had packed for them. There were also some cookies leftover as well. Gabrielle wasn't sure what they would eat tomorrow as all that was left were pickled beans and apple sauce. Hopefully the next place on the list would be more welcoming.

It was a long cold night. Gabrielle and Clara decided that they would take turns keeping watch to make sure no animals came into the shed. Everyone else slept close to each other to keep warm and thankfully the big blankets from the wagon helped somewhat. While doing her watch Gabrielle felt sorry for the horse that was stabled in a lean-to where the wind could blow in. She fed him an extra ration of the precious grain tonight and hoped he would be alright and ready to travel in the morning.

They were all awake as soon as it was light and packed back on the wagon ready to move on. Gabrielle did not want to knock on the door to the house so she found an old piece of paper and with a stick rubbed in the coals, wrote thank you and left the note stuck in the back door. She vowed she would never treat anyone like she had been treated if the situation was reversed

Gabrielle and Clara hoped to reach Phillipsburg by midday. John was unable to give them a name of someone who might give them lodging for the night, but Jacques knew a farmer friend who lived just on the outskirts of town. They had sold several cows to Jacques once and in return Jacques had sold François grain and corn. François and his wife Anabelle had six children and were a friendly, positive family who just loved farming and didn't care to get involved in politics. Jacques had written them a letter asking for a favour but he did not know if the letter ever arrived.

Shortly after the noon hour, the very hungry family of five arrived in Phillipsburg. They drove through the village and were amazed to see so many people coming and going. Gabrielle followed Jacques' directions and just at the end of the houses in town was a long lane leading to a farm. The barn was visible but no house was in site. Gabrielle turned the wagon into the lane, "I sure hope this is the place and if not I hope they are friendly."

Two large dogs came running from behind the barn barking as though they wanted to tear anyone who stepped from the wagon to pieces. They were followed by three boys of various ages and sizes.

Shortly behind them was a man who looked like he might be the owner. The dogs were quickly quieted and the man asked, "Can I help you?"

"I am Gabrielle St-Pierre, Jacques' wife and these girls are our family." My husband sent you a letter earlier this fall, but you may have not received it due to all the conflict. We have had to leave our farm in St. Denis due to fighting. We are on our way to Vermont and were hoping you could give us shelter for the night." She realized she had just said this whole sentence without taking a breath. She was anxious especially after last night.

"I am François and yes I did get your letter. We were wondering when you might arrive. Of course you may stay here. We are happy to have good friends visit us. Boys take the cases to the house and any other pieces needed. Pierre, take the horse and wagon to the barn and feed and water the horse. Put the wagon in the shed and let the horse lose in the barn yard for now. Later we will put him in a stall for the night. Come to the house and you can meet my wife Annabelle."

Clara realized she had been holding her breath and suddenly took a big gulp of air. Everyone relaxed and was relieved they had a place to stay.

The house was hidden behind a grove of trees that separated the barn from the house. It was a log home with several additions to the one end. As they entered the house a blast of warm air hit the travellers. After almost a day and a half in the freezing cold, it was a welcome feeling.

The warm kitchen also offered up an aroma of freshly baked bread and possibly a beef stew bubbling on the wood stove. Annabelle quickly came over to the door welcoming everyone with a hug. Three young girls about the age of Julie and Elodie were partially hidden behind a couch but kept peaking out at the visitors.

"Maria and Anna come here and take everyone's coats and put them in the hall. Josie you can come here and say hello. Josie is four and the girls are seven and eight. You probably met the boys outside. They are Pierre who is nine, Jean is six and Henri is five. Come and sit. You must need some tea. Girls show your new friends where the outhouse is and where to wash their hands."

After helping everyone find the outhouse, Gabrielle and Clara returned to the kitchen and sat on the couch while Annabelle worked away at making tea and a snack for the girls. Both women were not sure about sitting some more but the couch was much softer than the hard wagon seat.

"I hope we will not be causing any difficulties for you if we stay tonight," Gabrielle spoke between sips of warm tea. "My girls and I are quite used to sleeping on the floor, and we have a bed roll in the wagon that the three little ones can all fit on."

"Oh my heavens no," Annabelle laughed. "We have two extra rooms at the back where relatives stay when they visit in the summer from Quebec City. I will send someone to get the bed roll though as it may get wet and damp outside. As you see we have six children and we just had to keep adding more rooms to the house to have space for everyone. Now tell me more about why you had to leave and how long you have been travelling."

Clara began the story of the fighting in St-Denis and how they left five days ago.

Gabrielle chimed in, "We have been fortunate to be welcomed by some wonderful families except for the place last night in Clarenceville. I suspect the older couple who knew my brother were tired of having people wanting to stay and as they were older, were likely afraid of letting strangers in their house. We actually slept in their outdoor summer kitchen last night."

"Oh dear, you must have all just about froze to death. Well our house gets a bit cooler at night but we keep the two stoves going in the parts of the house all night. Now where is Jacques? He is such a nice person, always so friendly when he came to buy cows or sell your grain. I hope he is not fighting with the Patriots. François was talking to some men who were on their way to Vermont the other day and from what they said, we understand the situation is quite bad with many Patriot deaths."

A sudden gasp escaped from Gabrielle and her hand quickly covered her mouth. "We have not heard anything since we left. Jacques, Clara's brother Sean and our Louis stayed to fight in

St-Denis. I am very worried but I do not know how to find out any information about them."

"I am so sorry to upset you. After we get the children to bed we can all sit and chat as I know François has some information, though it may not tell you where Jacques is. We are having an early supper tonight as our noon meal was more of a snack than a meal. Let's get you all settled in your rooms and see what the girls are doing. They seemed to have become new fast friends."

Dinner was delicious and with four adults and nine children all talking and giggling it was quite loud. That night the girls all decided to sleep in the large bedroom. Three girls in one big bed and three others on the floor on the bed roll. The boys decided the girls were silly so went to their room as usual. Gabrielle and Clara would share the other room that had two beds in it. Gabrielle decided to move Marie in with her later in case she awakened in the night and did not know where she was. Once everyone was settled and the dishes done, the adults sat around the kitchen table to chat.

"François. Tell Gabrielle and Clara what the man told you the other day about St-Denis and St-Charles."

François began the story he heard. "The battle at St-Denis was a victory for the Patriots as the British were not ready to fight, but at St-Charles the Patriots were far outnumbered and it was a disaster for them. Apparently many Patriots were taken prisoners and marched to Montreal and put in jail. Quite a number were killed as well. I am so sorry to tell you this horrid news. The towns were burned to the ground and many women and children escaped but with only the clothes they were wearing."

Clara added, "We saw a lot of people walking but many turned and went toward Fort Chambly. There were only a few men going that direction."

"The fighting continued around that area as well. Many British troops have been stationed there," François added. "I did hear that Nelson and Papineau escaped and headed toward Vermont. The British went back to St-Denis to find Nelson as there were rumours habitants were hiding him. They did not find him so they burned the town to the ground. There are many British soldiers wandering around town here, all disguised as habitants. They are watching for deserters trying to cross the border."

"We were going to try and cross the border either tomorrow or the next day," Clara exclaimed.

"We think you should stay here with us for awhile," Annabelle said quickly.

"Yes," added François. "It would be dangerous right now for you to try. Do you have a place to stay there?"

"Not really, "Gabrielle said. "We have some names of people Jacques knows who went there earlier because they did not believe in fighting. We are hoping for the best and that luck is on our side."

"No. You must stay here with us until things settle down. François has room in the barn for your horse and wagon and we certainly have space in the house. There is lots of food stored away for winter and we can find plenty of work in the house to keep us busy. Besides it is the winter now and not a good time to be travelling across the countryside with small children."

Gabrielle began to cry softly. "You folks are the kindest people. I have been so worried, trying to be strong for everyone." She looked at Clara and saw she had large tears streaming down her cheeks. "Clara has been such a help, never complaining all the while thinking about how she had to escape with her parents from Ireland not that long ago. If we could stay here for awhile, that would be a big relief. I have some money and you must let me pay you for letting us stay."

"No we will not talk of money," said François firmly. "Now I think we have had enough excitement for tonight. Tomorrow I will talk again with a friend and see if we can find out where Jacques and his buddies are hiding. Good night everyone and sleep well tonight."

Everyone awoke the next morning to a winter wonderland. It had snowed about six inches overnight and now it was clear blue skies and cold crisp air. The trees and houses looked like they were covered in icing sugar and with no wind, the snow stayed in place. The snow was the topic of conversation for younger ones at breakfast as plans were being made to go out and build forts.

François commented to Gabrielle, "I see you loaded the runners on the wagon when you left St-Denis."

"I had not even noticed them. Is that what was wrapped up in the grain sacks? Jacques or one of the boys likely did that knowing we would need them soon."

"Pierre and I will have a go at it later today. This morning though I am going to see my friend and find out what else he knows. I do not know how or where he gets his information, and it is better not to ask too many questions these days."

After breakfast the girls all had small chores to do around the house and today they were very keen on getting them done quickly. Soon everyone was involved in finding warm clothes and boots for the outdoor adventure.

Annabelle announced that Maria would be in charge of outdoors and the three women would stay inside to organize a few things.

"I would like to write some letters to my brother and to a friend to see if they can help us find out where Jacques and the boys are. I brought the addresses and some writing paper with me so I could let Jacques know when we arrived in Vermont. Is it all right if I use your address here as a contact?"

"Of course it is as you will be here into the new year or maybe till spring if need be," answered Annabelle. "You know it does get lonely here on the farm. The men are always busy and the girls are still young, so I am going to enjoy some adult female company. Now Clara you can come with me to the kitchen and help me make bread. I would love to hear all about Ireland."

Gabrielle began to think about what she wanted to write in the letters. She could hear the friendly chatter in the kitchen and hoped Clara did not mind telling her story as parts of it were very sad, and Clara was only fifteen. Annabelle was a very empathetic listener.

First she would write to her brother in Toronto and then she would write to Justine and see if her brother Emile could help them.

Phillipsburg, Lower Canada
C/O François Tremblay
November 28, 1837

Dearest John

First of all, the girls and I are fine. We left St-Denis on November 23, when the fighting started. Jacques and Sean and Louis stayed behind to fight with the Patriots.

We are here in Phillipsburg with some friends of Jacques', and will be staying here for the winter rather than going to Vermont. They are so kinds to let all of us stay here. François has a friend who told him some of the things happening in the Valley. It is not good. The Patriots were victorious in St-Denis, but then lost terribly at St-Charles on November 25. The town was burned and many men were taken prisoner and marched to Montreal. Nelson and Papineau escaped and no one knows where they are. Because the British did not find Nelson, they returned to St-Denis and burned and looted the town. We may not have any farm to go back to.

Before I forget, thank you for giving us the names of friends where we could stay. The Hawley's and the Kelly's were such welcoming people. Just lovely. The friend in Clarenceville did say she knew you but was quite annoyed that we asked to stay overnight with so many children. We had to stay in the unheated summer kitchen, but we all survived and are now here in a warm friendly place. Françoise and Annabelle have six children of their own so the girls are thrilled to have playmates.

Do you think you would have any way of finding out if Jacques, Sean and Louis are in the prison in Montreal? The rumour is they could hang for treason so they might need a lawyer. I am also sending a letter to Justine to ask if her brother Emile might know something we don't.

François is talking to his friend to find out more details today, so I will add more later.

Good day again

François just came back and said his friend heard there are trouble spots near St-Benoit and St-Eustache.

There has been no serious fighting, just small skirmishes. The rumour is that Papineau has fled to the United States but Nelson is nowhere to be found. So really not much more news from here.

I still have money in cash from the bank account and have all our papers regarding the farm with me. They are in a safe spot. Do not worry about the girls and me. But maybe pray the boys are safe and alive.

Your loving sister, Gabrielle

~

Phillipsburg, Lower Canada
C/O Françoise Tremblay
November 28, 1837

Dear Justine

How are you my dear friend? I heard you are now living with your family in Montreal. I hope you are safe there as we heard there was some trouble in the city.

As you see by the address, the girls and I are in Phillipsburg. We were on your way to Vermont to get away from the fighting. We left on November 23 from St-Denis and travelled this far. We are staying with friends and they think it is safer to stay here for the winter rather than try to cross the border.

Jacques and Sean and Louis stayed behind to fight with the Patriots. At St- Charles we believe they may have been taken prisoner and taken to Montreal. That would be the best case scenario considering the circumstances. Of course the British went back to St-Denis and when Nelson could not be found, they looted and burnt the town. So we do not know if we have a farm to return to.

I was wondering if your brother Emile still worked for the Government. If so, is there any way he could find out if Jacques or Sean or Louis is in the Montreal prison?

It may be a long shot but if it endangers his person or job in any way, please do not have him ask.

How are you and Joseph doing? Is he staying in Montreal with you or is he in St-Eustache? I will always remember fondly the lovely visit we had at your parents' place, and how we met Jacques and Joseph. What fun that was. Also how is Sophie? She must be a lovely grown up women by now.

Give my best regards to you parents and Sophie.
Stay safe and well my friend.

Sincerely
Gabrielle Drummond-St. Pierre

~

Gabrielle had just stuffed the letters into the envelopes when she heard the laughter of seven happy children come into the kitchen. There were coats and boots and lots of puddles on the floor, but seeing the rosy cheeks and smiles on their faces was worth cleaning up the wet things. For a few moments the children were able to forget about what was happening around them and enjoy the fun of just being a child.

THIRTEEN

'PREPARE FOR THE WORST, BUT HOPE FOR THE BEST.'

Benjamin Disraeli

John Drummond was enjoying his new job, his new house and his new friends in Toronto. Life here was civilized, and his status as a lawyer with a prestigious firm gave him many opportunities to socialize with the elite of Upper Canada.

However, lately at some of these gatherings there was talk of discontent among many people living here. It seemed to be more prevalent in rural area, and poorer parts of the city.

John began thinking about a strange occurrence last week at a party he attended at a friend's home. Many of the well known names in the government of Upper Canada were also in attendance. One surprising guest was the former Mayor of Toronto, William Lyon Mackenzie. He was a red headed Scotsman and a journalist who once owned the first newspaper in Upper Canada. He did not mince words when it came to government affairs and tonight was no different.

Mackenzie felt the privileged families of Canada were running the country and growing rich on the backs of the hardworking people, only showing them contempt and insult.

Tonight, at this pre Christmas party, Mackenzie began his tirade and went on to say that very soon the farmers would be taking over the city by force if they had to.

Later John was talking to another guest and asked him. "Do you think he means what he says about an uprising? The Governor does not feel this way and in fact has sent all the troops to Lower Canada as that is where the threat of rebellion is right now. Governor Bond Head feels he has the situation under control."

Macaulay thought for a moment and said. "There are squads meeting at the edge of town with guns and are practising every night. It may not be long before we see a civil war as I believe these squads and Mackenzie are in correspondence with Papineau in Lower Canada. Both factions are infuriated as we heard Mackenzie state tonight. I do not see how any of this will end without resorting to taking up arms."

"And here I thought it would be peaceful and safe here. That was one reason I left Montreal." John was also thinking to himself that he needed to somehow get in touch with his sister as well as to have Helene check on his house.

The party continued, but the mood had been spoiled with many attending worrying about their future and their safety.

~

The community of Lloydtown was small enough that everyone in town knew everyone else as well as their business. The founder, Jesse Lloyd, had come from Pennsylvania as a non-militant Quaker and built and operated a sawmill supplying the new farmers with lumber to build houses. He then built a grist mill to grind their grain into flour. Over time, Lloyd became dissolutioned with the government and joined the ranks of William Lyon Mackenzie as one of his chief associates. By this time Lloyd had ceased to be a Quaker.

Lloyd spoke at many rallies convincing the young and older farmers to join the rebels and attack the capital of Upper Canada. Two brothers, Peter and Edward Brown, after hearing both Mackenzie and Lloyd speak at Lloyd's home, decided they needed to join the rebels in order to improve not only their lives but also the lives of their future families. It was exciting to train and drill preparing for attacks. But as the time grew closer to the actual attack, both Peter and Edward were starting to have doubts.

Peter said one night on their way home from drills, "Do you think we will really attack the elite of Toronto? I wonder when this will all happen. It's starting to be winter and marching in snow is not what I signed up for."

"I think we will be able to just scare them and then some negotiations will take place," answered his younger brother.

"Don't be so naive. Why do you think we have guns? Are you going to chicken out and quit?"

"Not a chance." Edward almost yelled the answer at his brother, but in his heart he really was having second thoughts. He now had a girlfriend who he hoped to marry one day getting killed or injured was not part of their plan.

"I think I heard Jesse and Mackenzie talking about sometime in early December as the date for the attack, but don't say anything as it is supposed to be a surprise."

The brothers were quiet for the rest of the walk home each thinking his own thoughts.

Mackenzie meanwhile was getting anxious and wanted to get the rebellion going. He and his leaders set a date. The rebellion would take place on December 7th. But as with most wars, communication and secrecy are an important step to achieving victory.

One of Mackenzie's friends in Toronto informed him that news of the attack had been leaked to the authorities in Toronto. He suggested the attack be moved up and as many troops as possible be gathered at the north end of the city but Mackenzie refused.

Confusion reigned, messages were sent to Mackenzie to retreat but he would not. The rebels assembled at Montgomery Tavern and waited for reinforcements coming from the west. Several men on both sides tried to ride horses through the lines, but were shot which only fuelled the intent to fight.

The rebels started their march down Yonge Street but were met by a truce party coming north offering the leaders complete amnesty if they returned home. Mackenzie demanded it in writing and eventually the offer was withdrawn. The rebels continued marching.

Peter and Edward were in the middle of the pack marching south to Toronto. Peter leaned over to his brother and said softly, "No one seems to be in charge of this attack and we haven't been told exactly what we are supposed to do."

"You're right. I think we should try to stay in the middle of the troops rather than at the front. I do not want to seem like a coward and I do believe in the cause but maybe not enough to get killed."

"Stick together brother and at some point we may decide to go our own way. Stay alert."

Many of the men in the group of rebels did not even have guns. They were carrying clubs and pitch forks. Peter and Edward noticed some of the other men talking quietly to the man beside them and looking off in the distance.

By late afternoon they were marching with a line of riflemen at the front. The front row would shoot and drop to their knees so the second row could shoot. It was beginning to get dark and there was smoke and the smell of gunpowder in the air. As darkness fell, many of the men were confused by the method of fighting so turned and ran into the woods and the darkness.

Demoralized they returned to Montgomery tavern to await orders. They stayed overnight and harassed and threatened the poor owner until he fed them. By now it was Wednesday afternoon and about fifteen hundred men were sitting around waiting to be told when to attack. The leaders were arguing about timing. Mackenzie would not listen to his sources in the city suggesting he retreat and call the whole thing off. During this time many men drifted off to their homes. By the next morning when some reinforcements arrived there were only about four hundred men remaining to fight with the rebels.

At noon on the Thursday, the sound of bagpipes from the south signalled the approach of the Loyalist troops. Three troops began firing with guns and canons and sent many of the rebels running to the north.

Peter and Edward had decided sometime in the middle of the night to leave the rebels and go back to Lloydtown. This did not seem like the best way to convince the government to allow equal representation for all parts and people in the province.

Two days later Peter was working in the barn and said to Edward, "I heard some news today from a couple of neighbours about the end of the battle at Montgomery tavern. The Loyalists burned the tavern and a couple of other of houses. Mackenzie and several other leaders including Mr. Lount escaped to Niagara and crossed the river to the United States. Many farm lads were led to believe fighting was the answer just as we were, but unfortunately they paid the price."

"I have no regrets Peter about leaving and coming home. Especially when I hear the leaders ran off to America. Who are the real cowards?"

~

John Drummond arrived at his office the morning after Mackenzie and his rebels had attacked. He had heard the fire bells ringing the day before and had seen black smoke drifting south. He had just hung up his coat when George Macaulay came into his office and shut the door.

"Did you hear what happened yesterday? Before John could answer, George continued. "Mackenzie tried to take over the government with his band of farmers brandishing clubs and pitch forks and some guns. Apparently word got out ahead of time and the Loyalists in Toronto marched out to meet him. He was easily defeated and some prisoners were taken. There were casualties on both sides, but the real news is Mackenzie escaped. They think he went to Niagara and crossed the border. He was not so smart though as he left behind all his notes with the names of everyone who participated."

"How did you find out all this information?"

"I would rather not say but my source is pretty reliable. They are going to arrest all the participants and charge them with treason."

John was pretty sure he knew who the source was but decided it would be better not to know for sure. "That will be a lot of trials with so many rebels involved."

George interrupted. "Oh, and I forgot to tell you Montgomery's Tavern was burned as was Gibson's house. Today should be an interesting day here in the office."

John had hoped for a quiet day with time to take care of some of his personal business. Last evening when he arrived home, there was a letter from Gabrielle explaining what was happening in her family. Today he hoped to contact friends in Montreal who might be able to help him. "It is interesting that this attack has gone down at the same time as Patriots attacking in Lower Canada. Do you think the leaders may have conspired?"

"I did hear about some fighting there but I do not know much about what happened," replied George. "Have you heard anything?"

John then told George about what was happening and relating some of the details Gabrielle had included in her letter. "We are worried that Gabrielle's husband and sons may have been taken prisoner and are in jail in Montreal. Today I am going to try and contact a few colleagues to try and find out answers. I have a number of letters to write today so as much as I would love to discuss this George, I must get to work."

"I totally understand," George said as he left the office. "Let me know if you need any help."

"Thanks." John knew that George had connections in the Governor's office through his father and if he needed some help it would be there. He wished he had connections like this in Lower Canada. He did have a few through the law office in Montreal, but wasn't sure it would be enough to free Jacques and Sean and Louis if they were indeed in jail. Treason was a serious charge punishable by hanging.

John decided to write first to Justine and her brother Emile. Justine would be happy to hear that Gabrielle was as safe as possible and with friends. Of course Justine would tell Joseph and Emile about the letter and if they could help, they would.

Toronto, Upper Canada
December 6, 1837

Dear Justine

I am writing a quick note to let you know some details of which I have just been made aware. I received a letter dated November 28, from Gabrielle. She and the three girls and Clara had to leave St-Denis in a hurry the day the fighting started. They are now safe in Phillipsburg with friends and plan on staying there for the winter. However, Jacques and Sean and Louis are nowhere to be found. It is surmised they were taken prisoner in St-Charles and may be in jail in Montreal.

If you or Emile or Joseph know of anyone who can find out if they are in jail, I will be forever grateful. And of course so will Gabrielle.

I hope you are safe in Montreal. Things have changed everywhere since I left. There was an attack here in Toronto in the past two days by rebels unhappy with the government's treatment of people. Most of us are choosing to stay at home and not venture out except for work. It is not the joyous Christmas season we expect.

I must go as I have several more letters to write.

Thanks in advance for any help you can arrange.

Sincerely
John Drummond

~

John wrote the next letter to his friend Helene explaining the situation and asking if she could contact the Richards who were caring for his home. He wanted to let them know there was a possibility that Gabrielle and the girls or even Jacques and Sean and Louis may be staying temporarily at his home. He knew that Helene would give the news to Mr. and Mrs. Richards in a gentle manner so as not upset or worry them.

His next letter was to his boss George Moffatt again explaining the situation, but asking more legal questions about the rights of anyone taken prisoner. He also hoped that George would reply giving him some inside information about what was happening in Montreal and surrounding areas. He would have to wait patiently for that answer.

John then took a break walking around the office several times as his shoulders were aching from sitting in one position writing what were not cordial letters.

The next letter was a harder on to write.

December 6
Toronto, Upper Canada

Dearest Gabrielle

I received your letter today and am glad you are all safe. You are wise to stay in Phillipsburg for the winter as travel will be difficult with the children and there are many dangers on the roads now. Going to the United States not knowing people would present more difficulties.

I have written to Justine, Emile and Joseph and asked them to seek out information regarding the Patriots in prison. I also sent a letter to George Moffatt at the Montreal office to help clarify what is happening there and about the rights of prisoners.

I notified my housekeeper through Helene that if needed you and the girls or Jacques and the boys would be staying at my home in Montreal. Maybe not right away, but you know you are always welcome to stay there if need be.

As soon as I find out any information from Montreal, I will let you know at the address you included in your letter.

Keep me informed of any changes. Stay safe and keep a low profile.

Your loving brother
John

~

John decided not to tell Gabrielle about the attack in Toronto by Mackenzie as she did not need anything else to worry about. He just hoped it would be good news when he wrote the next letter.

FOURTEEN

'HOPE IS THE WORD WHICH GOD HAS WRITTEN ON THE BROW OF EVERY MAN.'

Victor Hugo

John tried to wait patiently for a letter from Justine or Emile but he was a bit like a young boy waiting for Christmas Day to arrive and find the much wanted toy under the tree. In reality it was just two weeks until Christmas but the arrival of the news he hoped for was more important than any present he had received in the past.

Two days before Christmas he received a letter from Emile. His hands were shaking as he opened it, hoping for good news.

John

Please excuse the lack of formality in this letter but nothing is as it should be now.

As you may have heard, there was an attack by the British in St-Eustache several days ago. The British had been going from small town to small town all the way along the north shore of the river. In each town they killed or arrested any Patriot in their way. They looted then burned most homes, farms and churches. When they reached St-Eustache the Patriots thought the church would be spared so a number of them boarded themselves inside. The British actually attacked from both sides of the river so the Patriots never stood a chance. Fire was set to the church and any Patriot trying to escape from the upper windows was immediately shot. So terrible. Many killed, or badly injured or taken prisoner. They were then marched to Montreal by the British troops in the snow and cold and jailed in Le Pied du Courant. Any Patriot who did manage to get away is now being rounded up to be arrested. They are all being charged with treason.

However, there are at least fifteen hundred prisoners in the jail and the logistics of hanging that many men is not feasible.

The very sad news is that Joseph Paquet, Justine's husband was killed in the church. He died a hero along with about twelve other Patriots. Justine is inconsolable needless to say. She is still in Montreal with our family.

I do not know anything about Jacques' brother, but I did not see his name on the list of Patriots killed at the church.

I do have some better news for you though. I asked around, do not ask how, and obtained a list of names of prisoners captured at St-Charles. Jacques St- Pierre and Sean Ryan St-Pierre are listed as Patriots charged with treason. There is talk of prisoners being allowed to consult a solicitor and sign a paper admitting guilt. I am going to try and arrange to see them and of course not let them sign anything at this point. The Governor is beside himself with trying to solve the whole mess. They have actually stopped the troops from arresting any more men as they have no room to house them.

I will keep you informed of any developments regarding the prisoners. I did hear a rumour of some being given amnesty but no one really knows yet. Let Gabrielle know that at this point Jacques and Sean are alive and in prison. Do not go into the details of the ramifications of treason. Though knowing Gabrielle, she likely knows all that.

I hear you had a bit of a rebellion in Toronto a few days ago. Who is next?

Stay safe my friend and have as good a Christmas as possible. Our family will not be celebrating this year.

Your friend
Emile Dumont

~

John was numb after reading the letter. He never thought things would get this far out of control. Maybe there was some truth to the complaints the habitants and farmers had. Maybe they were not being treated fairly. Maybe the privileges of the elite and their influence on the government did not address the needs of everyone in the country. Maybe there did need to be reform in both Upper and Lower Canada. Possibly the British did not have this country's best interests at heart. How could this problem be solved?

John sat for a long time, sipping his scotch until he realized it was dark outside. He felt he needed to be able to talk to someone, but it was the holidays and the office was closed until after the new year. He had turned down an invitation to spend Christmas with the Jarvis family but now he wondered if he could change his mind. It would be comforting to be able to talk to someone else and the presence of excited children might be good for him. Tomorrow he would see if he could change his mind, hoping that it was not considered bad manners. He was pretty sure the Jarvis's would understand if they knew the circumstances.

John was able to contact his friend Samuel Jarvis who was more than thrilled that he would be spending Christmas Day with them. He also wanted to talk about the situation in Montreal with John as he knew some lawyers there that might be able to help. John was happy to hear this information and for the first time in at least a month he began to feel positive about Christmas.

Three days before Christmas a letter arrived from George Moffatt.

Christmas Greetings John

I received your letter and have been asking in confidence about your sister's family. My colleagues have informed me that decisions regarding prisoners in Montreal will be made sometime next year. At the moment the charges of treason still stand but there are presently over a thousand prisoners in a jail that was built to hold less than three hundred.

I have assigned one of our senior lawyers to find out if your brother-in-law and nephew are in the jail. He will attempt to visit them and find out details and he will correspond with you when he has information.

I am sorry this is not better news but we are working on just that.

I am hearing good things from our Toronto office so keep up the good work.

Try and enjoy Christmas.

Sincerely
George Moffatt

~

John let out the breath he had been holding. This information was not much but at least there was a glimmer of hope. Now with just two days left, he must get himself organized and do some Christmas shopping. He needed to purchase a house gift for the Jarvis family as well as gifts for the children.

Christmas Day at the Jarvis home was as peaceful as possible with four excited children trying out new toys and sneaking candies from the dishes put out for the guests. John did have time to talk to Samuel privately after lunch while the children were supposed to be napping.

"I have been thinking about what you told me about your sister's husband being in jail for treason," began Samuel. "I have a friend in the legislature who may know some people who can help you. I can contact him if you would like and see what he can find out and possibly fix the situation."

"I would certainly appreciate that Samuel. I have asked George Moffatt who has put one of our Montreal lawyers on the case to see what he can do, but I guess the more people trying the better our chances are of getting them released from prison. I did mention my nephew was possibly there as well."

"Write the details on this paper and I will contact them right after the new year."

As John was writing down names and descriptions he wondered about the many prisoners who were not lucky enough to have any contacts in elite positions to plead their cause.

The rest of the day was enjoyable and when the time came to walk home, John was glad he had the chance to walk off the excess of food he had consumed in one day. He also had time to think about what he would write in a letter to Gabrielle. Should he wait until he heard something positive from Montreal or should he tell her now the few details he knew? He did not want to worry her more than she already was, but he also did not want to give false hope.

By morning he had decided to write Gabrielle letting her know the details he had been given and the plan his friends had formulated to find Jacques and Sean. At least it sounded like there was hope.

~

Christmas in Phillipsburg with the Tremblay family was happy and loud despite the dark cloud hanging over Gabrielle and Clara's head. The younger children were happy playing games together and did not seem to worry about things. Everyone received small homemade gifts to play with and there were new clothes for the numerous growing bodies. The fabrics and materials may have been rescued from someone's previous coat or dress, but it was new to the recipient. Christmas dinner was a combination of many preserved vegetables and several geese from the barn. Maple syrup seemed to be the main ingredient in all the desserts. After the children went to bed, the adults talked while sitting close to the stove. With full stomachs and the warmth from the stove everyone was ready to fall asleep.

Once in bed Clara began to think of Sean and Jacques. What kind of a Christmas dinner would they have had? How cold was it in the prison? Were they safe from other prisoners who were still angry? Tears filled her eyes as this was not how their life was supposed to have turned out. It seemed as though every time she thought about their current situation, she began to cry. How could she believe in reform for the habitants if this is how they were treated? She finally fell asleep while questioning was she really still a Loyalist? She wasn't sure she was a Patriot.

New Years Day arrived with cold snowy weather. Everyone hoped that 1838 would be a better year than the past four years. The town of Phillipsburg and the surrounding area saw an increase in the people passing through. Many were women and children wearing thin wool coats and often begging for food. There was also an increase in the number of military men, probably British, hanging around the streets. François heard from his friends that several Patriots had come this way to escape to the Unites States and the

British were watching in particular for some of the leaders. They often stopped the farmers asking questions about their activities and who was staying at their home. Some did not give the answer the British liked, were arrested on the spot and sent to Montreal as traitors.

The troops particularly liked to stand around where the stage coach stopped and watched as the mail was delivered. Gabrielle decided that she should pick up the mail and if she was questioned she would resort to her best English accent. A woman was not as likely a suspect as was a man. Gabrielle had her story all prepared just in case. Hopefully the military would not be suspicious of a letter coming from Upper Canada.

Half way through January a letter did come from Toronto. As Gabrielle walked out with her letter she was stopped by a soldier. He put his gun in front of her and shouted "Stop!"

Gabrielle looked at him with surprise and pretended not to understand, all the while shaking inside. She hoped he would not see her hands holding the letter shaking. She to him in English, "What do you want?"

"Who is that letter for and where did it come from?"

"This is a letter from my brother in Toronto. It is probably wishing me Merry Christmas." She showed him the envelope with the return address of his home.

"Oh go home where you belong."

Gabrielle decided to not answer that remark and returned to the house, thinking how ashamed she was to be from the same country as this rude soldier. She did not dare open the letter in public and walked as fast as she could as she was dying to read it.

Once in the house she quickly opened the letter to see what John had to say. It was only one page and she was a bit disappointed to still not know the whereabouts of Jacques and Sean, but glad to hear several lawyers were investigating.

She went to the room where the children were playing to see if Clara was there. Finding her, she handed her the letter to read, saying "I guess that is as positive as we can hope for now. I am very sad to hear about Justine's husband. She must be devastated. I think I will wait until next month to write to her."

"Yes. It is not really the best news, but it is not bad news either."

~

One day about the middle of December, there was a lot of action at the prison. A huge number of men were brought to the prison. Rumours began to circulate of another battle closer to Montreal had taken place and once again the Patriots were defeated. Jacques heard the name St-Eustache mentioned and began to ask questions in case his brother was somewhere in this prison. The story was that Patriots had taken refuge in the church but the British had fired shots and eventually set fires in the church causing the Patriots to try and escape through the windows. Most were immediately shot by the British or perished in the fire. The town was burned and again many habitants were homeless and losing everything they owned as well as family members.

The small towns surrounding St-Eustache were pillaged and burned not only by the British but also by many neighbours of English descent. These farmers had been treated similar to the French habitants, but to hopefully retain their homes and farms, they sided with the British.

The prisoners again were marched to Montreal and joined the others where there were over five hundred men jammed into the cells. It was now mid December and winter was keeping the prison even colder.

In less than a month the Patriot leaders had been arrested or escaped to the United States. The Patriot numbers had been reduced from eight hundred to less than two hundred. There were over five hundred men in jail who could hang for treason. The number of homeless women and children was too large to count. The Patriot movement for reform and fairness had been defeated.

January proved to be a brutal month in the cramped prison. The humid air from the crowded bodies clung to the walls and often dripped to the floor. If anyone tried to lean against the wall while sitting on the damp floor, their clothes soon became wet. The worst part was the rancid smell throughout the prison. In the area where Jacques and Sean were confined, the freezing nights were long but constantly interrupted by at least half the men coughing. In the morning it was common to find out someone had died in the night. Jacques had taken to wearing his scarf over his face. As dirty as it was he hoped it might stop some of the germs from reaching him. He tried to keep his mood upbeat so Sean would not feel so depressed. He noticed Sean rarely spoke about anything now, but just sat hunched over lost in his own thoughts.

One morning after the meagre morning meal, a guard came to the cell and called out, "Jacques St-Pierre."

Jacques stood up, looked at Sean while putting his hand on Sean's shoulder, smiled briefly and walked over to the barred door.

This had happened before many times and only once had the prisoner returned to the cell. Everyone was watching to see what would happen.

"I am Jacques St-Pierre."

"You have been summoned to the main office. Come with me."

Jacques nodded and did as he was told; only turning back once to look at Sean.

The prisoner and the guard walked past several cells just as full and just as smelly as the one Jacques had left.

After what seemed like a mile, they reached another locked door. The large key clanged as the lock opened a metal door to reveal a new part of the building. It was now lighter, cleaner and smelled somewhat better. The men continued along a hallway until they reached an open office door. As he entered the room, Jacques heard a sharp intake of breath from one of the men.

Jacques instantly recognized Justine's brother, Emile. "Good day Emile. What a surprise to meet you here." Jacques realized he must be a site and also that he had lost a considerable amount of weight. No wonder Emile gasped when he saw him.

"Jacques I am pleased to have found you. Are you alone here or are there family members here as well?

Jacques desperately wanted to sit down as his legs were now trembling from the long walk but knew that was not an option. My son Sean St-Pierre is in the same cell as I am and I am not sure about my brother Henri St- Pierre."

The military person at the desk began shuffling through a thick stack of papers but shook his head. "I do not see that name, but many here have not been listed as guilty."

"Jacques we are working on this situation where everyone will be identified and given a chance to speak to a lawyer about the charges. You have been assigned a lawyer from George Moffatt's law office here in the city."

At the mention of the name Moffatt, the sergeant at the desk sat up, looked at his notes and cleared his throat. "I will see if we can locate Henri St-Pierre and he, your son and you will be seeing the same lawyer. Now you must return to your cell until we contact you again."

As Jacques was being marched out of the office to go back to the hell hole he turned and said "Thank you Emile."

"Be safe my friend."

Emile turned and started speaking with the sergeant in an authoritarian voice about what the next steps would be in this case. All Jacques could hear was the Sergeant saying repeatedly, "Yes sir."

Inwardly he was smiling but he kept his stone face as he was put back in the cell while several prisoners mumbled about how lucky he was to still be alive.

Of course others wanted to know why he was taken out so Jacques just said "They are checking who we are and want our real names for the record." He then laughed to lighten the mood and not be grilled too hard about what was said in the office.

Later on when, things were back to their dreary normal routine in the cell, Jacques took Sean's hand and squeezed it and whispered, "We will be ok."

It remained cold within the prison walls for several more months, but one day to everyone's surprise and fear, the prisoner were told to march in single file outside to the yard. Many thought this was the end and they would all be shot. There was no talking in the lines but sobbing and sniffing could be heard.

When they arrived outside to their surprise, it was a lovely sunny spring day. "Well it's a nice day to die," said someone. No one laughed.

"You have twenty minutes to walk around before we go back in." bellowed one of the many guards.

Sean and Jacques quickly walked around the fence keeping an eye out for anyone they knew. Jacques was telling Sean about the visit with Emile. He had not had a chance to tell him privately what he had learned from his visit to the Sergeant. A voice behind them suddenly spoke. "Is that you Jacques?"

Jacques turned to see his brother, Henri standing there. He was as thin and disheveled as the other two but they just acknowledged each other by speaking. They knew any physical contact would be considered fighting and the consequences were just not worth it

Jacques asked as they walked, "How long have you been here? Where were you captured? You remember Sean of course? We were taken at St-Charles last November."

"I was captured at St-Eustache. I was one of the lucky ones. So many killed and the whole town burned."

"Do you know anything about Justine's husband Joseph Paquet?"

"No I don't' but if he was in the church it is not likely good news. Any idea how long we are stuck here? I thought for awhile it was all over today."

Jacques looked over his shoulder to make sure no one was within hearing distance and then told both Sean and Henri about his visit with Emile and who was to represent them. "I think we may be lucky on this one. Do not tell anyone though."

A bell rang and the men were ordered to get in the line for their cell. The last few minutes of warm sun on their faces would have to last until whenever later was to be.

~

Gabrielle, Clara and the younger girls had settled into a very comfortable routine with the Tremblay family. Everyone got along with everyone. Even the children rarely fought over toys. Gabrielle was glad she decided to stay on this side of the border. There were a number of soldiers still hanging about in town but once they knew who was local, they rarely bothered you. François returned one day from town waving a letter as he walked into the kitchen. He handed it to Gabrielle and everyone in the room became quiet. Annabelle quickly herded the younger children out of the kitchen and into another room.

Gabrielle opened the latest letter from her brother and began to read aloud with Clara sitting beside her. She knew they were in prison but was glad to hear the lawyers were working on resolving the cases hopefully with good results. Mostly though she was thrilled to know they were still alive. The remainder of the letter explained what was happening with the lawyers and the courts regarding the serious charges. "I am glad to hear that Henri is alive. Hopefully the three have chances to see each other in that horrid place. It is just so hard to wait for news coming in bits and drabs. Shouldn't this war over by now? What do these legislators do all day? If this was how they run the country, they should all be sent home to England."

May arrived with cold rains and cloudy skies. Once again the few farmers that remained in the valley had trouble getting on the fields to plant their crops. There was little left in the granary to feed the animals. The grass in the fields was growing but slower than the animals ate it. Children of course kept growing and parents worried about how they were going to feed their families as well.

The third week of May though everything changed. The sun came out, the rain stopped; gentle breezes blew across the fields drying up the mud allowing the farmers to plant their crops.

Children were happy to go outdoors to do chores and play with each other if there was time. Walking through the village one day Gabrielle heard someone humming a tune. Sunshine always helped change the mood. She hoped and prayed that Jacques and Sean were still safe and they might still be allowed to go out into the fresh air.

As she was walking a group of men approached her and began to ask questions.

"Do you live here? Where is your husband? Do you have sons who are fourteen?"

How was she to answer if they just kept asking and not listening? "Yes I live here and my husband and son have been in prison since St-Charles. Why are you asking?"

"Never mind." And they moved on.

Gabrielle thought this whole scene was odd. She would ask Françoise about it later tonight.

After dinner when she told Françoise what had happened there was silence for a few minutes.

"There is a group of habitants in this area who are joining with some from the United States to start the fighting again. They are a secret society so it is hard to find out much about their plans, but they are trying to get locals to join up and be a part of the group. They approached me last week but I said no. They accepted that answer for now but it may not be the case at some point. Things are starting to heat up again."

"Just when we think things are getting better, it gets worse."

About a month later another letter arrived for Gabrielle and Clara.

June 1838
Montreal

Dear Gabrielle and Clara, Elodie, Julie and Marie

It has been awhile since I have written anything so please excuse my terrible handwriting. Sean and I are safely out of prison and living quite nicely at John's home. It is a long story so here goes.

As you know we were defeated at St-Charles and marched to prison in Montreal in the cold. The prison was fairly new but with over five hundred of us it was very crowded. I will not tell you about the conditions as they are a bad memory. Sean and I did discover that my brother was there as well but we only saw him when we were allowed outside.

Your brother arranged for Justine's brother to help us and he found a lawyer from Moffatt's office. We were given good treatment by them considering we were charged with insurrection. Unfortunately several men were hanged and they exiled twelve leaders including Wolfred Nelson to Bermuda. They let the rest of us go. Luc Gagnon the lawyer from Moffatt's did not think it wise to return to St-Denis area yet so Henri and Sean and I are living in luxury at John's house. We have been here two weeks and we still have to scrub off some more layers of dirt before we are descent again. It is lovely to sleep on a soft mattress instead of a hard floor.

John's housekeeper seems a bit afraid of us but she is a good cook and we are gradually putting on some of the weight we lost. We are winning her over by doing all the hard jobs for her.

Sean is fine, but he did not feel like writing anything. He sends his love especially to Clara.

I have not heard anything about Louis and am very worried we lost him in the battle at St-Charles. I do want to go back to check things out but everyone including John insists we stay here until next spring at least. I will soon have to find something to do as you know I can't sit and do nothing. We are helping the gardener grow a vegetable garden and keep the house fixed up. But you know I like to plant a whole field not just a row of something.

Please do not leave Phillipsburg and come to Montreal yet. There seems to be a second wave of the rebellion and it is organized by men in your area plus some from the United States. The government has suspended the Lower Canada Assembly, a new Governor in Chief has been sent from England, and he is to investigate the reasons for the rebellion. This is not the time to be travelling even though I know you are really good at it now. Your brother is sending you a letter soon as well with more information.

I will sign off for now but will write later. I miss you and love you and so want to be with you. We have endured this long so we can wait some more. Give all the girls big hugs.

All our love
Jacques and Sean. And Henri sends his love too.

~

Gabrielle just wanted to keep reading the letter over and over. She and Clara hugged each other amidst tears of joy. There were really no words that could express their relief and joy in knowing Jacques and Sean were alive and safe. They both jumped up and hurried into the other room to tell the girls and the Tremblays about their good news.

It was an exciting evening in the house knowing this great news. In a time where there was so much bad news this was just the thing to renew one's faith in the world.

Gabrielle really just wanted to grab the horse and wagon and go directly to Montreal. "I think I could get there without too much trouble, though it has been awhile since I was in Montreal. Clara you could stay here with the children and help Anabelle. Eventually Jacques and I could come back together to get you."

There was silence in the room. After a few moments François spoke. "At the very least you need to sleep on this decision. You read that there is a second wave of the rebellion starting and you do not want to get trapped somewhere and not be safe. Also I think you need to wait until you have a letter from your brother as he may have important information for you."

Gabrielle sighed. "I guess you are right but here he is so close but so far. We cannot stay here forever. I will think about it overnight."

Clara had never seen Gabrielle so adamant about doing something so dangerous. She was quite worried as she did not want to lose Gabrielle. She had already lost two parents and that was enough. "Gabrielle you know I would do anything you asked me to, but please reconsider. Remember how worried we have been for months now thinking we may have lost both Sean and Jacques. I will be just as worried if you leave and not know if you are safe. The girls still need you as a mother." Clara knew she was using emotion to get Gabrielle not to go, but she could think of no other way at the moment.

The two families went to bed that night each with their own thoughts about what was the right and safe thing to do versus what your heart was telling you to do.

FIFTEEN

'WAR HAS NEVER HURT ANYBODY EXCEPT THE PEOPLE WHO DIE.'

Salvador Dali

The City of Toronto was in turmoil. Mackenzie had escaped in December to just across the river from Niagara. From there he continued attacks but most were ineffective. In the jail in Toronto were several hundred prisoners awaiting trial for treason or insurrection as a result of the battle at Montgomery Tavern. A hundred and fifty men, including Peter and Edward Brown, had already been convicted and exiled to a penal colony in Australia. Two men, Samuel Lount and Peter Matthews had been found guilty of treason and were sentenced to hang. Both men had been loyal followers of Mackenzie and the lawyers felt they were instrumental along with Mackenzie in organizing the attack.

The hanging was scheduled for April. Weeks before, citizens came to watch the scaffolding for the gallows being built. On the day of the hanging over a thousand people gathered to watch the grisly affair. In the crowd were two friends Andrew Hunt and Robert Brown. They were both thinking of their visit to Lloydtown and Kettleby several years ago. They recalled the posters advertising meetings with Mackenzie, but never thought that things would get this far out of hand. As the two prisoners were marched out of the jail to the gallows the crowds began whistling and jeering. It was obviously a Loyalist crowd. Andrew and Robert decided they could not watch this and walked away.

In his law office, John was having trouble concentrating. He was aware of what was happening a few blocks away. He did not think hanging a man was the answer to solving political reform, but unfortunately that was the law. He was also thinking about the new uprisings in Lower Canada. He was relieved to know Jacques and Sean were being represented by an excellent lawyer and would likely be released from prison very soon. Several rebels had already been hanged in Montreal, but with over five hundred rebels awaiting trials, he knew hanging them all was not feasible. The rumour around the Montreal office was they would all be released to go back to their villages or at least what was left of them.

John was pleased when his friend Samuel Jarvis came into the office. "Thank you for distracting me. It is hard to work today knowing what is going on up the road. There is so much upheaval in this country right now. Tell me what you hear about things in Montreal."

Samuel sat in the chair opposite John, made himself comfortable, and began to tell him the latest news. "Robert Nelson is an angry man. His brother, who truly believed political reform was necessary to help the French in Lower Canada, has of course been found guilty and is to be deported to Bermuda. Now Robert must take up the cause. He escaped just in time across the border into United States and knows there is a price on his head. He cannot return so is part of the group welcoming rebels to the United States. They provide the refugees with shelter, food and supplies. At this time there was also a group of Americans somewhat unhappy with some of the ways their government is ruling. They have organized themselves into groups called lodges. They are a secret society and feel they can help liberate the French of Lower Canada from British tyranny. The President of the United States is not happy about these lodges interfering with the neutrality of the border so has sent militia to stop any interference. Often though, the militia has sided with the rebels causing more problems. Nelson has helped establish what are called Hunter's Lodges along the border and he has about six hundred men continuing raids against the British. Many of these raids take place on the shores of Lake Ontario and along the river. They attacked and were defeated at Amherstburg in January. This spring one group of Hunter's Lodge disguised themselves as natives and captured and destroyed a British steamer travelling from Montreal to Toronto. All the passengers and crew were released before the ship was pillaged and burned. Needless to say the Governor is not happy so has sent reinforcements to border areas."

"Well I did not know it was that bad. I guess I have been wrapped up in what is happening here and also what will happen to the prisoners in Montreal. You know my brother-in-law and nephew are in the prison there."

"Yes I do remember you telling me that. Any word on what will happen?"

"I think and hope they will all be released as some have already been hanged but there are over five hundred prisoners. I believe a verdict is coming soon. We just have to hope."

"Of course with the new Governor Lord Durham now in charge, things may be different. He suspended the constitution and put in the special council with appointed members but it still seems somewhat authoritarian. So really, not much has changed. He is supposed to be writing a report about the reasons for this whole rebellion."

"Well time will tell. We just have to do as we are told and keep our heads down," laughed John.

~

Clara was sitting under a large maple tree reading a book she found in the house. The summer had turned very hot and humid in the last week. This morning the laundry to be done seemed endless. It had taken her until lunch time to get it all washed, rinsed and hung on the line to dry. The younger girls were washing the dishes from lunch; Gabrielle and Annabelle were in the garden picking beans, so this was a good chance to sit in the shade before collecting the dry laundry. She was trying to read but her mind kept wandering. She would turn sixteen in a few months and wondered what would happen next in her life. She knew many girls her age were already married and some even had babies of their own. She had met some boys at parties in the community but really most of them were silly and only cared about guns and hunting. She thought back to the time John sent her books to read and wished she had them now but she knew that was just being selfish. She wondered if there were schools in Montreal where she could attend and learn to be a teacher. Would anyone let her attend a school? Would she have to learn everything in French? Would anyone want to hire her as a teacher? Maybe there were places she could go in Toronto where John lived, but that would seem like she was asking for favours. She understood the concerns of the Patriots about being treated fairly, but she also still felt some loyalty to her Irish background. Would she be accepted as a Patriot or considered Loyalist. It was impossible to see a path she might take in the future. Of course the immediate task was helping the St-Pierre family reunite and re-establish a home. Her time alone to think was over as the young girls came running over, asking Clara to come with them berry picking at the back field.

The hot dry summer continued once again leaving crops withering and dying in the fields. Insects continued to plague the area, and most creeks dried up. At times the amount of water in the river was too shallow to allow boat travel for transporting supplies. The habitants in the lower Richelieu Valley would once again have meagre crops to see them through the winter.

There was still talk of rebellion though. The Hunter's Lodges continued their raids frustrating the British as no information could be extracted from locals to know their plans. The secret society was true to their name. At several raids though, the Patriots did not have the advantage of surprise and many members of the Lodge were taken prisoner by the British. Once again the prison in Montreal began to fill up with Patriot rebels. The war games continued on through the fall.

One afternoon François came into the house and started talking about a battle on the St. Lawrence River. Annabelle and Gabrielle were only half listening as he was always coming in with stories about what was happening. When they heard the words '*the rebellion is over,*' they stopped and sat down to listen.

"I have just heard from my friend that there was a battle near Prescott in Upper Canada at a windmill. There were over two hundred men that tried to capture the windmill but after fighting for two days they were defeated by a large militia and a marine unit from Kingston. The rebels, who had hoped the local farmers would join in the battle, finally surrendered when the farmers refused to fight with them. At least a hundred were taken prisoner, and over fifty killed and many wounded. But there will be no more fighting as Nelson has once again fled to the United States. There are many men in prison as well as some leaders. Everyone thinks this time the government will not be so kind to the prisoners and let them go.

"Oh my." Gabrielle had her mouth covered and as though she was afraid to speak the words. "Do you think Jacques and Sean will be able to return to the valley now?"

"It seems like it might be a possibility but maybe we should wait to hear from your brother before we do anything. Winter is almost upon us and you have no food stored up for the winter. You do not even know if your farm is still there," said Françoise.

"Yes. You are right again," she laughed. "I will write a letter to John to see what he thinks will happen."

That evening Gabrielle wrote to John asking what he thought would happen and if Jacques should come to Phillipsburg or if she should go to Montreal. The next day it was in the post and on its way to Montreal. Now she just had to be patient and wait for a reply.

It took three long weeks before an answer came.

Toronto
November 30, 1838

Dear Gabrielle

I know you are impatient to see Jacques and Sean but you must still wait until the new year at least. The authorities in Montreal are very angry this time and are in the streets in Montreal watching everyone. Men who are just walking are being arrested and thrown in jail. I have recommended that Jacques and Sean stay indoors at all times. There have even been some women arrested as they think they might be carrying information to the prisoners.

I think it would be prudent to wait until early spring before we plan anything. I know this is difficult but the farm may have been burned, you have no food for winter and everyone is safe where they are at the moment.

My colleagues in Montreal feel thing will be settled regarding the Patriots by spring one way or another. They feel the leaders will be severely punished.

One thing you and Jacques may want to consider is living in my house in Montreal for awhile. Jacques may want to go to St-Denis at some point to check out the situation but you and the girls are welcome to stay in Montreal. The girls could go to school and Clara needs to do something with her life. I know Sean really wants to be a farmer like Jacques and that can be pursued. Now may be the chance. Think about it and write to Jacques.

Stay safe and Merry Christmas
Love John

~

Gabrielle showed the letter to Clara, and then to Annabelle and Francoise as she wanted to make sure they were ready to have the whole family stay in Phillipsburg for another winter.

"We have enough food stored away for the winter, the children all act like brothers and sisters now so let's start planning for a Joyuex Noel. Everyone is safe and well and our future is looking bright at last," said Annabelle.

PART III

PEACE ORDER AND GOOD GOVERNANCE

Section 91: British North America Act

SIXTEEN

'LIKE BRANCHES ON A TREE, OUR LIVES MAY GROW IN DIFFERENT DIRECTIONS, YET OUR ROOTS REMAIN AS ONE.'

Author Unknown

"Why do we have to wear these uncomfortable clothes today? I know you said our grandparents are coming but really, we will only be sitting in a chair." Gabby was annoyed because she really just wanted to read her book in her room. Sitting in the parlour listening to old people was not her idea of fun.

"You will do as you are asked and your Grandmother sent you that dress so I insist that you wear it. May I also remind you that you are just ten years old and your Father and I are still in charge." Marie-Claire was appalled at her daughter's rudeness and wondered what was happening to this generation. She watched as Gabby stomped off to her room too change. Her thoughts went back to her Mother who was also ten when she arrived in this country from Ireland. So much had happened in the past fifty years.

~

Life in Montreal for Clara was pleasant, comfortable and enjoyable now compared to the years before she moved there permanently. She lived in her brother's house with her husband Jean. Clara had three children but their son and second daughter had both died. Marie-Claire their only daughter and her husband lived in Kingston. She had five grandchildren who brought her great joy. They all had their own personality and what she called spunk.

Her dreams of being a teacher never really came true, but now she had great hopes for her grandchildren, especially Gabrielle or Gabby as she was called by her parents and brothers. Clara was excited about visiting Marie-Claire and her family in Kingston this week. She and Jean were travelling by train tomorrow and would stay for several weeks. Gabby had three younger brothers who she bossed around continuously. The newest addition to the family was only three months and Clara looked forward to cuddling a newborn once again. It would be an enjoyable trip but likely exhausting. She had purchased gifts for all the children. There were new toys and games and of course clothes. It was nice to have the money to buy the things you wanted, not just what you needed. She remembered making baby clothes for her sisters from old clothes the others had outgrown. At one point Clara remembered making clothes for the twins from Gabrielle's wedding dress. It certainly was a different time.

Clara thought back to her fifty years in Canada. First losing her parents to cholera just after arriving from Ireland and then having to escape the rebellion were some of the worst times. There were also good times though. Having been adopted by Gabrielle and Jacques and living with them was a wonderful memory. Going to live in Montreal with her sisters at Uncle John's house was the point when her life changed.

Clara was attempting to pack her clothes in a leather suitcase but it seemed each piece of clothing brought back a different memory. She thought back to staying with the Tremblay family after they escaped from St-Denis just as the British were arriving to try and defeat the Patriots. She, Gabrielle and the three younger girls had stayed there for almost two years and still kept in touch with them every Christmas. After Jacques and Sean were released from prison, they stayed in Montreal until it was safe to travel back to the Richelieu Valley. This had been a difficult time for Gabrielle as she just wanted to be with Jacques. Clara recalled spending more time than ever with the girls as their Mother was so quiet and withdrawn.

Finally in the early summer of 1839 the women gathered together their belongings and said goodbye to the Tremblays to begin their journey to Montreal and finally join Sean and Jacques at John's home. It was a long journey but broken up with a visit to Jacques' sister's near St-Hilaire. Clara remembered their first night in Lower Canada staying at their place and sleeping in the barn. This time they were welcomed into the house. Marie and Jean had been very lucky during the Patriots war. Their farm was not really close to the fighting and had been spared the looting and burning done by the British after every battle.

The second day about noon at St-Hilaire, a carriage could be heard coming down the road. Everyone's ears perked up listening as it got closer. Even now there was still uneasiness about someone coming along the road. The horse and carriage turned into the lane and continued toward the house. By now the entire family was outside watching. Jean was just about to go back onto the porch to pick up his gun when he recognized the person driving.

"Bonjour mes Amis!" The voice said.

Gabrielle in an instant was down the steps running toward the horse and carriage. She would know that voice anywhere. "Oh Jacques," was all she could manage to say.

Jacques had decided to go as far as his sister's house to meet the women. He would accompany them back to Montreal. It was a very happy reunion for the rest of the day. The youngest Marie was not quite sure who this stranger was who just wanted to hug everyone, as she had been only three when she last saw her father. The St-Pierre family stayed another day and then left to continue their journey to Montreal.

Clara recalled having to drive the wagon accompanied by Elodie and Julie while Gabrielle and Jacques and Marie travelled in the carriage. She also remembered getting strange looks as she drove the horse and battered wagon through the posh neighbourhood to John's house. It was another joyful reunion when they arrived and saw Sean at the house. Clara often spoke of how this was one of her happiest days since going to live with the St-Pierre's.

The family stayed in Montreal for several months before Jacques and Sean ventured to St-Denis to see if anything was left of the farm. They stayed in St-Denis for two months as what had greeted them was not good news. The barn had been burned and the timber half of the house was destroyed. Of course there were no farm animals around, but the barn could be rebuilt on the old foundation. They spent some time repairing the stone section of the house which involved chasing out a number of critters who had taken up residence. It was now livable. One day as they were working a man rode in on a horse. Jacques noticed he only had one arm but managed the horse quite well. As he came closer to the house Jacques realized it was Louis. After all the greetings Louis told his story. He had been separated at St- Charles from the rest of the men as he had been assigned to watch for British in the woods. As a part of the militia came from behind there was gunfire and he was hit in the shoulder. The militia kept going deciding he along with several other Patriots were either dead or not worth taking as prisoners at that point. After all the fighting had stopped and under the cover of darkness, he and one friend escaped back through the woods to his parents' old farm. As it was isolated, no one came looking for them. Eventually they found help, were bandaged up, and they returned to the farm to hide. When the fighting stopped temporarily, Louis found medical help but had to have his arm amputated.

"I am fine now and have managed to fix up the old house so it is livable. My friend stays with us and is my farm helper, and I have even managed to take a wife and we have one boy. I am doing what I always planned to do. I often ride down here hoping to find you have returned and today is my lucky day. Where are Gabrielle and Clara and the girls?"

Sean and Jacques told their stories of prison and the girls stories of escape. "We are starting to rebuild here as you can see. It will be a slow process but now that we know you are close by, we are excited to start over," remarked Sean. "Brothers again."

The return to Montreal was again happy when the story of finding Louis was told to everyone. John had come to Montreal for a visit as he knew everyone but Louis would be there. He thought Louis was dead and was thrilled to hear otherwise. "I have made some major decisions regarding this family and I want everyone to hear. We can tell Louis when we see him next," said John. The whole family and his loyal housekeeper and gardener were all sitting in the parlour.

"I have decided that I will stay in Toronto and I do not need this house in Montreal anymore. There was a quiet gasp from Gabrielle. "I am reassigning the ownership to Clara. Now Clara gasped. "I have put aside a sum of money for Sean, Louis, Elodie, Julie and Marie. It is enough for them to attend a good school and buy a modest home for themselves if this is what they wish. Sean I know you want to farm so that too is an acceptable choice. Clara there is enough money to keep this house, employ my loyal friends to help you and go to school if you wish. I have no need for all this money and have a comfortable place in Toronto. Now you may have to allow me to stay here if I come to visit." John laughed and looked over at Gabrielle and Jacques. I invested the money you left with me Gabrielle and it has increased quite nicely. You and Jacques will have enough money to rebuild the farm or start over wherever you want to locate. We all might as well enjoy this while we are alive and all of us are still together as a family. There has been enough trouble and hardship over the past few years, so let us be happy now."

Later that night after the celebrating had ended, John took Clara aside and said, "I would like you to make sure you and your sisters go to school and you stay here to help them. Young women need to have an education as well as boys in today's world."

Clara could only nod her head as there seemed to be a large lump in her throat that might result in tears. She finally managed to say, "Thank you Uncle John. I will see that we all go to school."

She made sure her sisters went to school and helped run the household when John was in Toronto. Gabrielle and Jacques and Sean had gone back to St-Denis and rebuilt the partially burnt home and farm. A second home had been built for Sean when he married a local girl, and he was still living there and continuing to farm. Louis of course stayed on the family farm and reinvested his money in the property and shared it with his war time friend.

~

Clara was waiting at the front door for the carriage to come around the front. Her bags for the trip were sitting alongside Jean's.

"Are you sure we need this many bags, "asked Jean? "I could wear my dark suit wherever we go."

"Oh Jean. You are not working at the bank anymore. You need to wear something other than a dark suit with a white shirt and tie. Things are not quite as formal as they used to be."

Jean had retired a few years ago but still insisted dressing like a banker. He and Clara had been happily married for thirty seven years. They knew each other's likes and dislikes, tolerated each others' friends, and loved to entertain friends and family especially at Christmas.

Clara had met Jean at a party given by a school friend's parents one Christmas. The friendship got off to a poor start when Jean's friend made fun of Clara's French accent. She still put a bit of Irish brogue into some of her French words. Jean tried to stop his friend from making a scene but in the end joined in the laughter with the other boys. Clara stomped off to the other room, but her face was flushed and she was quite embarrassed and angry. The next week Jean came to visit her at the house carrying a bouquet of flowers. He apologized and invited her to his parents' home later that week for dinner. He also had a note to give her from his mother confirming the invitation. Clara accepted and the relationship continued for two years when they married and Jean moved into Clara's house. These were odd circumstances at the time, but everyone agreed it was the best thing to do as Marie was now finishing up her schooling and was about to become a nurse.

The carriage arrived to deliver them to the train station for their trip. The train was still relatively new to the country and in fact one could just about travel right across the country by train now thanks to the hard work of the government and many men who came from foreign countries to complete the dangerous work.

Clara and Jean were travelling first class so had a small room for the two of them. As Clara watched out the window she saw new buildings, new towns and many more people than were around when she first arrived in Canada. She remembered Uncle John telling her about his first trip to Toronto. The landscape still looked like that but with more people and buildings.

The regular clack of the wheels on the track was enough to lull Clara into a light slumber. She was suddenly transported back to County Cork. The rolling green hills dotted with sheep was an idyllic picture for a few moments but a small croft house made of stone with smoke coming from the chimney told another story. Clara was washing clothes in a tub of grey water and then placing them over rocks or scrubby bushes to dry. Often they never really dried. Sean had gone with his father to try to sell the peat they had cut but not many farmers had money to buy anything. Clara's mother was standing at the stove looking into a pot of stew that had no meat or potatoes in it. Everything in the picture had now gone dark with no sun shining anywhere. Clara was not enjoying this dream anymore but it seemed to continue on and on. A whistle blew and she was jolted awake. They were in Kingston. Clara decided not to tell Jean the dream. She stood up, stretched a little, gathered up her purse, and followed Jean out of their room. He was busy directing a porter to take their bags to the platform to meet their ride.

Marie-Claire's husband James was waiting on the platform. He was easy to spot as he looked quite official in his military uniform. He had just been appointed as the Head Master at the new Royal

Military College. Clara whispered to Jean as they stepped from the train," I guess we are in Loyalist country now."

"Welcome to Kingston." And then to the porter he almost commanded, "I have a carriage waiting for us at the end of the platform."

Kingston was an interesting town. It was settled as far back as the 1600's but really became a populated town in the 1840's. After Upper and Lower Canada became united with the BNA Act in 1841 Kingston was the first capital. But being close to the American border and subject to possible attacks the capital was moved to Montreal. It was a town of wooden buildings as lumber was plentiful until a fire destroyed the entire town. It was then decided all important buildings would be constructed of Limestone which was plentiful in the area.

Clara and Jean were amazed at the beautiful stone structures dominating the landscape. "These buildings and homes are beautiful. Is your home made of stone as well?"

"Yes. We have a square stone home that goes down to the waterfront. Finally we have some large trees that give us shade in the summer."

Clara did not have to wait long as after travelling along a tree lined street, the horse and carriage turned and passed through large stone gates and along a curved gravel path. At the end was a large two story house with at least six windows across the front on both levels. The centre front black doorway enhanced the Georgian architecture. A large veranda spread across the front of the house where chairs and benches were placed. It looked very welcoming in the late afternoon sunshine.

They family must have been watching for them as suddenly the door burst open and four children of various sizes emerged all at once followed by their mother carrying the baby.

"Welcome Grandmother and Grandfather," four voices all said at once. The children stopped at the top step as if suddenly remembering their manners and how they were to act when they arrived. Robert, who was just two, quickly stepped behind his Mother's long skirt hiding from these strange people.

Marie-Claire went quickly down the stairs and greeted her parents. Hugs and kisses were exchanged, almost squishing the baby. The children were soon down the stairs to be part of the welcoming. Gabby was the only one who really remembered her grandparents as it had been two years since their last visit.

"My goodness," said Clara. "I would hardly recognize any of you as you have all grown so much. What are your parents feeding you to make you grow so tall?"

Gabby was amazed her Grandmother was so friendly. She had met some of her school friends' grandparents, and they were stuffy and not friendly. They really did not seem to want to talk to children at all. Before she knew what was happening Clara had taken her hand and they were walking together into the house. This was going to be a good visit after all.

The inside of the house was even more amazing than the exterior. There was a wide hall with stairs leading straight up to the bedroom level. The parlour was on the right and the dining room was on the left. Both had wide double doors with beautiful mahogany casings around the opening. The trim around the windows and the baseboard was quite substantial mahogany as well. Toward the back of the house was a hallway that led to the kitchen and a large room that looked out to the lake. This would be a beautiful house to explore thought Clara and she knew just the person to take her on this tour.

The luggage was in the front hall and a man suddenly appeared and asked to which room it should be delivered.

Marie-Claire handed the baby to a young woman who called the children to come with her and suggested. "Let's get you settled Mother and Father so you can freshen up and then come down to the sunroom for tea."

Clara felt as though this was another dream and it was nothing like the one she was in during the train ride.

The sunroom was on the south side of the house facing the lake. Several islands could be seen from the shore but in looking past the islands, the lake seemed to go on forever. The gardens leading down to the lake were in full bloom with colourful perennials. Close to the lake was a summer gazebo inviting enough to just sit and stare at the lake.

"That looks like a nice place to sit and relax," suggested Clara.

"It is but with the baby and the others, I do not get much time to relax. Yes I do have lots of help in the house but I really like to spend time with the children."

"I have some gifts for the children," said Clara. "Can I give them out now?"

"Oh, of course. Let's call them in here." Marie-Claire rang a bell and a maid appeared and was given the request to bring the children to the sunroom.

Clara thought to herself that she and Gabrielle would never have believed it if someone told them years ago this is how their children and grandchildren would be living.

The noise began quietly but picked up intensity as the children raced along the hall. They entered all at once laughing and talking over each other and came to an abrupt stop in front of their mother.

"Please sit on the floor as your Grandmother has something to tell you."

They all did as they were told but there was whispering when they saw the stack of presents on the couch beside their grandmother.

Clara handed out the presents, one at a time and waited for each to open it while the others watched. It was as though there was an electric current travelling along the floor creating wiggling and laughing and joy. All the children said thank you and gave hugs to their Grandmother, and then the boys asked if they could take their toys out on the lawn. Permission was given and off they ran. Gabby though hung back and sat beside her Grandmother.

"I love to read books. Do you think you and I could start reading this tonight before I go to bed?"

Clara was thrilled with the request. "We certainly will. This is a new book I found about a girl almost your age. I hope you like it. I haven't read it either. The author wrote Alice in Wonderland about twenty years ago. My friends told me it was a good story with interesting characters."

SEVENTEEN

'PROGRESS IS IMPOSSIBLE WITHOUT CHANGE, AND THOSE WHO CAN NOT CHANGE THEIR MINDS CAN NOT CHANGE ANYTHING.'

George Bernard Shaw

The next few weeks were busy visiting places in Kingston, spending time by the water on hot days and of course each night reading another chapter about Alice and her many adventures.

One sunny day the family packed a picnic and took the carriage along the lake to the harbour. It was here that the new canal had been built. It allowed lumber from the north to travel down the Rideau Canal from Ottawa to the St. Lawrence River and Lake Ontario. This day the family were lucky enough to see many logs floating down through the locks of the canal toward the lake.

"Look boys," their father called to them. "See the lumberjacks walking on top of the logs directing them to go the right direction."

"That looks dangerous," announced Grandfather.

"Oh I think that looks like fun," said Thomas who was just eight. "We have logs floating into our shore sometimes. John you and I could try that next time we find one."

Their Father quickly and sternly answered, "I do not think any of you will be trying to be a lumberjack in the near future."

The boys grumbled that they could do it and began practising on the grass with a make-believe log.

The picnic outing lasted almost to supper time and there were five tired children riding home in the carriage that evening. The adults sat on the front porch after dinner enjoying the last bit of sunset to the west. Just before dark a city worker walked along the street and lit the gaslights on the street. These were a fairly new addition to the city and the citizens were proud to be one of the first cities in Canada to have gaslights.

The two weeks sped by with many outings and it was soon time for Grandfather and Grandmother to return to Montreal.

"Grandmother you can't go home yet as we are not finished the book," said Gabby.

"Well my dear you keep reading and you can write me a letter to tell me what happens."

"Can I get a stamp?" Gabby turned to her mother to see if she would allow this. She had never written a letter to anyone before.

"Yes Gabby. We can arrange that. In fact you can go to the post office with me when you have the letter ready to send."

Good byes were said, the boys did not seem to mind being hugged by Grandmother and Gabby thought to herself that this trip was so much more fun than she had originally thought.

~

Clara and Jean's trip home to Montreal was pleasant but uneventful. When they reached their house and Clara looked at the facade she mentioned to Jean, "Our house is looking very outdated compared to Marie-Claire's."

"Yes, but it is our home. We will not be moving to a newer one. I know you like some of the stone houses being built just up the street, but they are not built nearly as well as ours. I hear that in the winter the stones expand and crack creating structural problems in the homes. John had the best engineers and carpenters build this house. In fact they were sent here from France by Louis XIV to build not only the houses but the city plan as well. We have gardens and large areas with stable blocks and out buildings that rival any in the city. This is one of the few homes with fine wood carvings both inside and out. You only see this type of carving in churches now. Today the carpenters are building fast rather than building quality."

"I know Jean. This is a wonderful old house with many historic details that need to be kept. Maybe we could change some of the colours and furnishings inside instead. I am getting tired of the dark colours and all the dust catchers in the rooms."

"Well that could be a possibility. The markets are starting to improve so we may have some money to upgrade a few things. But we certainly must be careful how much we invest in this place."

Clara decided to leave the conversation about improvement for now and do some scouting of ideas on her own. She would approach Jean at a later time. He will always be a banker, she thought.

The house had been built in the 1820's and was well constructed as Jean acknowledged. There had been a new kitchen added with water available inside as well as a room for bathing upstairs and a water closet on both floors. The house still used oil lamps and candles for lighting which often left dark smudges on the wall. The fabrics used were all dark and heavy. The thickness of the fabrics helped keep the cold of winter and the blazing summer heat out of the house, but it also made the rooms very dark and often gave a depressing feeling to the house. Clara got to thinking that if she painted the rooms some of those lovely but outdated pale Georgian colours and had light weight fabric curtains made, the whole house would be improved. She might keep the heavy draperies hanging at the edges of the windows so they could close on cold nights. She would think about this as her summer and fall project.

Two nights later a house just down the street caught fire and burned. By morning there was only charred rubble on the ground. It was a wood frame house built about the same time as Clara's and Jean's. At breakfast it was the topic of conversation between Clara and Jean.

"I do worry Jean about our house catching fire. It would be terrible and there is always the possibility of someone dying in the fire."

"Yes that is a possibility. We do try to be careful about the lamps and candles but we do not know how careful the staff is. I am going to call some people today about ways we can protect ourselves. I have heard there are some new advancements in fire protection that we may want to consider."

Montreal was one of the cities that boasted updated fire houses throughout the city and there were now regulations as to building and maintaining the buildings. This was a result of a fire in 1849 that burned down the parliament buildings while the assembly members were sitting discussing government business. The latest piece of safety equipment was a chemical cart. It was a tank containing chemical fire retardant mounted on wheels. It was designed for large estates and would help stop a fire before the hook and ladder wagons arrived. Also many estates had a water pumper of their own to use.

Jean felt these two items might be just the thing to allay Clara's fears regarding fire. There would be quite a cost involved but it would be less than selling this house and buying a new one. He was definitely against moving to one of those new stone homes. Jean also decided to build a large pond at the back of the property so they would have their own water source for the pumper. It would improve the property and with some landscaping it could be quite attractive.

Several weeks later when Jean had arranged all the details of the work to be done, he told Clara his plans.

"Well that is welcome news Jean. I think I will feel much safer. I have also been thinking of some improvements as well for the inside of the house."

Clara told Jean of her plan to redecorate and change the colour schemes. She even had several sample of colours and fabrics to show him. Jean had the feeling he had been upstaged, but if Clara would be happy to stay in this house, then he would just have to agree with her.

"Well it is going to be a busy place over the next few months," replied Jean.

All this talk of fire protection had Clara thinking back to the spring of 1849. She had been living in Montreal now for almost nine years and had been married to Jean for four years. Jean was a banker at the Bank of Montreal on Place d'Armes. Julie and Elodie had finished school and had both returned to the Richelieu Valley area. They were qualified to be teachers but only the cities offered regular school to children so were working as live in governesses with some wealthy families. Marie was still living with Clara and Jean and attending nursing school at the Grey Nuns hospital. That evening she and Marie and a friend were sitting in the sunroom after dinner and Clara began to tell the story of the night of April 25th.

"After the rebellions in 1837 and 1838 ended and an Act of Union was proclaimed in 1841 uniting the colonies of Upper Canada and Lower Canada and creating the Province of Canada. A single parliament was established with an equal number of seats for each region called Canada East and Canada West. The debts were consolidated, the French language was banished for government use and certain French Institutions like education and civil law were suspended. Needless to say there was opposition by the French political leaders and the Catholic Church. In time because of economic prosperity, growth and responsible government, changes were made to try and appease everyone. Unfortunately, there were still hard feelings. The inhabitants of Lower Canada or Canada East were still waiting for their claims of loss during the rebellion to be settled. The amount the government wanted to give as compensation was considerably less than what was demanded. The Tories who were mostly Loyalists and in the minority in the legislature, felt the rebels who fought against the government should not be rewarded for their actions. There was much discussion and debate and motions often leading to physical violence in the house. Several votes were taken and finally the Rebellion Losses Bill was passed and only needed royal assent by the Governor. Late in the afternoon of April 25th, the Governor decided that since he was in town to give assent to a new tariff bill, he would just include some forty one other bills awaiting his assent including the Rebellion Losses bill. People and visitors in the galleries were taken by surprise and the protests began. The Governor apparently tried to quickly escape back to his residence but was attacked by egg and rock throwing protesters along his route home.

In the next few hours alarm bells rang throughout the city and someone actually rode through the streets to announce a public meeting at 8:00 pm on Place d'Armes. It was said that between 1200 and 1500 men attended the meeting to listen to speeches given by the opposition demanding the governor be recalled by Her Majesty. A petition was drafted but the captain of the volunteer corps of firemen lit his hat and the petition on fire and asked the crowd to follow him to the Parliament buildings. Of course the mood of the crowd was whipped up by this time because of the speeches. Along the way windows were broken and damage was done to several buildings. When the crowd arrived at the legislature, the lights were on inside as a committee was still meeting. The rioters broke into the building by breaking down the doors using a ladder from the fire wagon as a battering ram. The members of the committee withdrew to safety as the outside of the building had now been set on fire. When the rioters entered the house, they began to vandalize the chamber. Fire from outside had now spread to inside as gas lights were knocked over and the mob left in haste. Only the ceremonial mace and a portrait of Queen Victoria were saved. The fire consumed the two libraries, parts of the archives from Upper and Lower Canada and thousands of volumes of public documents.

Several adjacent buildings and warehouses were also lost in the fire as well as the general hospital of the Grey Nuns. I have never been so happy to know you were home that night and not working at the hospital. I was also worried as Jean was still at the bank when this all began and he was in quite a state when he arrived home for dinner. There were mobs making their way to the where the bank was located but they ended up meeting at another location for the speeches. Who knows what would have happened to the bank and the Place d'Armes if they had met there."

"Was anyone arrested for destroying property?" asked Clara's friend Jane.

"Oh yes. Five of the speakers at the meeting were arrested the next morning but Lafontaine who was the Attorney General managed to have them released two days later. Meetings and riots continued in Montreal for some time. Sunday was the only day when it was safe to go outside. Jean did not go to work and as the hospital had burned Marie you were home here as well. The governor tried to resign, but Britain said no and eventually he decided not to leave his home and someone else had to take his place and make decisions. Houses and buildings were set on fire and several men were killed by rocks and gunfire. It was a very unsettling time. In May it was proposed to move the Parliament to Toronto and later that month the decision was made to prorogue parliament and not reconvene for a year. I guess the government hoped all the problems would just be forgotten."

"Nothing was really accomplished as several motions to disallow the Rebellion Losses Act were made to British Parliament but they were always defeated."

EIGHTEEN

'EVEN THE DARKEST NIGHT WILL END AND THE SUN WILL RISE.'

Victor Hugo

Gabrielle and Jacques were quite happy living outside, cooking over an open fire and sleeping under a canvas when they returned to St-Denis. The land continued to be owned by the St-Pierre family and having buried important papers before the rebellion made it easy for Jacques to reclaim his land. Sean had accompanied Jacques and Gabrielle and was a great help while the rebuilding project was underway during the summer. It was a warm summer with only timely rains making it perfect for farming and building. Jacques and Sean managed to plant some crops with the help of Louis and Gabrielle planted a large vegetable garden hoping to harvest food for winter.

There were many French farmers returning after the rebellion who were not so fortunate. They could not reclaim their land because they did not have the proper documents and most records in the municipalities had been burned. Many stayed in Montreal trying to find work forcing entire families to live on the streets and beg for food to survive. Private land was often taken over by wealthy owners as their own and then rented back to farmers for unreasonable sums of money.

Jacques and Gabrielle were very fortunate to have funds from other sources allowing them to purchase a few necessities for the farm. Jacques also often hired local men needing work to help rebuild his house and barn.

It was the first week in October and the trees were beginning to show their scarlet and orange colours. "Tonight is the first time we will be sleeping in a solid house again," commented Gabrielle as she carried in another basket of squash. "The nights are starting to get cold, so our timing is good. We were lucky to find this wood burning stove for the house that is still usable."

"It is not in perfect shape but hopefully it will last this winter and next year we can try to find a better one. Our house is much smaller than before, but we have fewer people living here now than before. We still have work to do to complete it, but it was smart to keep the stone part and finish the new part in stone as well. This house will not burn from the outside. We may have to build another house soon though as I noticed Sean talking to one of the Bissett girls on a regular basis. She often comes over with cold drinks or a fresh baking but always manages to give it to Sean."

"I have noticed that as well. Time does move on. Our girls are all in school; Clara is finished and watching over all of them. It would be nice if we could travel to Montreal for Christmas and maybe stay awhile to visit. Maybe Louis could watch our small herd of three cows while we are away."

All Jacques said was "Hmm."

Gabrielle hoped that might mean yes.

As it turned out Jacques and Gabrielle did go to Montreal a few days before Christmas. The weather stayed warmer than normal and with only a skiff of snow, travelling was easy. Jacques did put the runners in the carriage though as he would likely need the sleigh on the way back. Sean decided not to go with them and said he would stay at the farm to care for the animals. Apparently he had already been invited to spend Christmas day at the Bissett farm. Gabrielle would leave him supplies for meals but she suspected he would likely be eating more meals at the Bissett home.

It was fun to see the girls and as an extra surprise John had returned home from Toronto for a few days. Christmas was truly a family holiday except for Sean and Louis not being there. The past few years had been stressful dealing with famine, crop failures, war and prison. This year though there was delicious food, carol singing, a tall Christmas tree with real candles and presents for everyone. Gabrielle and the girls decided to go to midnight mass on Christmas Eve and as they left the church, it began to snow.

"How perfect," said Gabrielle. "I will make a wish on the snowflakes for peace in our world and happiness for us all next year and always."

The four girls in unison replied, "Amen."

The new year, 1841, was rung in with bells ringing throughout the city. There were a few political issues needing resolving, but best of all there was no fighting at the moment. This would be the year the country would come together and be a union. It had to be accepted by the British Parliament and listening to the rumours going around, it sounded like it would pass. In the country farming and forestry were flourishing. There were new canals being built so trade could expand. The only complaint by a few was that the French were being overlooked and their culture and language were trying to be repressed. Hopefully this was just a rumour.

Before Gabrielle and Jacques left Montreal they were able to visit Justine and her parents who now lived in Montreal. It was a different visit though as this was the first time she and Justine had met since Joseph had been killed at St-Eustache. They then returned to St-Denis a few days after New Years. There was a break in the weather so they figured it was a good time to travel. They stopped at his brother's place near St-Eustache for a night or two to visit. This had been such a lovely visit this Christmas Gabrielle thought maybe they should do this every year. The stress of the past few years was behind them and the future looked bright for the St-Pierre family.

Their return home had some excitement to offer the family. The moment they walked into the house, Sean jumped up from the table where he was reading a book. "I have good news for you two. I am engaged to be married to Catherine Bissett and we are going to be married next Christmas but we might move it up to April. We don't want to wait a long time and there is a small cabin behind their house where we can live for the summer. It may not be good in winter but we will work something out."

Gabrielle was smiling the whole time Sean was speaking. This was only the second time she had ever heard Sean say so much at once. "Sean. We are so pleased. We knew she was special to you and she is a very nice girl. Congratulations. I am sure you two will be very happy." As she went to hug him she reminded him, "We always have room here for both of you.

Jacques shook his hand and said, "Congratulations. Well done. You can stay here if need be as I still need you here on the farm. Remember, some day this farm will be yours and now Catherine's as well."

That evening there was much talk of future plans for the young couple. Jacques mostly listened but at one point he added, "I think a small cabin at the end of the garden would be a perfect first home for you and Catherine. We have a number of logs from cutting down trees at the back of the property that would work for a cabin. I think you and I are going to be busy this winter with a building project."

"That is a great idea. Thanks. I can hardly wait to get started," replied Sean.

"Now we need to set a date when Catherine and her parents can come over for dinner to celebrate this good news. Any time is good for us so you and Catherine figure out a time after talking to her parents," said Gabrielle as she was writing down notes for planning this event.

Later while lying in bed, Gabrielle was much too keyed up to sleep and began thinking about the first time she met Sean. He had been just fourteen and was trying to be very brave and protective of his sister. She knew he was sad as he had just lost his parents to cholera, but he tried to hide it by being the brave one. He only said a few words when spoken to but over time he watched every move Jacques made. He even began to imitate his walk. Sean was a quick learner and very soon became quite competent at many skills needed to be a farmer. It was hard to believe he was now twenty-four and about to be a married man. Gabrielle knew Jacques loved Sean as a son and was so proud of all the things he had learned. Jacques had also told Gabrielle that when he and Sean were in prison, Sean showed toughness not common among many others his age. Sean never said much but his actions and behaviour spoke volumes.

She drifted off to sleep thinking about the future with Sean and Catherine and the children they might have and how she might soon be a Grandmother. What pleasant thoughts.

Several weeks later the Bissetts came over for lunch and spent the rest of the afternoon at the St-Pierre farm. Lily and Gabrielle of course were already friends so that made conversation easy. Catherine was quite pretty with long dark hair and a lovely smile. She seemed quite shy and only spoke when asked a question. Apparently she was just eighteen but being the oldest in the family was very mature and knew how to run a household.

Gabrielle tried to engage her in conversation and asked, "How long did you stay in St-Charles after we dropped you off that day we all fled? We were worried about you as the fight in St-Charles was quite intense."

Catherine looked at her Mother and began the story when she saw her mother nod her head. "We stayed the night in a relative's barn near St-Charles, but the next day everyone was leaving as the rumours were that the British were coming. There were the five of us and also four of our cousins plus our Aunt. We walked as fast as we could toward the east hoping to get to a small town and find some shelter. Along the way we encountered some men who were going to fight the British in St-Charles. They pointed us in the direction of a woods and said on the other side was a small cabin they had just left. Because of the woods they said it would be safe. When we got there it was almost dark and when we opened the cabin door the smell was disgusting. The place was a mess and some animals had been in it leaving rotten food all over the floor. We sort of cleaned up, huddled together in the two beds to keep warm and spent the night there hoping no animals would return. In the morning when we could see better we did a bit of cleaning up, thinking we would be staying there for awhile. That day and all through the next two nights we could see flames and smoke coming from the St-Charles area. We stayed there for five days before going back to our Aunt's place in the country near St-Charles. She was lucky as the British had not gone that direction and her place was not burned. We stayed there for the winter. The next summer we went back to St-Denis to find our house and barns all burned. Our dad was also lucky as he escaped to the woods and was not captured and put in prison. He and some of my cousins have helped to rebuild the farm."

Lily looked at Gabrielle and nodded. "It was quite a bad time in our life. Sean told us about your journey as well. It must have been quite scary driving the horse and wagon on the roads not knowing who you would meet. But now it is better times and we are so happy that Sean and Catherine are getting married. We are trying to convince them to wait till next Christmas as that is the old tradition in these parts."

"I think it would be a good idea to wait as well. It will give Jacques and Sean time to build the log cabin here," replied Gabrielle.

The conversation continued all afternoon until dusk and the Bissetts rose to leave before it was too dark for travelling. It looked like the wedding would be just after Christmas and it would be a traditional celebration.

It seemed like a long time to wait to be married, but both Sean and Catherine knew there was much to do to get ready for a big celebration as well as all the regular farm work in the spring, summer and fall The rest of the winter Jacques and Sean hauled the logs from the back of the property to beside the house. The logs had to be stripped of their bark and notched at the ends to fit the pieces together for the cabin. When it came time in early spring to raise the logs for the cabin Sean was surprised as Louis had told most of the village about the building and every able man came to help. Men who were no longer strong enough to help sat on the sidelines and offered instructions and comments. The women also came later in the day with food to feed everyone. It turned out to be a pre wedding party of sorts. By the end of the day the log cabin walls were fitted together, the roof trusses were attached ready for the roof boards. Only the chinking between the logs was needed to make it weather proof. Louis promised Sean he would help him do that as he had fixed his log house and knew exactly what to do.

One Sunday a month or so later, Sean brought Catherine to see the house. "Now close your eyes and I will lead you into the cabin."

Catherine did as she was told and entered the cabin holding on to Sean. She then opened her eyes when Sean told her to. "Oh my. It is wonderful. I can't believe you did all this."

"I had some help. Look at this part. This is where we will have a kitchen and eat our meals." Sean led Catherine around the cabin pointing out all the features. "We have made two bedrooms. One bedroom is for us and one for our children when they arrive. We even made a small room for washing up and it could be a toilet room in the winter.

Catherine couldn't speak but just kept smiling. Finally she said, "This is more than I ever dreamt of. I did not want to wait till Christmas but now I see it really is the right thing to do. I think I can start making curtains for the windows and quilts for the beds. Where will we find some furniture?"

"Have you seen my Father's workshop? It is full of furniture just needing a bit of repair. I bet your parents have a few things we could use as well. The one thing we need right away is a stove to heat the place and for cooking. I will talk to Louis. He seems to know a person who can find just about anything you need and for the right price."

They continued looking around the cabin seeing all the details that made it a house. They knew they loved each other enough to make it a home.

The farming chores continued with planting the spring crops, tending the kitchen garden, and feeding the animals. There was a new farm job this year as Jacques decided to try and raise sheep. Spring of course was lambing season so many nights were spent in the barn helping the ewes birth the lambs. "I am not sure but I may be too old to be staying up all night sitting in the barn waiting for baby lambs," said Jacques trying to stifle a yawn at breakfast one morning. We may build another sheep barn and you can be in charge of lambs Sean."

"But you do such a good job Jacques; I don't want to take it away from you."

Everyone laughed but there were still about three more ewes that had not had their lambs yet. There would be more sleepless nights.

The fall of 1840 saw a record crop with more wheat and hay than was needed. The governments had been working together to build canals allowing the farmers to ship their goods to markets further afield. Forestry and farming were booming. There was more immigration at this time as well but it had more of a negative effect on the economy than expected. The need for more land to allow more farming blocked some expansion for certain industries.

Jacques had just returned from the village one day and at lunch he reported the latest news. "I have just heard that all of us who experienced losses during the rebellion should make claims against the government and be compensated for these losses. There is going to be an inquiry about it and we are all to send in our claims for losses. I am going to figure the cost of building a new barn and part of the house as well as the cost of having to purchase new livestock and the feed for them. If everyone does this the total amount will be tremendous. It may be years before anyone sees it, but we have to try. I heard that those who suffered losses in Upper Canada have submitted claims and some have already received their claim money."

"How will you ever figure out an amount," asked Sean?

"I have kept track of all the money I have had to spend to buy materials and animals as replacements."

"Maybe we should charge for the years we could not farm and produce crops and for our time in prison. That was definitely loss and suffering."

"I agree with that."

Since returning to St-Denis from Montreal and the winter spent in a cold prison, Gabrielle had noticed Jacques was walking with more of a limp and often was rubbing his knees when he thought no one was looking. Some mornings it was hard for him to get moving and he seemed to stop working outdoors earlier in the day than he used to. The cold and damp and poor nutrition had taken its toll on his forty year old body. She now realized the reason Jacques insisted on installing a wood burning stove in the upstairs hallway in the house. If they left their bedroom door open, the warmth from the fire heated their room nicely.

Here it was fall and they were facing another winter of cold and snow, but maybe the wedding celebrations would warm everyone this winter.

Christmas was a bit of a whirl this year as the wedding was to be held January 4th and there were many last minute details to complete. The log cabin was complete and was furnished using furniture the two sets of parents donated. There were dishes ready for cooking and eating and Gabrielle had even stored food in the cold cellar ready for the newlyweds.

The usual plan for these celebrations was that there really was no plan. The first party was held at the bride's parent home and at that point someone would suggest where the next party would take place. Often the partying went on for a least a week. Gabrielle and Jacques had not had all the parties when they were married and Sean agreed with them in thinking it was a bit too much. But Catherine and her family wanted to stick to tradition so that's how it would be. The only certainty was the second party was to be held at the St-Pierre farm.

Jacques had slaughtered a pig and the meat was smoked ready for the feast. Gabrielle had been cooking for what seemed like weeks and had many goodies stored in the cold room. One never knew exactly how many people would show up for the party or stay overnight if the weather turned snowy. Just before December Jacques had picked up a copy of the new Farmer's Almanac at the general store in St. Charles. He had immediately consulted it to check the weather for the time of the wedding.

"The Farmer's Almanac says it will be fair weather for the first week of January but about mid month we are to get an intense snow storm that will almost be a blizzard."

Gabrielle turned from the stove and asked, "How can they know what the weather will be like so far in advance? They must be just guessing"

"Well, they have been putting this book out for over twenty years now and as wild as it sounds they are mostly correct in their predictions. You know I always use it to know when to plant the crops and only once did it not work out to be the right time. I guess the grasshoppers did not read the book that year so came anyway and ate everything," said Jacques with a smile on his face. Gabrielle just smiled at him.

The day finally arrived and the wedding was beautiful. It was held in the local church and then everyone went back to the Bissett home for lunch. The real partying would begin about dinner time. The snow cooperated and just gave a light dusting that day. Catherine was the centre of attention as she entered the church wearing pale blue long dress made of a fine silk taffeta. Apparently the dress had belonged to a distant relative and Lily had remade it beautifully into a fitted bodice with gathering at the V shaped waist. The scooped neck was decorated with white lace matching the lace and button details on the sleeves. Many dresses these days were quite full with pleats and gathers at the waist, but Lily and Catherine had made a statement by reducing the bulk of fabric from the skirt. Catherine had several small evergreen and holly branches wound together in a halo like crown that she wore in her hair giving a festive but angelic look. As she walked down the aisle with her father, Gabrielle saw that Sean was trying to hide the tears that were surfacing in his eyes. Lily was dabbing her eyes as were many more in the congregation. Gabrielle hoped she would see her daughters look so lovely and happy some day when they might be married.

Clara, Elodie, Julie and Marie had come to St-Denis for Christmas this year and of course stayed for the wedding. It was the first time they had all been together as a family in St-Denis since the Patriote War. It truly was a joyous occasion.

John Drummond had taken his sleigh as far as St-Hilaire and continued to St-Denis with Jacques' sister Marie and her husband Jean. They arrived for the wedding the day before. After the party at

Jacques and Gabrielle's home the girls decided they would ride back with their Uncle Jean and Aunt Marie as far as St-Hilaire and then continue on to Montreal with their Uncle John. The weather was cold but still not much snow on the ground so the sleigh skimmed nicely along the road. There was a lot to talk about as everyone had a different story to tell about the people they had met at the parties.

Two days after the party at the St-Pierre farm a third party was to take place at Lily's sister's home in St-Charles. Around noon that day it started snowing and by late afternoon a foot of snow was on the ground and one could not see from the house to the log cabin. There was no sign of the snow stopping any time soon and the wind was getting stronger, blowing the snow into drifts around anything located on the ground.

Jacques came into the house after tending to the livestock and said to Gabrielle, "I do not think we will be going to the party tonight. I have talked to Sean and he agrees it is too dangerous to be out in a sleigh with the horse today. He and Catherine are not going either."

"I am so glad you said that as I do not want to go out in this either. Also I am ready to stay home after so much going on since Christmas. A nice cozy night at home by the fire will be perfect."

"I think Sean and Catherine are ready for the partying to stop as well. They can enjoy a night in their new log cabin as well. You see Gabrielle, the Farmer's Almanac was right.

Just as the Almanac said there was heavy snow and blizzard like winds for four days piling snow up to the roof of the log cabin and filling in the pathway to the barn. The snow was too deep at first for the horse to plow through it and clear a path so Sean and Jacques had to dig a path by hand to the barn. After four days of digging and having the horse pull the scraper, the snow along the sides of the path was as high as the horse's head. Bringing wood into the house to keep the stoves going was a monumental task each day as was first finding the pump and then digging around it to get water for the house and the barn. Every morning Sean had to chop through the ice in the water troughs so the animals could get a drink. It was going to be a long winter if this kept up.

One day as they were trying to find a spot to pile up the manure from the barn, Sean asked Jacques, "What does that Almanac predicted for spring? Will it be late or early? We are running out of space in this barn and we really can't get out the back door yet."

"I haven't wanted to look yet as we don't need any bad news. You and Catherine come over for dinner tonight and we will read it together."

"Sounds good to me. Is that snow at the back still too hard to shovel through?" The snow on the north side of the barn had blown against the door and was now a hard packed drift at least ten feet deep.

"Well it's sunny today so when we are done here let's go around and see if we can dig through it. It may take us several days."

The only way to dig through the drift was for Sean to climb on top of the drift and begin to dig down, while Jacques shovelled around the bottom where Sean threw the snow. They could almost make blocks of snow that were strong enough for building.

"To bad we couldn't figure out a way to keep these blocks of snow for watering in the summer when we don't get rain. I know they do it for ice but have never heard of it for snow," said Jacques as he leaned on the shovel taking a rest.

"What if we put them in the cistern and they melted," asked Sean?

"Well we usually get lots of rain in the spring and it might overflow into the house. But we can look up rainfall amounts for this spring tonight in the Almanac."

It took three days to shovel the drift, but finally they were able to get the doors open and now had a large pile of snow that would be sitting next to the new stack of manure from the barn.

Spring did come early that next year and the crops were all planted with just the right amount of needed rain. One day Sean and Catherine walked over to the stone house to talk to Gabrielle and Jacques. They rarely did this so Gabrielle was worried when she saw them coming. She was always worried they would want to leave and find another farm away from the St- Pierre property.

Sean began as they sat on the porch steps. "We have some news to tell you. Don't worry. It is good news. We are going to have a baby and he or she will arrive around Christmas. We are very excited and we hope you are too."

Gabrielle jumped up and rushed over to Catherine to give her a hug. "I was afraid you were going to tell us you were moving somewhere else. I know you and Jacques have been out looking at other properties."

Jacques stood up and shook Sean's hand congratulating him on soon becoming a father. "Yes we have been out looking but mostly at newer equipment for this farm."

"Yes. Catherine and I are never leaving. We plan on living here forever."

Catherine added, "We love it here being close to you two and not far from my parents. This is the perfect place and we want our child to be near grandparents too."

"Oh my," said Gabrielle. "Jacques we are going to be grandparents."

Life in St-Denis the next few years rolled along with very few bumps. Sean and Catherine had a baby boy in early December making Christmas for everyone a very happy time.

During the next five or six years the crops grew well and farmers were able to sell their crops to towns and countries farther away because of canals and new rail lines. Sean and Catherine had a girl two years after their son Connor was born. Life on the St-Pierre farm was a busy time.

There were still rumblings in what was now called Canada East about the treatment of the French Canadians being not equal to those of English background living in Canada West. The claims against the government by the residents in Canada East for compensation of lost property in 1837 were still not settled. New areas wanted to join both Canada East and West which upset the representation in the Assembly. The present 1840 Act of Union did not seem practical anymore for a growing and expanding country but Britain seemed indifferent to any suggestions.

NINETEEN

'LET US BE ENGLISH OR LET US BE FRENCH AND ABOVE ALL LET US BE CANADIANS.'

Sir John A. Macdonald

John Drummond was enjoying the train trip from Toronto to Montreal. It was certainly better than taking a steamer and then a horse and carriage as he had on his first trip to Toronto. He was also thinking about the reason for this trip. He was now fifty-eight years old and was contemplating retiring from law.

His boss George Moffatt had retired from the law firm a number of years ago and had served three terms in the legislature and had definite opinions about how the country should progress. Since he still had contacts with political decision makers, he had suggested that they include John Drummond in their project for a federation. His comments to Joseph Taché were "John is well versed in the law for Canada East and Canada West as he has lived and worked in both."

So here was John on his way back to Montreal to start a new job. He would be travelling to Ottawa frequently, as it was now the capital, but working the majority of time from his old office in Montreal. He was also pleased to be staying once again in his home on St. Catherine Street. Clara and Jean had done a number of upgrades to the home but with the expansive grounds surrounding the house, it still always seemed like home. Clara now had two children still at home. Marie Claire was now nine and Sheila was just four. Her oldest child, a boy, unfortunately died before he was one. It would be delightful to see his great nieces and Clara and Jean again.

John had also kept up to date on the proposal for a federation in Canada replacing the Union Act and he felt he could offer practical legal advice. This could be the start of a whole new political way of life for Canada but the steps would likely tred on both the English and the French so caution must be paramount.

John arrived at the train station and found a carriage waiting to take him home. It was a short ride as a new road had been added making it a much quicker. Clara and Jean greeted him warmly at the door and since the children were still at school they enjoyed a quiet visit together in the living room. John began telling them what his new job might entail and both seemed amazed and enthusiastic at the prospect of not being governed by Britain.

Jean then asked, "Do you think now is a wise time though to try and get both East and West as well as the maritime provinces together? All three Atlantic Provinces are thinking of forming a union together to help with trade. We have had two depressions in the past ten years so everyone's economy is still shaky. And there is a big debt from the railway expansion."

"Well, said John, "when the U.S. failed to renew the Reciprocity Treaty the provinces began to trade with one another so maybe the same would happen with an Atlantic union. More trade would help pay off the railway debt. Halifax does have an ice-free winter port, but we would need more intercolonial railways to reach Halifax from Montreal."

"I do see those possibilities," replied Jean. "But what about the French demands for church run schools? The Catholic Church want state supported schools but the West want non denomination schools. Will they ever agree on that?"

Clara suddenly spoke up asking, "The big question may be will Britain want to let Canada be anything other than a colony?"

"They already lost that battle once in 1776 south of the border. We need to be stronger here to prevent the United States from trying to annex us. I am not sure Britain would be ready to step in again and fight to keep a colony," replied John.

The front door suddenly burst open and in ran two girls calling out before reaching the room. "Is he here yet?"

The conversation ended and chaos ensued and the girls were quickly asking for some of his famous stories about Toronto.

The next few years developed into a pattern. John would travel to Ottawa for a week and then return to Montreal. He always carried a big satchel of papers with him where ever he went. He did tell the girls stories when he was home but this time they were about what was happening in Canada. He would talk about people with names like Macdonald, Cartier, Tupper and Brown and told the girls that these were names they should remember.

This travelling continued for almost five years. John did go back to Toronto for part of one year, but returned with news that he had sold his house in Toronto and as soon as all the government negotiations were completed he would be retiring and staying in Montreal. "I will soon be looking for a lot to build a small home where I will live and Marie-Claire and Sheila will visit every day to cook and clean for me," he said with that familiar grin on his face.

Christmas was always the best time as Elodie and Julie and Marie would come and stay for the holiday festivities. Usually they could be convinced to go sledding or snowshoeing if there was snow. But the absolute best was when Grandmother Gabrielle and Grandfather Jacques came to visit. Sometimes in the evenings there would be a musical concert where everyone had to play a Christmas carol on an instrument. Grandfather Jacques and Uncle John always picked a wind instrument and made up the song as they went along. And it was always terrible. Marie-Claire and Sheila were expected to play the piano nicely with no wrong notes before they could try another instrument.

Uncle John always did his political quiz. He would say a name and if you knew who the person was, you wrote it down on a slate with chalk. "It is a good thing that he has been telling us all those stories because now we know the answers," said Sheila.

Clara always enjoyed seeing everyone having so much fun. There had been many Christmas days when food was scarce and a small practical present was all there was for the children. She looked over at Gabrielle and the two shared a smile and were likely sharing the same thoughts.

By 1864, John Drummond had a new house just down the street from his original home. He sometimes enjoyed the peace and quiet but he often could be found on a Sunday afternoon back at Number 24 playing games or just listening to Marie-Claire and Sheila retelling all the gossip and activities happening at their school.

Life at work was most often a frenzy of getting things done on time or rewriting proposal drafts. This spring there was to be a conference in Charlottetown and John was to be part of the delegation.

When John returned from Charlottetown he was telling Clara and Jean the exciting news about the future of the country. "Originally the three Atlantic Provinces were contemplating a union but an up and coming lawyer and member of the legislature asked if the Province of Canada could be included in the negotiations. John A. Macdonald and several others suggested a union of the three Atlantic Provinces with both Canada East and West. Financial arrangements for this union were presented and what a united government might look like. It took several days for all proposals to be heard but in the end there was enough interest and concerns it was decided to hold another conference in Quebec City this fall. I will be attending that one as well. Really I just sit there and when asked tell them yes this is legal or no it is not. It is exciting listening to all these ideas from politicians. This John A. Macdonald fellow is quite the speaker. He really tries to dominate the group with his ideas. Also there is a fellow from Lower Canada, George-Étienne Cartier, who

I believe was a Patriot during the rebellion. I think he spent a lot of time with Papineau and Nelson. He must have been very young then. We should mention his name to Jacques as he may know him"

"Oh John you aren't feeling old are you, "asked Clara?

"Well he and I were likely the oldest ones there. I think when this is all completed I will retire here in my little house and let my sister take care of me."

Clara later said to Jean that evening, "I am sure John is enjoying this new challenge immensely. With all this excitement about the future he may find retirement dull and boring."

"You are most likely right Clara. I myself do not think I will ever retire from the bank. They will have to carry me out of that building."

"Jean, do not even say anything like that. You know it will be nice to stop work and maybe travel to the continent together."

John attended the Quebec Conference in October and had returned to Montreal for Christmas that year. As usual Jacques and Gabrielle and the three girls spent some time at Number 24 that year. It was a special time as Sean and Catherine and their children also came for two days.

"Clara pulled Sean aside after dinner on Christmas Eve and asked, "Is Jacques all right? He seems to be a bit off colour and has no energy."

"He has me worried. He tires very easily and often has a nap after lunch and does not come back outside until late afternoon. I don't mind doing the farm work but I did ask Gabrielle and she says he is just getting older. I am not sure though."

"He is only sixty-five."

"I know Clara but you know he is a very private person so there is not much I can do other than get to the job ahead of him to do the heavy things before he tries. I think being in prison may have damaged something. I was much younger so I am fine."

"Maybe you should try and find someone looking for a job to help on the farm."

"We do have one of Catherine's younger brothers helping us, but you know Jacques." Sean just shrugged his shoulders and returned to the other room to help Catherine dress the children for sledding.

Christmas was much quieter this year as the children were older as were the adults. If anyone noticed Jacques' lack of energy, no one mentioned it. When everyone departed for home after Christmas, there were tears as the girls said goodbye to their parents. Extra hugs were given to Gabrielle and Jacques and returned. Clara knew others had the same quiet thoughts as she did.

Three months later a man arrived at the door of Number 24 with a letter from Sean. Jacques had had a heart attack and had not survived. Gabrielle was at his side when he died. There would be a funeral in St-Charles and he would be buried in the graveyard where many of his fellow Patriots were buried. As it was still winter Sean suggested they have a small service now and one later in the summer when more of the family could safely come. At the bottom of the letter Sean had added.

Since Jacques was such an advocate of the Farmer's Almanac, I checked the weather for next week and we are to have a late winter storm with at least ten to twelve inches of blowing snow. Not good for travel.

Clara began sending out messages to the family. She invited the girls to come and stay a few days with her and Jean. She also wrote letters to Jacques' brother in St-Eustache and also to Justine who still lived in Montreal. She was sure Sean had sent a message to the family in St-Hilaire. Then she had to write the hardest letter of all.

My Dearest Mama

I am so sorry to hear about Jacques. This must be so very difficult for you to realize he is no longer here with you. He was the best father, French teacher and carriage driver I ever knew. The kindness both you and Jacques showed when Sean and I arrived here will always stay with us. We both felt so safe with you in your home. We will all miss him terribly, but there are so many good memories we have it will seem like he is just in the other room. Everything we do now is somehow connected to him.

The girls are here with us for a few days, and John is in town right now too. You know you are welcome to come here for a visit and stay as long as you wish anytime you want to. In fact I really want you to come and stay with us for awhile.

All my love
Your daughter
Clara Ryan-St. Pierre

~

A family service for Jacques was held in May that year at the cemetery in St-Charles. Clara, Jean and the girls all travelled together on the train that now ran between Montreal and Quebec City. They were able to leave the train at a station quite close to St-Denis and this made the trip so much easier. Later in the week John and Gabrielle's friend Justine would also be arriving. The twenty-fourth of May that year turned out to be a sunny and warm day in the valley. John remarked that this was Queen Victoria's birthday and maybe someday we would celebrate it here in Canada East and West as she might just become our sovereign leader at some point. Sheila looked at Marie-Claire and whispered as she rolled her eyes, "Here we go again. Remember that. There may be a quiz later."

"I saw that," said Uncle John.

Gabrielle decided two days later that she would pack some things and return to Montreal with Clara and the others. "Now that there is a train it is much easier to travel. Justine and I can have a lovely visit while travelling; only this time it will be much more comfortable than our first trip together."

Sean and Catherine were sad to see her leave but knew it would be good for her to get away for a bit. The grandchildren were in tears but Catherine assured them she would comeback soon. "She is only taking summer clothes so she will be back by the fall," Catherine reassured the children.

As it turned out Gabrielle had to send a letter to Catherine and ask her to pack some cold weather clothes in a trunk and ship it by train to Montreal. She was enjoying her time visiting with Clara, Jean and the girls, Justine and John. There were also concerts and functions to attend as well as places to go for tea in the afternoon. She suddenly realized she had missed all this while living on a farm. One day she told Justine, "As much as I loved living on the farm, it was really because Jacques was there too. Now that he is not there it is not as delightful. I am thinking of moving back here to Montreal. There are many rooms in Number 24 so I am sure Clara would not mind. John as well has an extra room in his place and I could stay there when he is away. Or I could actually find a small place of my own."

"Gabrielle it would be lovely to have you close by again. But think about it carefully and promise me you will not make a decision until after Christmas. Talk to everyone first before you decide."

"Of course, and you can help me look for a new house if I decide to go that route."

That evening Gabrielle gathered up her courage and approached Clara and Jean about moving there permanently.

"Oh what a coincidence. Jean and I were just saying that you should move here. You have looked so happy these past few months. We have also been thinking of adding a small addition to the back of the house. It could be a kitchen, a living area and bedroom and bathroom just for you. Of course you could eat meals with us whenever you wanted to. And it would be all on one floor with no stairs."

"Now be careful. I am not old and crippled yet, though my knees do hurt occasionally especially when it rains. Jacques always said that and said that is why he read the Farmer's Almanac so he would know when to complain."

Jean then added in his best banker voice, "I have the perfect man for the job and he has done work for the bank so I know he is good. I will contact him tomorrow and we can start planning."

The work on the new place began before it was too cold to dig in the ground and was very exciting to watch the progress. John came over one Sunday for dinner and announced, "I have a proposal for you Gabrielle. I am going to London for the conference when we present our resolutions to the Queen. I will be away for Christmas this year as I am staying over in London to help work on the draft in January. I may not be back until spring. Why don't you stay in my house so that it is occupied during the winter? You will be close enough to watch the progress on your place and I have arranged for someone to care for all the things that may go wrong in a house while I am away. They will even shovel snow and light the fireplace for you."

"You may be sorry as I may never leave and Clara and Jean will have to rent the new place out."

John left for London three weeks before Christmas. Elodie and Julie announced they were invited to a friend's country house for the holidays and would be away until after New Years. Clara and Gabrielle both privately thought there were likely boys invited for the parties, but they were both adults and working at good jobs so it was inevitable that they would someday have their own lives. Marie said if her sisters were not going to be around she might as well work at the hospital and earn extra money. Clara had received a letter from Sean telling her they would not be able to visit this Christmas as they were to go to Catherine's family this year.

"Well I guess it will just be the three of us and Marie-Claire and Sheila this year. Maybe we should go out for dinner or have someone make it for us this year," said Clara.

"Good idea Clara, I know the perfect person to make that for you. We often use this company if we work through the dinner hour. Let me contact him and it will be my Christmas gift to you," said John.

"Just make sure they have mince pie and plum pudding with sauce," said Jean.

"It will all be taken care of."

Christmas did turn out to be quiet but lovely. It had been a difficult and busy year for everyone so a peaceful Christmas season and wishes for a Happy New Year were granted. John had made an excellent choice of the caterers and the dinner menu and everyone was feeling stuffed after dinner. Jean had his pie and pudding with sauce so he was happy. John had picked an extra present for Marie and Marie-Claire and Sheila. He always managed to find the latest fashion or trend as gifts. Gabrielle and Clara both received a soft cashmere scarf and Jean found an excellent bottle of scotch under the tree. Elodie and Julie would find a present under the tree as well when they returned from partying. He was the best brother and Uncle in the world.

~

John was enjoying being in London. He hadn't been there for years and seeing all the familiar buildings and scenery brought back pleasant memories of his childhood in London. With Queen Victoria on the throne, the city was transformed into a Christmas wonderland of decorations. The colourful gas lights reflected in the silvery ornaments along the streets and shop windows. There was no snow as at home and it felt almost warm to John as he walked each night back to his hotel. Even in the rain the lights of the city sparkled. He knew though that he was residing in an affluent area that was safe to walk at night. Many parts of London were dark and dangerous for a stranger to walk alone. There were also many adults and children who worked in factories all day and went home to a cold house and likely not enough food for the whole family.

John sincerely hoped that changing the structure of the government in Canada East and West would improve the standard of living for many who were now barely able to exist whether living in the rural areas or in the cities. He hoped that having a central authority controlling jurisdictions, representation by population with a two house system and responsible government at federal and provincial levels while preserving ties with Great Britain would be the best change for the country.

Their group completed the drafts of the British North America Act in early February and it was presented to Queen Victoria for approval. The Act passed quickly through the various levels of British Parliament and on March 29, 1867 it received royal assent. Queen Victoria proclaimed that day that the provinces of Canada, Nova Scotia, and New Brunswick would come together and be One Dominion under the name of Canada effective July 1, 1867.

The delegation had chosen the name Dominion of Canada and also decided Canada East would be renamed Quebec and Canada West be called Ontario. The election of delegates representing the various areas would not take place until six months after the original proclamation. There was a euphoric feeling among the delegates and much celebrating in London on that March evening. It had been a long process and all but a few felt it quite worthwhile.

John returned home in the spring but spent much of his time in Ottawa that summer and fall helping draft new laws reflecting confederation so he encouraged Gabrielle to stay at his house while he travelled. Gabrielle was enjoying her time living in John's house down the street from Clara and Jean not feeling guilty at all about taking over his home. She had become quite involved again with Justine working with organizations to help new immigrants adjust and survive. It was work she had loved before and once again found a niche where she could help as a volunteer.

July 1st of course was a big celebration for the Dominion of Canada, but a more private and elaborate celebration took place in Ottawa in November that year for the opening of the now Dominion of Canada's first Parliament.

John stopped in at Clara's place one afternoon carrying two large white envelopes with elegant hand lettering on the front. It looked like an official gold seal on the back.

"I have in my hand the invitation to the party of the century and I need to find someone who might be interested in attending."

Marie-Claire, who was just seventeen, quickly turned and said, "I'II go. What is it for and where is the party? Will I need a new dress?"

Clara looked horrified at the boldness of her daughter, but said "Tell us John. What is being celebrating?"

"I have received these invitations from the Prime Minister, Sir John A. Macdonald, to attend the opening of the first Parliament in Ottawa. It is in November and I am allowed to bring three guests. Now I have to ask Gabrielle or she may not let me back in the house. I would like you Clara to come as well to this historic event. As for the third person I could be either Jean or…"

John hesitated, looked around the room until his eyes rested on Marie-Claire. "Oh yes," she said. "Pick me. Dad won't mind."

Everyone laughed. The front door opened at that point and Jean came strolling into the house. "What is so funny? Never mind. I have exciting news. I have received an invitation to represent the bank at the opening of parliament in November." Jean said as he waived a similar white envelope in front of everyone.

Laughing again, John showed his white envelopes to Jean. "I guess we are all going to the party together. Marie-Claire you will definitely need a grown up gown for this party."

Preparing for this historic event took up much of everyone's time over the next few months. They had to arrange a place to stay, book the steamer from Montreal to Kingston and then the train to Ottawa. Most important to the women was the purchase of the clothing they would need. It was all very exciting. Marie-Claire was the envy of all her school friends when they discovered why she would miss a week of school.

Hotels were a scarcity in Ottawa for the event and as luck would have it, John had a friend who owned a country home just outside of Ottawa and had offered it to John and the family as he was staying at his home in town that week. The home came with a staff and carriages and drivers. This would be luxury. Clara and Gabrielle thought back to living only on the food they could grow and finding the drinking water with ice on top of the pail in the kitchen because the fire had gone out in the stove over night. They knew some people still probably lived in those conditions. Hopefully a new form of government would make things more equitable for everyone.

Finally the day arrived to board the steamer to Kingston. Jean was horrified when he saw the number of trunks that would be travelling with them. He was glad that one staff person was coming with them to help carry and load the trunks.

Clara and Marie-Claire hoped they remembered to pack everything they needed and each had a journal with them to write down all their recollections of each event.

Gabrielle tried to pack lightly but the crinolines that were worn under the dress styles of the day took up an enormous amount of space in the trunk. She would just have to wear the same one under every dress.

John had travelled ahead of the group and arranged a place to stay overnight in Kingston so they would arrive in Ottawa during the day rather than very late at night. He had arranged transport as well from the steamer upon arrival and to the train the next day. He had done this trip many times over the past few months so he knew all the tricks and all the right people to call.

The family were taken by driver directly to the country home, and arrived mid afternoon. Tonight there was a reception for delegates and John would be attending by himself. He would stay overnight in Ottawa rather than travel back alone late at night. The next afternoon was the opening of Parliament and the family had reserved seats in the gallery. A reception with dinner would take place somewhere near the Parliament buildings. The buildings themselves were not yet completed so other arrangements had been made for all events.

Clara had chosen a scooped neck evening dress made of bronze satin with bands of black trim on the skirt. She accessorized it with a waist length black wool jacket that could be removed for the evening event. As was the custom the dresses were worn over a hoop frame to give the wide skirt look. Long gloves would be worn in the evening as the dress had short sleeves but short gloves were the custom during the day.

The three women had coordinated their dress colours, and Gabrielle had chosen an evening dress of gray striped satin in the skirt with a white voile low cut top. A matching jacket trimmed in contrasting fabric with full sleeves was worn over the dress during the day.

When Marie-Claire entered the parlour dressed in her newest dress, the conversation stopped. Her dress was white linen with an overlay of sheer fabric called illusion. It had long sleeves of the sheer fabric and a higher neckline. It was fitted to the waistline but flowed to the floor as it was worn without a crinoline or hoops. Her hair was long past her shoulders with loose curls around her face. She was a vision of beauty.

Clara and Jean could not believe she was so grown up. Marie-Claire was their oldest daughter and they were very proud of her. Their first born son had lived only a year and it was such a loss for them. Marie-Claire was born next and was a robust active child. Her sister Sheila had stayed at home in Montreal much to her annoyance. She was just too young to attend such an event. Today they would enjoy the pleasure of seeing Marie-Claire attend her first important function celebrating the birth of a new nation.

The opening of the Parliament was held in an adjoining building next to all the construction of the new centre block. It was now November and of course the past week had been quite rainy. To disguise the mud path and to avoid any mishaps, the workers had laid boards along the way. There was still mud on the boards but it was better than no boards. The ladies all lifted their skirts to prevent the mud from sticking to the satin fabric.

Once inside, they were greeted and directed to the gallery by very efficient government workers. The house began to fill not only with guests, but also with the newly elected members of both houses of parliament. There certainly was an electric feeling in the room. Suddenly there was a banging on the door and a gentleman carrying a large ceremonial mace entered and laid it on the clerk's desk in front of the speaker's chair. It became very quiet. A parade of men entered one after the other. There was the Governor General, Viscount Monck, who was to be sworn in today, then Prime Minister Sir John A. Macdonald, followed by a stream of well dressed men all smiling and congratulating each other. Among those men was Uncle John who looked up at Marie-Claire in the gallery and gave her a slight nod of his head.

The Prime Minister had been appointed earlier by the Queen, and Viscount Monck was previously the Governor General of the Province of Canada and had been asked by Macdonald to become the first Governor General of the Dominion of Canada.

After he was officially sworn in with much pomp and circumstance, Viscount Monck read a speech while sitting on what looked like a throne to Marie-Claire. She thought it was quite a long speech with too many words. The prime minister spoke as well and it seemed every sentence was heartily cheered by the group. Today they were all friends. But in one corner of the room sat three men who constantly exchanged words quietly even during the speeches. It was obvious when they did not stand up to cheer the words of the Prime Minister that they were not completely happy with Confederation.

Later when Marie-Claire asked Uncle John who were the three men, he told her, "They are the representatives from Nova Scotia and I will tell you more about it later."

The reception that followed was very crowded and hard to see anything as some folks were chatting in groups with waiters trying to pass food and drinks around. Because of the circumference of the women's skirts there was little space to move about the room. Finally a bell rang and most of the men left the room. The other guests were directed to a group of rooms that had chairs arranged in conversational groupings. Clara and Gabrielle found a corner with three chairs and quickly sat down. Marie-Claire followed their example.

"We have been standing for ages and this chair is quite comfortable. I may just stay sitting here forever," Gabrielle declared.

Before anyone could say another word, a line of trolleys pushed by uniformed men were rolled into the room. Tea and cakes were being served to the guests.

"So this is how the government people live," whispered Clara to the others.

That evening the dinner was also held in the reception tent and it had now been transformed into a banquet hall. There were gas lights hanging from the tent ceiling as well as others along the side walls giving the room a lovely golden glow. Clara and Jean and Marie-Claire and Gabrielle were in a group talking with John when a gentleman with dark curly hair in a dark waist coat and light trousers came over to the group.

"John. This must be your family we so often hear about."

"Yes Prime Minister. Let me introduce you to my sister Gabrielle, my niece Clara and her husband Jean, and my great niece Marie-Claire. May I present the Honourable Sir John A. Macdonald?"

Marie-Claire was almost speechless but quickly remembered a question she had wanted to ask. "Do you think there will soon be schools for all children to attend? I am fortunate, but on my way to school, I see many children younger than I am who seem to be going somewhere other than school. Shouldn't everyone learn to read and write? Will your government help these children?"

"My you have very grown up thoughts for such a young lady. Yes we hope to improve this situation." And with that statement the Prime Minister turned and greeted another group of people waiting to have his attention.

Clara leaned over and said, "Maybe you should not have asked that question Marie-Claire."

John quickly stated, "Oh no. Mr. Macdonald does not mind questions at all and that was a very good one. His mind is always working overtime and if a suggestion is put to him at some point, he may recall it at a later date and work on it."

Gabrielle had been looking around the room at the splendour of the surroundings when her eye caught a face returning her glance. She felt she should know this person but did not know from where. Suddenly the man was approaching them.

"John. Who is this man coming towards us?"

"Oh. That is a friend from St-Denis days. You and Jacques both knew him. It is George-Étienne Cartier. Good Evening George. You must remember my sister Gabrielle."

"Yes of course. We are old friends. I was sorry to hear about Jacques. He was a good man and one we could always count on when needed. Your brother and I have been spending too much time together working on this Confederation. So much writing and rewriting. Now John, introduce me to the rest of your family."

Introductions were made and a pleasant conversation ensued until a bell rang announcing dinner.

Dinner was very Canadian with a variety of entrees from various parts of the country. There was fish from the Maritime Provinces, fruit pies and breads from Quebec, and several kinds of meat from Ontario. No one went home hungry that evening.

It was a late night ride back to the house that night with the festivities still continuing in the Capital. The next day it was just pleasant to relax in this wonderful home talking about last night's spectacular event and knowing you did not have to go anywhere until tomorrow.

TWENTY

'OUR GREATEST HAPPINESS DOES NOT DEPEND THE CONDITION OF LIFE IN WHICH CHANCE HAS PASSED US, BUT IS ALWAYS THE RESULT OF A GOOD CONSCIENCE, GOOD HEALTH, OCCUPATION AND FREEDOM IN ALL JUST PURSUITS.'

Thomas Jefferson

Life in the new Dominion of Canada continued on as before. Not many people saw much difference in their lives except for the newly elected members of Parliament. There were still disagreements between areas. Several newly populated area of the country decided to join the Confederation as provinces. Nova Scotia decided to stay as a Province and not try to leave and in the end, that was the best decision for them.

~

Just up the street from Number 24 was an area known as the Golden Square Mile. It had all started when a fur trader named James McGill had purchased forty-seven acres and built a very large expensive home for his family called Burnside. Soon other wealthy industrialists purchased land and built their own mansions and the Golden Square mile over the next twenty years became a very prestigious place to live. When McGill died he stated in his will that the Burnside estate of forty-seven acres and ten thousand pounds be used for the establishment of a University or college for the purpose of education and the advancement of learning in the Province of Quebec.

The University and a Grammar School were located at the end of St. Catherine Street. Marie-Claire attended this school until she had completed all the grades offered to young women. At this point women were to find a husband, marry, and stay home and raise a family. There was a school in the Eastern Townships called Bishop's College School where young women could attend and learn about teaching in schools. Marie-Claire decided teaching was what she really wanted to do. At the age of eighteen, Marie-Claire packed her belongings in a trunk and moved away to school several hours from the only home she had known. She would be living in a home with one of the professors and attending classes daily. There were very strict codes of to adhere to and she was not allowed to go home for a visit until Christmas.

Marie-Claire fell in love with learning and before she knew it December had arrived and she was packing to go home for a visit. She had so much to tell everyone but she could hardly wait to return as this term would be a practical exercise where she would observe children in a classroom.

The second year of the program actually had students teaching in classrooms while the lead teacher watched. It all seemed so easy until it was the day for Marie-Claire to teach her first class on her own. In her classroom were grades four, five and six. She would have to have two grades doing some assigned work while she taught a lesson to the third group. Marie-Claire assigned the grade six class a set of mathematic questions printed on the board. The grade fours were to copy a poem from the board and write on their slate what they thought it meant. She would work on some new mathematics problems with grade five.

It all seemed as though it should work out well, but she had not factored in the boys in grade six. They often liked to quietly tell funny stories making the others laugh out loud. Within five minutes several boys were laughing and giggling on the one side of the room. Marie-Claire stopped her lesson and addressed the situation asking the boys to stop and get back to work. The disruption continued and now the grade four class and some of the grade fives were laughing as well. She stopped the lesson, walked over to the three boys she knew started the disruption and made them stand in separate corners of the room facing the wall. As she attempted to continue the lesson, one boy in the corner at the front of the room turned around and began making faces. The entire room went silent. The regular teacher went over to the boy, took him by the ear and walked him to her desk. She opened a drawer and pulled out a leather strap.

"Miss Marchand. This young man has defied authority and must be strapped. Four times on each hand. You must strap him. I will show you how. She asked the boy to hold out his hand and put the other behind his back. He did as he was told and seem to know the routine as he had obviously experienced this punishment before. The teach raised her hand with the strap and with a resounding whack brought it directly onto his palm.

"Now you may continue."

Marie Claire took the strap but was not sure if she was shaking more that the boy. He was quiet but she could see tears in his eyes. Several girls in grade one were sobbing.

Marie-Claire managed to complete the punishment and then sent the boy to the cloak room to collect his coat and go home. She knew when he arrived home he would likely receive an even harsher punishment from his father.

The lead teacher called recess for the rest of the students much to Marie-Claire's relief. She had to get a drink of water and sit down for awhile as her legs were shaking. Maybe being a teacher was not as easy as she had anticipated.

Not a word was mentioned about the incident by anyone for the rest of the day; but the children all worked hard and completed all the tasks she assigned quietly.

At the end of the day, the lead teacher sat Marie-Claire down and explained why she made her strap the boy. "If I had done it and you had not, those boys would be bad everyday you are here. They cause trouble for me as well and they are really only putting in time until they can leave school. In the spring when it is planting time they will not be here as they will be working on the farm. You did very well today and I think you will be an excellent teacher."

"Thank you. Let's hope tomorrow is better."

"Oh it will be. George will not likely be here and no one else is likely to take a chance on repeating the same silliness."

Marie Claire became more proficient at controlling the class behaviour during her time as a student teacher and the students, especially the girls, enjoyed all the days when she was at the school.

Her second year as a student teacher was spent in two different schools. One was in the city in Montreal where many of the students came from homes where food was not always available and attendance was inconsistent. Education was a privilege and not always considered important by the parents. She seemed to be constantly helping students catch up on lessons they had missed due to absenteeism. Teaching at this school allowed Marie-Claire to live at home in her old room. She knew her dinner would be made for her every night and a delicious lunch ready in the morning to take with her to school.

The second school assigned to her was in a rural area near Sherbrook. She had to board with one of the families in the small town. The family were kind and welcomed her to their home, but she felt she caused some disruption as two of the girls had to move out of their room so Marie-Claire could sleep in their room. Four of the six children in the house also attended the one room school which made for interesting walks to and from school each day.

The lead teacher at first assigned just the two lower grades to Marie-Claire while she taught the remaining six grades. Gradually she was assigned extra grades and after five weeks, Marie-Claire was teaching all eight grades every day for the next month. She never thought she would be able to accomplish it, but she did and according to her lead teacher she did a very good job.

When June arrived, she said good bye to her students and her host family and returned to college for the last few weeks. Her time at Bishops had been successful and at graduation she was honoured to receive the highest marks in her class. Clara and Jean had never been more proud.

Marie-Claire was watching the mail arrive every day during July that year. One day a large white envelope arrived as Marie-Claire was sitting in the front hall awaiting the post. She quickly tore open the top and scanned the letter.

"Mom." She ran all the way to the back garden as she was calling. "It came. I got the job I wanted. I am going to be a teacher just down the street at the grammar school. I can live at home and walk to school."

"Oh Marie-Claire. That is so wonderful. I was so worried you would be far away somewhere and we would rarely see you. What grades are you teaching?"

"I haven't even read that far yet," she laughed. Again she read the second page of the letter. "I will be teaching grade four girls. How perfect is that. I was worried I would get grade six boys."

"I must run down the street and tell Uncle John and Grandmother the good news."

This school was a prestigious school in Montreal where girls and boys classes were separated and where many children from wealthy families attended. She also realized often these children were given most things they asked for and were often demanding of others. She would have to make lessons very interesting to keep the girls engaged. She had a whole month to plan before school started.

September came, school started, her class for the most part were quite lovely young ladies and happy to be back at school. The biggest problem in class was the chattiness of the girls. Marie-Claire soon devised a reward system for the class if there was no talking during work time. The special outings she planned for the class were just the incentive needed and her class soon became the envy of other classes in the school.

One of the rules teachers had to follow was to remain unmarried. At first Marie-Claire was so busy planning lessons and teaching, she had no time in her life for any social events. At a Christmas concert in her first year of teaching, she met a young man who was an uncle of one of her students. He had come to the classroom to pickup his niece after the concert. The talked briefly and before he left, he invited her to a concert in town the following week. Without consulting her parents, Marie-Claire accepted the invitation and James asked her address and said he would meet her at her home about seven.

When Marie-Claire arrived home that evening, she knew she must tell her parents. “Mother and Father I have been invited by James Armand to attend a concert next week. He is a family member of one of my students. I have accepted his invitation.”

Her statement left no room for discussion and Clara knew eventually her daughter would meet someone. She just always hoped he would be a nice young man. “How wonderful. Will we get to meet this young man?”

“Yes he is picking me up her before the concert.” Marie-Claire decided she did not need to give out any more information so excused herself and went to her apartment. Since Gabrielle had moved into John’s house, Marie-Claire now occupied the small addition at the back of the house. It was nice having her own space but she still enjoyed dinner with her parents every night.

Marie-Claire noticed the week seemed to drag while she waited the night she would attend the concert with James. Finally Saturday came. James arrived and was very polite and friendly when he met her parents. He also seemed even more handsome than she remembered from a week ago.

The concert was all Christmas music and was set in a unique wooden church lit by candlelight. It was just the setting to be inspired for Christmas. James and Marie-Claire enjoyed the concert and Marie-Claire invited James back to her parents place for a late evening meal. Clara had arranged delicious Christmas goodies in the dining room and she and Jean stayed for a short time and the politely excused themselves to allow the young people to chat on their own.

Several other outing were arranged and as Christmas holidays were about to start, Marie-Claire had more free time for socializing instead of work. In fact the two spent almost part of everyday for the next two weeks together. By the time school started again in January, they decided they were perfect for each other and had declared their love for each other.

James was a student at McGill University, finishing work on his Masters degree in Science and Education. He had completed his undergraduate work at Royal Military College in Kingston and was hoping to obtain a teaching job there when he finished at McGill. Every few months James had to go to Kingston for a week and participate in military manoeuvres and so he did spend some time away from Montreal. Marie-Claire was busy at school but did miss James when he was not visiting her almost every day.

At Easter James invited her to his parent's home for dinner. It was a bit stressful meeting his parents for longer than just a passing moment. As schools had a week off at Easter, the couple were able to spend more time together. One afternoon it was unseasonably warm and the couple were enjoying the warmth of the sun while sitting on a bench near Mount Royal overlooking the city. James suddenly stood up and then knelt down in front of Marie-Claire.

"Marie-Claire. I love you so much. Will you marry me?"

"Oh my goodness! I was not expecting this. I thought you lost something. Yes I will James. You are the best thing that has ever happened in my life and I do love you. Yes! Yes! Yes!"

James slipped a beautiful antique diamond ring on Marie-Claire's finger and of course it was the perfect size. He stood up and put his arms around her and the two hugged.

"I have already asked your Father for your hand in marriage and he has agreed. And your Mother gave me one of your rings to use to get the right size."

"When did you do that? You are tricky. Do your parents know yet?"

"Yes. I told them yesterday. In fact we are to go for dinner at my parent's house tonight, and your parents will be there as well."

Do my Grandmother and my Uncle know as well?"

"No. I thought you might like to tell them yourself."

"Can we stop there on the way to my house? I do need to change for dinner."

"Of course we can. Let's walk down the hill and go there now."

"James this is a beautiful ring. It looks antique."

"It is. It was my grandmother's on my Mother's side of the family."

The couple walked hand in hand down the hill to visit Uncle John and Grandmother Gabrielle to tell them the good news.

The minute James and Marie-Claire entered the small cottage; Gabrielle looked at her and quickly said, "I knew it. You two are getting married."

"How did you know that?"

Marie-Claire you look like you just swallowed all the candy in one bite. I know that look anywhere."

James and Marie-Claire told Gabrielle and John that she was right. They just became engaged and wanted to be married at Christmas.

"I am so pleased for both of you," said John. "Where do you think you will be living?"

James told John about his hopes for a job teaching in Kingston and they would just have to wait until May or June to know the answer to that question. I have applied for a job, but will not know until after I graduate this spring.

John left the room and returned with a bottle of champagne. "I think we have something to celebrate today."

"Tonight we are having dinner with Mr. and Mrs. Armand and Mother and Father, so we should not drink too much," laughed Marie-Claire.

It was exciting chatting with Gabrielle and John; telling them how James proposed and all their plans for the future. John and Gabrielle were enthusiastic listeners and asked all the right questions without being too intrusive.

Later in the evening at James parents' home, the atmosphere was very happy but a bit more formal. Marie-Claire was very thankful her Mother had taught her table manners fit for dining with royalty. She knew when to begin eating and which piece of cutlery to use with each course. By the end of the evening, she realized her cheeks were somewhat stiff from smiling so much.

After dinner James walked Marie-Claire home and they talked all the way about the future. Marie-Claire was so happy to be marrying James but she would have to resign her position as a teacher once she was married. This was the only part she regretted.

"Maybe I can convince someone to hire a married woman at a school in Kingston," she said. "That rule needs to change anyway."

"We will see," James said as he drew her near and kissed her goodnight.

Marie-Claire didn't answer. She just returned the kiss and leaned into his embrace.

The next few months were a whirlwind of activity. The wedding plans were being arranged for a Christmas wedding in Montreal. There would be many guests invited. John had a list of friends from both Toronto and Montreal he wanted to attend. Gabrielle had many friends she wanted to invite. Marie-Claire's Aunts all had spouses and friends to invite and of course Clara and Jean had many friends both from their social circle and from Jean's workplace to invite. And that was just Marie-Claire's side of the family. Once the names were all collected from both families, the list numbered over two hundred. They would need to find a large hall for the reception.

After waiting well into June, James finally heard he had been accepted as the new Science Professor for chemistry at Royal Military College. The newlyweds would be starting their life together in Kingston. His job started in September.

Marie-Claire did tell her Principal that she was to be married at Christmas and would be resigning from her teaching position. Her Principal was saddened to hear the news and asked if she would stay on until Christmas break. He even offered to let her stop a week early if she started the fall term.

"I wanted to start a new program this fall for the girls in the upper grades and I had planned on asking you to head it up. We want to give the girls an extra course in building confidence. Girls need to be prepared to go farther even if they do get married. It would also involve having a place where their young children could be cared for while they learn and work."

"Oh, that is quite progressive." Then Marie-Claire quickly added, "I would be thrilled to help develop a program like that. Possibly if two of us could work on it, the other leader could take over when I leave."

"I have already thought of someone I am sure you could work with. Jane Matheson is quite interested in new ideas and I think you two have worked together before."

"Yes we have and she is a wonderful collaborator."

"Deal done. You can come back in the fall and leave the week before Christmas break. Now we may call on you for ideas after you are married. You can always come back to visit your parents and stop in to see us," he laughed.

Marie-Claire felt a bit better about leaving teaching knowing she would have the chance to start something very new and ahead of its time.

James went off to Kingston in September to start his new post. Since it was a live-in college, the professors were given a small house to live in. He and Marie-Claire had taken some time in the summer to collect furnishings from the storage building at the back of the property. Most of the pieces were in good shape, just dusty. They had belonged to Gabrielle and Jacques, Aunt Marie, Clara and Jean and of course Uncle John. The two decided they would call the style "Early Relatives" It was all nicely set up with pictures on the wall and a few dishes in the cupboards. Their wedding gifts would fill the other spots after December.

Gabrielle consulted the Farmer's Almanac and it predicted a sunny but cold day with no snow in the next two weeks. Perfect. Grandpa Jacques would be pleased.

Marie-Claire had chosen an antique white dress of silk with lace overlays. The sleeves were just lace and ended in a point at her wrist. The skirt was long and draped to the floor in soft folds. Something New. The neckline was scooped and she wore an antique necklace Gabrielle had lent her. Something Borrowed. Her slippers were a soft white rough satin with tiny blue bows on the front. Something Blue. And of course the Something Old was her antique engagement ring. She looked stunning. So much so that Jean had tears in eyes when he was ready to walk her down the aisle.

Sheila was her Maid of Honour and looked perfect dressed in a floor length gown of hunter green. Both bouquets had sprigs of holly and mistletoe mixed among the white carnations and green foliage.

Clara wore a delightful floor length wool crepe dress in a dusty blue colour. The colour suited her Irish complexion perfectly.

The church was full, and the reception followed at a large hotel in the city. It was all decorated for the holiday season and by the end of the evening, everyone was in a festive mood.

The newlyweds decided they did not want to travel far as both had to return to Kingston before New Year's Day. They spent several days at Auberge de Lachine on the outskirts of Montreal.

They had only a few days at Clara and Jean's home to pack their belongings which seem to have multiplied. Most of their things were being shipped to Kingston by steamer and delivered to their new place later. James and Marie-Claire would travel by steamer as well on the last day of the year.

It was hard to say goodbye to the family but it was a new adventure and an exciting time in their life.

TWENTY-ONE

'MY ROOTS ARE IN THE PAST: MY HOPES ARE IN THE FUTURE.'

George Bernard Shaw

Very quickly life in Kingston began to follow a pattern. James went to the school each day and Marie-Claire unpacked their boxes of wedding gifts and found a spot to put them. She kept quite busy but she still missed her work at the Grammar School. She hoped she would get used to being at home cooking and cleaning and sometimes reading. It was mid April and spring had arrived. The weather was somewhat better allowing her to get out and walk around the campus. Lately though she had no energy and often felt quite nauseous. Several weeks later as it continued, James insisted she consult a doctor.

James came home after school one day and found her lying on the couch. He was very concerned until she told him, "We are going to be parents by Christmas. I am not sick. I am expecting a baby."

James was speechless. He just kept looking at her with a strange look on his face. Finally he managed to say," Really? I can't believe it. Really?"

"Yes James. Really! It will be our Christmas present to each other."

"We must tell our parents. My Mother will be thrilled as she really wants grandchildren. We can send a letter this week or we can go to Montreal for Easter and tell them then."

"I like the Easter idea better. Maybe by then I will be feeling better. The doctor said I might feel ill for several months, but it should get better."

"Good idea. Can I make dinner tonight?"

"Sure. You will just have to put the dish in the oven as it is all prepared and ready to cook. Aren't you lucky?"

By Easter Marie-Claire was feeling better and quite enjoyed the trip back to Montreal. Their parents were thrilled to have them home and even more excited when they were told the news of a new grandchild by Christmas. Gabrielle could not believe she was going to be a Great Grandmother and John felt the same about being a Great Uncle.

"Really though, "John said in his best official voice. "You all know that I am a 'great' Uncle and always have been."

Clara just walked around all weekend with a smile on her face.

It was decided this far ahead that Christmas would not be in Montreal. Instead it would be in Kingston. Rooms at a hotel would be arranged for all that travelled and the parents would arrange for dinner to be ordered from the hotel and served in a private dining room there. Jean reminded everyone not to forget the mince pie and Christmas pudding. This was truly advanced planning.

Marie-Claire was thrilled about being a mother and a bit nervous at the same time. She was able to go to Montreal in the summer while James was working and visit with her mother and grandmother for several weeks. She was also very curious about whether they would have a son or a daughter. Secretly she hoped for a girl, but knew as long as the baby was healthy, it did not really matter. Either would be loved and welcomed.

The visits also gave her a chance to ask her mother and grandmother many questions about babies.

Gabrielle recounted the time Clara almost had to deliver her sister. "I was never so happy to see Mrs. Simard arrive at the house that day," said Clara. "Do you remember the boys kept bring in pails of water to heat on the stove? It is all funny now, but then it was quite scary."

"Clara you were so good with the twins and with Marie. I always relied on you so much so I could do the other farm work. And Marie-Claire, I think you will be a natural just like your Mother."

"I remember John telling Sean and me when he said we were going to live with you and Jacques that we would have to help around the farm and take care of children. I had always been the baby in the family and was absolutely petrified I would drop one of the girls or do something wrong. I always watched you so closely Gabrielle to see how you did things."

"And it all worked out just fine Clara."

Marie-Claire returned to Kingston feeling a bit more confident about taking care of children and knew she could always have her Mother come and stay for awhile if she needed her.

It seemed like forever but finally December arrived. Two days before the family were to arrive Marie-Claire went into labour and within sixteen hours she and James had a perfect little girl. There was no need to write a letter or send a telegram as the family would arrive the next day. It would be good to have her mother to help as she was supposed to stay in bed for a week. James was at the top of the world when he met the family at the pier.

"Congratulations to all. You are Grandparents, Great Grandmothers, Great Uncles and Aunts. We have a precious little girl. Born yesterday and everyone is doing fine. We are naming her Gabrielle but I think she will go by Gabby."

"We have hired a nurse to be at the house for awhile so let's get you to the hotel and tomorrow you can all come for a visit. The nurse is a bit strict about not allowing more than one visitor in but maybe we will give her the day off tomorrow. She doesn't need to know."

There was a lot of excitement in the group and they all wanted to go right away to see the baby, but knew they must wait until tomorrow. Gabrielle in particular was thrilled to know the baby had been named after her. She said a quiet prayer to Jacques telling him everyone down here was fine. She hoped he was looking down on the group at this moment.

The next day was busy. The family had to take turns visiting Marie-Claire and the baby. The nurse somehow heard that the family was coming to visit and decided not to take the day off. Instead she stood guard at the door only letting one person in at a time and then after the fifteen minute visit there had to be an hour resting time for Marie-Claire. No was allowed to hold the baby, just look at her in the bassinette. She did make an exception for Gabrielle when she realized the baby was named after her Great Grandmother. She actually was allowed to hold the baby for a few minutes. Clara was somewhat put out by all the rules as she felt she should be allowed in any time she wanted.

On Christmas day the family arrived at the house early so they could organize dinner. The chef at the hotel had agreed to make the dinner and have it delivered to the house about an hour before dinner. He said he had never done this for anyone before and he hoped dinner would not be ruined by the wait. The young man who delivered dinner had a list of instructions two pages long from the chef about how it should be kept warm and for what length of time. Clara and Gabrielle hoped the chef would not show up later to check if they had followed his instructions.

The nurse decided she could take the day off as James suggested. She now felt comfortable seeing how Clara and Gabrielle took such care with the baby, and that they would know what to do every minute of the day. As soon as she left, Marie-Claire said she could not lay in bed another minute and moved downstairs to the living room to be part of the family. James and Jean carried the baby's bed, blankets, clothing and diapers plus any other needs down the stairs and established a new nursery spot at one end of the living room. It was a bit crowded but they were now altogether for Christmas Day.

It was a wonderful day for everyone. Marie-Claire had been quite organized and all the presents had been purchased well ahead of December. They were all wrapped and put under the tree as well. Everyone had a grand time unwrapping gifts and the smallest member of the family, who slept through the whole event, seemed to have the largest number of gifts.

Gabrielle, John, Sheila and Jean left for Montreal two days after Christmas, while Clara decided to stay in Kingston to help Marie-Claire for a few weeks. It was a wonderful time for Clara as not only was she a great help, but also at the end of January when she left to go home, she felt she had really bonded with Gabby.

The happy household soon settled into a routine ruled by the wants and needs of young Gabby. She knew how to get her Father's attention and have him play with her or read a story. Marie-Claire thought she was in charge of the daily routine, but actually it was Gabby who really ran the show.

When James had some holiday time in the summer, the family all went to Montreal for a visit. Unfortunately while they were there, John Drummond passed away. He was seventy-four and his heart just gave out one day while walking up the street to see Clara and Jean. Everyone was shocked and saddened by the loss. John had been such an important part of everyone's' life. He had arranged for Clara and Sean and Louis to be part of the St-Pierre family. He knew the right people to help Jacques and Sean find their freedom after the rebellion. He had given so much to help Clara and the three girls continue their education and give them places to live. Gabrielle especially was devastated to lose her older brother. They had been very close after the death of their parents and always looked out for each other.

Condolences arrived from so many who were part of his work and social life. The day of the funeral, a note arrived from Sir John A. Macdonald stating how saddened he was to hear of John's passing. He noted John's contribution to helping Canada become a self governing country would always be remembered.

~

The next decade there would be as much joy as sadness for this family. Marie-Claire would give birth to four more children, all boys. Clara and Jean were thrilled. Sean and Catherine only had the two children who were now in their teens and thinking about starting lives of their own. There was always laughter and games and new adventures whenever the children were present.

Unfortunately, generations exist because some are older than others. In 1881, Gabrielle died at the age of seventy-six. She had lived a remarkable life, but for Clara it was hard to say good-bye to the Mother who had taken in the ten year old orphan and raised her as her own.

Four years later Clara once again was devastated to lose the love of her life, Jean. He had been such a bright light in her life. They lived through some difficult times together, but they always remained a true partnership in a time when men still were the head of the household. They had seen real change during their marriage not only in lifestyle but also in how a country can change politically.

In 1900 just as the world was changing and making life easier, Clara's youngest daughter Sheila was tragically killed in an accident involving two sleds. For months Clara could not bring herself to leave the house or entertain visitors. Her three younger sisters tried to console her but to no avail. Clara felt she would be the next to die as she was now the oldest. In the darkness of her living room, she sat thinking about the past. She started as a Loyalist coming from Ireland to a new country. It was intended she would live in a Loyalist area, but instead ended up in a part of the country more loyal to France than England. She was raised alongside Patriots and endured the Patriote War all the while still believing Loyalist ideas. She had one Loyalist name and two French names. Clara sometimes really did not know who she was.

Six months later Marie-Claire decided she had to somehow help her mother. She hired a housekeeper, left the four boys at home with James and took Gabby to Montreal to stay at the house on St. Catherine Street. Gabby was almost twenty-five and had just completed her last year of University. She wasn't sure what she wanted to do next year, though a trip to see her Grandmother would be all right.

Marie-Claire was astounded when seeing her Mother in such a depressed state. The first thing she did was open all the drapes to let some light into the house. She then looked in the icebox and found no edible food. What had her mother been eating? She sent Gabby to the store with a list of items to purchase. She then began to clean the house and put away the many things that had just been dropped when not needed. It took the better part of two days for Marie-Claire and Gabby to put the house back into some semblance of order. The entire time they were sweeping, dusting, doing laundry and scrubbing surfaces Clara sat in her chair and watched without saying anything. Marie Claire suspected Clara had been sleeping either in the chair or on the sofa.

"We will make a nice dinner tonight Gabby and eat it in the sunroom. It is warm enough tonight to do that."

"How are we going to get Gran out of her chair, change her disgusting clothes and get to eat something," asked Gabby?

"Marie is coming over and bringing a friend who works at the hospital with patients who are depressed. She may know some strategies."

At four that afternoon Marie and her friend Judith arrived. Marie-Claire explained what had been happening in the house for the past few weeks and had laid some clean towels and clothes on Clara's bed.

Judith was amazing. She never really asked Clara if she wanted to do something but instead just said, "Clara we are going upstairs now." She then took Clara's arm and steered her toward the stairs. She continued this approach for the next hour. There did not seem too much of a protest going on upstairs, so Marie, Gabby and Marie-Claire remained in the kitchen getting dinner ready.

The next thing they saw was Clara coming downstairs, neatly dressed in clean clothes, hair nicely washed and combed and holding on to Judith's arm. There was still no expression on her face but she was looking around the room. She saw Gabby standing by the window and said, "Oh you have finally come home."

Gabby wasn't sure what she should say so just smiled and said, "Yes I have come for a visit Gran."

Dinner that night was somewhat subdued with some conversation between the women, but mostly watching Clara to see if she would join in. Clara did eat a bit of dinner but said nothing.

Judith suggested they hire a nurse to look after her physical well being and she would contact a person at the hospital to come and try to bring her out of the depression. The standard treatment at this time was to put the patient in a locked hospital room and leave them alone. No one wanted that to happen to Clara.

The next day a nurse arrived to help Clara during the day. Another nurse would be coming to spend the night making sure Clara slept in her bed. The person Judith contacted to come and work with Clara arrived after two days and began immediately to talk to Clara as if everything was as usual. Hazel took Clara for walks around the property on nice days and joined the family for lunch. She was a very calm pleasant women and Clara immediately accepted her help.

Marie-Claire also decided there needed to be new caretakers on the property. Mr. and Mrs. Richards had passed away several years ago and there was no one taking care of the property. She was lucky to have the names of another couple who could step in. James had contacted his parents and they were excellent at supplying names for different jobs.

It had been two weeks now since Gabby and Marie-Claire had arrived at the house. One evening after dinner the two were sitting in the sunroom and Marie-Claire decided this as good a time as any to approach the subject.

"Gabby. I have been thinking you may be just the answer to our problem. I really need to get back home to the boys and your father, but it is not the time to just leave and hope all the help we have employed will continue to do what we expect them to. Do you think you could stay here and run the household while I go home? I could come back in a few weeks to see how it is going."

"I'm not sure. I know what we do every day, but do you think the workers would believe that I was in charge? As well I might go crazy here myself with no one to talk to or visit with."

"What if you asked your friend Elizabeth to come and stay with you? She did not have a summer job this year did she?"

"No. We were going to do some things together in Kingston this summer. Would we have to stay at the house and property all the time, or could we sometimes go into the city to visit places? We wouldn't stay out late."

"I am sure you would use your best judgement about when and where you go out, so I can see no reason for you not to."

"Can I call Elizabeth today and ask her?"

"Certainly. Tell her James will arrange and pay for her train trip as she will be doing us a huge favour."

The arrangements were all made and as soon as Elizabeth arrived, Marie-Claire would leave for Kingston.

Clara seemed to be improving bit by bit. She would now talk to Gabby for a short time but still seemed to lose her concentration and drift away to the lonely place in her mind. The nurse was pleased that Clara was now bathing and dressing herself with encouragement. She seemed to be enjoying her meals a little more but rarely finished the food on her plate. It was going to be a long slow process.

Gabby really wished Gabrielle was still alive, as she would know exactly what to do. She could tell Clara a story about the past and bring her mind to another place. Gabby had often see the two of them look at each other as though they were reading each other's minds. Maybe Marie might know something that could help.

The days were organized into small chunks. Clara would come down for breakfast and the nurse and Gabby would casually chat and try to include her in the conversation. There were walks and reading after breakfast and then lunch with everyone at the table again. Afternoons were long as Clara had a nap and then more walks tea and dinner after six pm.

Gabby and Elizabeth decided the best time to go out were right after lunch until dinner time. They began exploring different parts of the city. At first they stayed in what was called the upper city.

There were lots of paths and parks with shady trees to explore. They often walked by a club that had a golf course and some tennis courts. Gabby decided to ask her parents if it was possible to join the private club and learn to play tennis. Besides, they had seen some handsome boys there playing tennis.

One day though they decided to go down to what was called the city below the hill. The girls could not believe what they saw. The houses were crooked with broken windows and looked as though a good wind would blow them over. Behind the houses were outhouses and some were shared by several houses. It was unclear how many people lived in each house as there were numerous children running in and out. Some of the children were not wearing garments on top while other lacked bottoms. Elizabeth and Gabby had never seen anyone living in these conditions before. Clara's house had indoor plumbing and running water installed several years ago. Both girls were living a privileged life but had not really thought about it much. They had just taken everything they had for granted.

"I bet these children do not have enough to eat ever," remarked Gabby.

"They obviously don't have enough clothes or clean clothes either, "said Elizabeth. "Why doesn't the city help them out? Surely there is some department that does that kind of thing."

"We need to ask Clara's nurse. I bet she might know about that. Let's ask her tonight at dinner."

The girls returned to the house and during dinner that night asked many questions about the conditions they had seen.

"Where you went today is likely a place your parents would not want you to be; but good for you recognizing a real need in this city. There are courses at McGill in which students are enrolled leading to careers in social welfare. These are exactly the people they help. I can get some information for you if you are interested."

Before anyone could reply, Clara spoke. "Before Gabrielle was married, she and her friend did that exact thing in the poor areas of Montreal. They would deliver food and find medical help if someone needed it. Uncle John did not like her doing it but she and Justine apparently stayed safe. Justine's parents did not know that she was doing it."

Clara went back to eating her dinner and did not say another word that night. But everyone else at the table knew there had been a break through. Now if they could just recall some other things Gabrielle had been involved in and had told Clara.

The next day Gabby called on Marie to ask for her help. "Did she remember anything eventful in their lives growing up in St-Denis?"

Marie thought for awhile and then replied. "I was quite young so I do not remember all the details, but Elodie and Julie use to tell about riding in the wagon going very fast to get away from the fighting. It was when the British attacked the Patriots in the Richelieu Valley. I remember being cold all the time so it must have been winter. Every night we had to stay with a different family. One night we had to stay in an outdoor shed. It was really cold and we had no food. But another night we stayed in a really nice house. We used to pretend we were princesses at that house and played that game afterwards. We stayed at another place that was great as there were a whole lot of children to play with and we did not have to leave for a long time. I am sorry I do not remember details as I must have been only about three."

"That's all right. Maybe we can work out some questions to ask Clara about those times. Too bad Elodie and Julie are not closer, but they may not want to travel anymore. I wonder if Sean remembers anything that might help; though he was in prison so that may not be a good memory for Gran or Sean."

That night at dinner Elizabeth and Gabby decided rather than ask direct questions, they would talk to each other about how people had to escape their homes during the Patriote Wars. Of course the nurse had been told of their plan and involved herself in the discussion.

Gabby commented to Elizabeth that she heard people had to flee with just the clothes on their backs and often on foot to escape being killed by the British.

"We were lucky," said Clara as she put down her fork filled with potatoes. "Gabrielle had everything packed and ready to go in a moment's notice. We also had a horse and wagon to take. The girls rode in the back and Gabrielle and I took turns driving. I was really afraid the wagon would tip over if I drove the horse too fast."

"Marie said you stayed at different homes along the way," added Gabby.

"Yes. John had given us names of people that would take us in for a night. Most were good but one was sad. They didn't want us so we stayed out in the shed and all slept together to keep warm. It was November. I always remember eating pickled beans and dried bread. I do not like beans now."

Gabby thought to herself to remind the cook never to serve beans to Clara.

Clara added a few more bits of information but soon it was obvious she was becoming tired. They would save more questions for another day.

After Clara had gone to bed the three women decided what they were doing was helping to start Clara on the road to recovery. She would still have to address the reality that Jean and Sheila had both died and she would be alone now.

Over the next few weeks, Clara had talked more about their escape from St-Denis and always waiting to hear about Jacques, Sean and Louis. A few times she initiated the conversation and seemed happy to answer the girls' questions.

It was early July when Marie-Claire and James arrived for a few weeks to stay at Number 24, St. Catharine Street with Gabby, Elizabeth and Clara. Marie-Claire was amazed and pleased with the progress Clara had made.

"Now that you are here Mom, maybe you can begin the conversation with Clara about Jean and Sheila. I just can't bring myself to do that. She is doing so well I don't want to see her go backward."

"You and Elizabeth have been wonderful and I think Gran is pleased to have you here. We have been thinking about the tennis you asked about. Your Father will go with you two today to see if something can be arranged."

"Oh that's great isn't it Elizabeth. We have been able to go a couple of times as a guest with the neighbour, but we don't like to always ask him."

"Thank you Mrs. Armand. I really appreciate what you are doing for me."

Later after James had managed to convince the manager of the club that Gabby and Elizabeth would be suitable tennis members, they all had lunch in the dining room. It was a treat to eat out and not have the same sandwiches they were served at home every day for lunch.

Gabby waited until dessert to ask her Father the question she had been thinking about for a few weeks. "Dad, did you know that there are many children living here in Montreal that do not have enough clothes or food and often do not go to school?"

"I am not really surprised as it has been like that for a long time. Why do you ask?"

"Elizabeth and I have been doing some research and there is a course at McGill offered to students who already have a degree but want to become involved in the welfare of the people who want to improve their living conditions. We, at least I would like to apply but of course I need your approval and some financial help. Elizabeth is going to talk to her parents as well."

"Well. That is a big decision. We will have to talk it over with your Mother as well."

There was more discussion over lunch as the girls told James everything they had discovered about the course and about Montreal. They were very persuasive and James was quite impressed with their research.

Marie-Claire had managed to begin talking to Clara about the losses she had suffered and Clara began to express her feelings about it. There were many days of tears and some silence, but over the two weeks there was enough improvement that both the day and night nurse was cancelled while Hazel still came every morning to spend the day with Clara.

The new housekeeper also enjoyed talking to Clara and always came in after breakfast to ask about the menu for lunch and dinner and if there was any mending or laundry needing to be done. She and Clara also enjoyed a cup of tea in late afternoon when they discussed the many changes in the neighbourhood. Hazel felt she might be able to spend only half a day with Clara very soon.

James and Marie-Claire were preparing to go back to Kingston in a few days and had a proposal to offer Gabby and Elizabeth. They had decided continuing her education was a wise decision and Gabby should apply to McGill for the course she wanted to take. Elizabeth had also convinced her parents that she should apply as well.

"Now girls, here is where it gets interesting," said James. "Since McGill is just up the street and you both need somewhere to stay, Gran has suggested you both stay here with her. As you know there is a small apartment in the back and she thinks you would like it as your own. Of course you would be welcome to eat meals with her any time you wish. The only thing we ask is you check in on her once every day to make sure she has everything she needs. You also may keep your tennis membership at the club even though I don't think you will have time for tennis. Elizabeth I have already contacted your parents about this deal. They think it is great but the decision is yours to make."

Elizabeth and Gabby jumped up, hugged each other while trying to quietly yell hooray.

Gabby then turned and hugged first her Father and then her Mother. "Of course we would love to do that wouldn't we Elizabeth."

"Oh yes. Mr. and Mrs. Armand you are just the best parents and friends ever."

Tomorrow they would order a huge bouquet of flowers for Gran as a thank you.

Now they just had to complete the paper work and hope they would be accepted. Three weeks later both girls were accepted into the program and would be starting in September. They had become serious about tennis and went almost every day to play at the club. There were always a number of young people either playing tennis or golf, and they soon became part of a group that met on a regular basis. Two young men in particular were soon walking them home after every match.

Clara was happy that Gabby would be living with her at Number 24. It reminded her of when she returned to Montreal to live in John's house and attend school with her sisters. It was hard to believe she had once been as young as Gabby. Her life had been very different from the life Gabby and Elizabeth lived. They had not seen the results of war or had to decide whether to be a Loyalist or a Patriot.

Clara eventually met the two young men who walked the girls home from the club and could see there was an attraction between Gabby and one of the men. They often were invited to Sunday lunch at Clara's. Both gentlemen were students at McGill as were the girls. At lunch the talk was often about the school events and the course work they were completing. One day though the talk turned to events taking place in Europe.

"I think there might be a war in Europe very soon," commented Gabby's friend Adrian. "I will never sign up if we are called up as we would be fighting for the British."

"Me either," said his friend. "The British have done nothing for us so why should we support them. France either. They did not come to our rescue before. My Grandfather died fighting the British at St-Benoit."

The room became silent until Clara said, "My father and two brothers fought the British as well and spent a long time in prison for defending their rights. But as time passes we have to believe we are one country working for the good of everyone. Let's hope there is no war."

The subject quickly changed to a more pleasant one and the outbursts were forgotten by all but Clara.

That evening, as Clara sat in the living room watching the sun go down, she hoped there would not be another war. She also hoped Canada, her home for many years, would not be divided again. There were still those who felt Loyalist or Patriot blood running through their veins and would want to make a choice.

References

Carter, R. T. (2011). *Stories of Newmarket: An Old Ontario Town.* Toronto, Ontario: Dundurn Press.

Craig, G. M. (1977). *Upper Canada: The formative years, 1784-1841.* Toronto, Ontario: McClelland and Stewart.

Dali, Salvador Quotes. [n.d.] Brainyquotes.com. Retrieved September 4, 2020, from http://www.brainyquote.com/quotes/salvador_dali_10125.

Disraeli, Benjamin Quotes. [n.d.] Brainyquotes.com. Retrieved September 4, 2020, from http://www.brainyquotes.com/quote/benjamin_disraeli_2966.

Emerson, Ralph Waldo Quotes. Wikiquote.org. Retrieved August 26, 2020. from http://www.en.m.wikiquote.org

Flint, D. (1971). *William Lyon Mackenzie: Rebel Against Authority.* Toronto, Ontario: Oxford University Press.

Franklin, Benjamin Quotes. Wikiquote.org. Retrieved August 29, 2020. from http://www.en.m.wikiquote.org

Gillham, E. M. (1975). *Early settlements of King Township, Ontario.* King City, Ont., Ontario: Municipality of the Township of King.

Greer, A. (1993). *The Patriots and the People: The Rebellion of 1837 in Rural Lower Canada.* Toronto, Ontario: University of Toronto Press.

Hugo, Victor Quotes. [n.d.] Brainyquotes.com. Retrieved September 4, 2020, from http://www.brainyquotes.com/quote/victor hugo .

Ingles, P., Burnstien, A., & Jasmin, M. (2001). CBC Canada: A People's History. Retrieved July 12, 2020, from https://www.cbc.ca/history/EPISHOMEEP7LE.htm l

Jefferson, Thomas Quotes. Wikiquote.org. Retrieved September 9, 2020. from http://www.en.m.wikiquote.org

Roosevelt, Eleanor Quotes. Wikiquote.org. Retrieved Sept 7, 2020. from https://www.en.m.wikiquote.org

Saul, J. R. (2010). *Louis-Hippolyte LaFontaine and Robert Baldwin.* Toronto, Canada: Penguin Canada.

Schull, .J. (1971). *Rebellion: The Rising in French Canada 1837.* Toronto, Ontario: Macmillan of Canada.

Shaw, George Bernard Quotes. Wikiquote.org. Retrieved May 16, 2020. From http://www.en.m.wikiquote.org

Waite, P. (2013). Confederation. Retrieved May 19, 2020 from https://www.thecanadianencyclopedia.ca/en/article/confederation

Printed in the United States
By Bookmasters